"Look who's here." Brody's gaze flicked toward the doorway. Officer Jenny assumed her regular stool and stared at Ronnie.

Although Jenny's presence was part of Ronnie's routine, Jenny's deepening interest in commitment made Ronnie uneasy. She merely wanted some fun, not a gay wedding, rings or a joint checking account. What she wanted was hot sex, and Officer Jenny certainly accommodated, as evidenced by the bruises on Ronnie's wrists. Ronnie winced as she lifted the full bottle of vodka, the price for a night of bondage with Jenny handcuffing her to the bed. It had been a new experience for Ronnie, who had found herself tethered to the headboard while the good officer did everything imaginable to her.

Jenny had excited Ronnie immensely because she was a risk taker and knew no boundaries, compared to Ronnie's other liaisons. Their first sexual encounter had occurred in a bathroom stall at Jenny's precinct, with Jenny's unsuspecting sergeant right outside, talking on her cell phone and primping at the vanity mirror. While Ronnie hovered over Jenny's mouth enjoying the officer's talented tongue all over her wetness, she simultaneously learned of the sergeant's impending divorce and scheming husband. The orgasm exploded into silence and the sergeant left as Ronnie fell into a heap on top of Jenny.

Visit

Bella Books

at

BellaBooks.com

or call our toll-free number

1-800-729-4992

Brilliant

Ann Roberts

Bella
BOOKS
2007

Bella Books, Inc.
P.O. Box 10543
Tallahassee, FL 32302

Printed in the United States of America on acid-free paper
First Edition

Editor: Christi Cassidy
Cover designer: LA Callaghan

ISBN-10: 1-59493-115-1
ISBN-13: 978-1-59493-115-4

Acknowledgments

Some stories write themselves and others take years to finish. This was the latter. Life and its distractions tended to pull me away, but fortunately, others appeared who helped bring this story into focus. I am always grateful to my son, the ultimate distraction, and the reason my life is so interesting. He has taught me much patience, something necessary with an old story. I must acknowledge Teresa Moore, an Australian University doctoral student who coined the term "phallocentric smog." I have never met the woman or read her complete dissertation, but I found the abstract fascinating. Christi Cassidy, my editor, caught all of my stupid mistakes, tightened up all the wobbly places and kept me honest when I looked for shortcuts.

Most of all, I could never imagine writing a romance without experiencing real love each day—*this one's for Amy.*

About the Author

Ann Roberts is the author of *Paid in Full* and *Furthest from the Gate*. She lives in Arizona with her family.

1. Ronnie Moves to L.A.

White highway stripes whipped past the car, vanishing almost as fast as they appeared. Ronnie Frost cracked a grin when she glanced at the speedometer. One hundred miles per hour and the '66 Mustang convertible wasn't protesting at all. The rebuilt engine could handle up to 120 miles per hour, and she pressed the gas pedal down just a bit more, watching the needle creep up to 105.

She was flying, strands of her long, blond hair floating behind her freely from underneath her baseball cap. The scorching heat baked her face and made it difficult to breathe, but there was no way she would put the top up, even if it meant sacrificing air conditioning. She loved the feeling of an open ride, and if she couldn't cruise down the road on her Harley, the Mustang was a pleasant substitute. Actually, she lamented, it wasn't *her* Harley, but her ex's, and it would be a long time before she could afford a bike.

Ronnie reached across the seat and flipped open a small cooler, pulling a Coke from the melted, icy water. She held the can against her cheek and neck, letting tendrils of water slide between her breasts, enjoying the momentary pleasure a cold shiver could provide.

She glanced at the speedometer again, realizing she'd accelerated to 110. It felt good to go fast. There was hardly anyone on Interstate 10, all of the tourists and truckers already having arrived at their Labor Day destinations. While everyone else enjoyed their barbeques, Ronnie savored the open road.

It was two o'clock and she'd just passed Palm Springs. She was making great time and hadn't stopped once—except when the nice highway patrolman caught her doing ninety outside of Quartzite. He asked her to get out of the car, and when his eyes weren't probing every inch of her body, they were admiring the Mustang. Usually Ronnie didn't use her sex appeal to her advantage, but in Arizona a ticket for ninety miles an hour would be close to two hundred dollars.

Ronnie guessed he was about twenty-six, just four years older than she, and when he didn't immediately reach for his ticket book, she flashed a smile that was both seductive and repentant. His baby face reacted instantly, giving her hope for a warning. He asked her if she knew how fast she was going, and she told the truth, but she loved to drive fast, the highway was so boring, and sometimes she couldn't help it. She promised to slow down, and he nodded, considering her sincerity.

It didn't hurt that she wore very little. A pink spaghetti tank top and denim cutoffs revealed more than they covered, including a silver belly ring, long, tanned legs and suggestive cleavage. When his gaze finally returned to her face, she stared into his eyes. He looked away first, asked her again to slow down and returned to his car.

Now seventy miles out of the patrolman's jurisdiction, she'd broken her promise. Ronnie let the car slide back under one hundred, feeling a little guilty. Suddenly, red and white lights flickered in her rearview mirror again. *Shit*. The California Highway Patrolman must have been hiding behind the overpass she'd just whizzed through. She decelerated and stopped on the shoulder. She had no idea how much a California ticket would be, but if it was like everything else, it would be *more* expensive.

She looked in her side mirror at the cruiser behind her, but no one emerged. *Great*, she thought. This guy meant business and he was already checking her plates. She tapped the steering wheel nervously, hoping she could talk her way out of another fine and most likely a court appearance.

She heard the door open and watched a pair of uniformed legs approach. "License and registration, please," an official voice asked.

Ronnie glanced up at an incredibly gorgeous redhead. The woman was petite, and despite the drab brown polyester pants and tan shirt, her curvaceous figure was apparent. Dark shades masked her heart-shaped face, but the full lips that pursed in disapproval fascinated Ronnie.

Ronnie swallowed hard and opened the glove compartment, fishing out her registration. Finding her license would be more difficult since she wasn't sure where her purse had landed when she'd flung it into the Mustang that morning with everything else she owned. She climbed over the seat and started sifting through her belongings, well aware that the redhead was only inches away.

"Moving to California?" the patrolwoman asked with a flat, uninterested tone.

"I'm going to grad school at Carlson University," Ronnie replied, finally pulling her purse out from under a stack of clothes.

"Excellent school," the officer commented. "What are you studying?"

"Sociology," Ronnie replied. She smiled slightly and handed her license to Officer J. Knight, as her gold nametag stated.

Officer Knight began the paperwork necessary to cite Ronnie's violation. When she strolled behind the Mustang to write down Ronnie's license plate number, Ronnie couldn't help but notice her incredible ass in the rearview mirror. Ronnie's libido kicked into overdrive as the good patrolwoman offered Ronnie a great view of her profile. The sun wasn't the only thing that was hot on this stretch of highway.

Officer Knight retreated to her air-conditioned cruiser while Ronnie sat on the side of the highway imagining what the two of them could be doing in the back of the patrol car beneath the underpass.

Once the patrolwoman's gun belt was discarded tongues and hands went everywhere. Ronnie caressed the CHP's buttocks and reached for her zipper, but she swatted her hand away.

"Sorry, darlin', I'm on duty. Besides, this is about you, not me."

Officer Jenny Knight's mouth, for Ronnie was sure the "J" was for Jenny, busily sucked Ronnie's breasts, pulling at the ring that pierced her left nipple. Only when Jenny bit too hard did Ronnie cry out, and the patrolwoman kissed the crimson aureole lightly. Taking control, she pushed Ronnie down on the seat and quickly peeled off the tiny denim cutoffs and tank top, leaving Ronnie clad only in her pink thong. Jenny's gaze wandered over Ronnie's naked body as though she were inspecting a suspect.

Ronnie felt her heartbeat quicken. Jenny loomed over her, staring but not touching. Suddenly Ronnie felt vulnerable. Jenny remained fully clothed, fully in control, while goose pimples burst over Ronnie's flesh from the icy air conditioning that filled the cruiser. Yet Jenny did nothing but stare. When Jenny did finally put her hands on Ronnie's knees, Ronnie took an audible breath as Jenny parted her legs and smiled.

Ronnie longed for the patrolwoman to touch her, but Officer Jenny clearly possessed great restraint. She traced the outline of Ronnie's lips and slid her middle finger inside Ronnie's mouth. In and out the finger came, mimicking what Ronnie yearned to feel between her legs. When Ronnie arched her back in pleading, Jennie let her hand trail down Ronnie's abdomen, stopping at the thin waistband of her thong.

"Are you wet?" Jenny sneered.

Ronnie whimpered, unable to answer, her eyes glued to the finger that caressed the pink fabric.

Ronnie's fantasy was abruptly interrupted by the very real figure of Officer Knight towering over her with a ticket. "I won't bother to ask you if you know why I stopped you or how fast you were going. If you're going to Carlson University, you must be very bright and those questions would be insulting to us both."

Ronnie nodded pleasantly. She expected no-nonsense Officer Knight to hand her the citation and go, but the woman just stood there, her eyes fixed on Ronnie's face.

Ronnie felt the need to fill the void with conversation. "I take it you know a lot about Carlson?"

"I live in L.A., about ten miles from the school. Today I'm just covering for a buddy, working the boonies, catching speeders such as yourself."

Ronnie couldn't help but smile, and she thought Officer Knight's stony expression softened just a bit. "I apologize, officer. I understand that I should slow down, and I intend to, starting now." And she really meant it.

She reached for the ticket and her license and registration, but Officer Knight still held them in a tight grip, out of reach. Ronnie's fingers brushed against hers and neither of them moved. "That's an incredible tattoo you have," Officer Knight said, as her shaded eyes motioned to the large labrys that covered Ronnie's left shoulder.

"Thanks."

Officer Knight released her grip on the documents and walked away, leaving Ronnie dazed and lightheaded. She sat there until the patrol car eased back on the highway, and when she finally looked down at the ticket, she smiled. Written across all of the official jargon, empty spaces and boxes was a simple note in black marker.

CALL ME. 555-7341—JENNY.

"Jenny. I knew it."

2. A Proposition for Ronnie

Ronnie's conscience added an extra half-hour to her drive as the speedometer never again wavered above eighty, and she avoided another confrontation with Officer Jenny or her colleagues. Eventually towns and cities merged together, while small subdivisions and random strip malls displaced the dismal shrubbery, giving Ronnie more color and scenery to observe. The buildings grew dense, the highway narrowed and Ronnie's fingers tightened on the wheel as the traffic congestion increased, signaling her entrance into the City of Angels.

Weekend traffic in L.A. was not what Ronnie expected. In Phoenix it was easier to navigate the freeways and surface streets on Saturdays and Sundays, but Ronnie quickly realized that in L.A., the weekend meant everyone was out, not holed up in the skyscrapers that surrounded her, the sun bouncing off their glass windows. Traffic was at a standstill, the three lanes of the 101 bumper to bumper with people enjoying the holiday. She stretched her arms over her head and took a deep breath, basking in the sunshine and the light breeze that kissed her body, the heat of the desert forgotten.

Any other time she would have been impatient, swearing at other drivers and their incompetence, looking at her watch, but in California, the cool weather mellowed her temperament. She rested two fingers on the steering wheel, her attention diverted to the massive billboards hovering above her, announcing several movie premiers and L.A.'s "favorite soft drink," Fanta Orange.

Beethoven's Fifth suddenly erupted in the open car, and Ronnie pulled her cell phone from its holster. "Hi, Mom. I'm not dead, and the car is still running, so don't worry." For the past month, Ronnie had listened to her mother's daily harangue about the stupidity of driving a classic car across the desert in hot weather.

"Really, Ronnie, is that an appropriate way to start a conversation? I just wanted to check in with you. We haven't spoken in nearly a week, you know." Doris Frost's offended tone was apparent, honed from years of practice.

Ronnie was well aware of that fact, and she bit her tongue, lest she tell her mother that one phone call a week was plenty of familial contact from her perspective. "I know, Mom. And I was planning on calling you and Dad this evening once I got settled."

"Where are you staying? Do you know yet?"

"Yeah, it's cool," Ronnie lied. Her original plan to stay with a friend had fizzled, and she wasn't sure what she would do at nightfall, but she wasn't worried.

"Now I hope it's safe. You need to be careful, Ronnie. A young woman as incredibly beautiful as you are needs to look out for herself. Women *and* men will look to take advantage of you."

Ronnie closed her eyes and resisted the urge to press the END button on her phone. Her mother meant well, but she could increase Ronnie's blood pressure by uttering a single sentence. "I've gotta go, Mom. Tell Dad I love him, and I'll call you in a few days."

"You said you'd call later today."

"I would have, Mom, but you beat me to it."

"You could still call, you know. It would be all right to speak with your parents more than once a day. The sun wouldn't stop shining if that happened."

"I know, Mom. But I've got a lot to do. I need to go. I love you."

Ronnie closed the phone and took a deep cleansing breath. She loved her parents and considered her father a friend, but her mother still tried to run her life, much as she had through Ronnie's youth. She escaped from the small town of Globe, Arizona, to the huge metropolis of Tucson and the University of Arizona just one week after her graduation from Globe High School. A softball scholarship guaranteed four years of freedom from her parents, who remained nearly one hundred miles away—close enough to call for help but distant enough to breathe. She sighed and holstered the phone again. It could be worse, she thought. They could have disowned her for being gay.

A Saab convertible pulled up alongside her and a deep voice said, "Hey."

Ronnie turned toward dark sunglasses and perfectly bleached teeth. "Hey," she said back with a polite smile.

"Just moved here?" he asked, loud enough to be heard over the engines.

"That's right."

"I'd be happy to show you the sights."

Ronnie laughed at the unoriginal line. "Thanks, but I think I can handle it."

He nodded and revved his engine to move forward. "See you around."

Ronnie waved good-bye and watched his taillights advance. Thank goodness most guys were pretty cool. She'd met a few jerks over the years, but in general the majority of the men took the rejection fairly well. Some had to be hit over the head with the words, "I'm a *lesbian*," before they gave up. Then they were usually speechless, but guys, unlike women, were much less likely to pitch a fit when told no.

Ronnie yanked the ball cap off her head and shook her unruly hair free, her eyes focused on the overpass sign up ahead. She saw her exit and signaled to move over. A black Jaguar with tinted windows drew up beside her and they continued to advance down the road side by side. Ronnie couldn't see the driver, but if the Jag didn't speed up or slow down, she was going to miss her exit. She braked, almost coming to a dead stop, hoping she could sneak in behind the Jaguar, but when she stopped, so did the Jag. Ronnie turned to the driver and gestured as if to say, "What the hell are you doing?"

The expensive ride remained parallel to the Mustang, the smoky windows shielding the motorist from Ronnie's wrath. *Damn California drivers!* Traffic in her lane sped up and Ronnie hit the gas, trying to pass in front of the Jag. Just as she turned the wheel to change lanes, the Jag pulled up next to her and she reflexively jerked back.

"Shit!" she yelled as the traffic passed the Carlson exit. She took a deep breath and smacked her brakes. Everyone was at a standstill again. She put the car in park, unbuckled her seat belt and leaned across the passenger seat, glaring at the Jag's side window, her reflection staring back at her against the black tint. Traffic started to move again, but Ronnie ignored the honking horns from those behind her and kept her gaze fixed on the Jaguar, which also remained motionless.

A few drivers veered around her, some flipping her off. She was about to give up when the Jag's window descended and Ronnie locked eyes with the driver. The woman was probably pushing fifty, her enormous black hair tumbling from her head, and she wore a low-cut dress that matched the Jag's exterior. The woman unnerved Ronnie, studying her, apparently unaware of the traffic backup behind her. If this was a come-on, it was certainly the strangest Ronnie had ever experienced. Ruby red lips mouthed, "Follow me," and the woman gunned the engine.

Ronnie debated whether to ditch the Jag or not, but natural curiosity compelled her to slide behind the sleek, black car. They exited half a mile later and turned into a strip mall parking lot.

Before Ronnie could shut off her engine the woman stormed out of the Jag and stood in front of her.

"Where did you learn to drive?" Ronnie demanded.

The woman leaned across the steering wheel and turned off the ignition, her breasts straining to stay inside the top of her dress. The car silenced, she faced Ronnie. "You are incredibly beautiful," she said, her voice devoid of any sexual interest.

"What?" Ronnie was dumbfounded.

The woman ignored her comment and looked around the car, sizing up the situation. "It's obvious you've been traveling all day, no attention to your makeup—or attire," she added with a note of disapproval. "I can only imagine what you'd look like when you tried."

Ronnie shook her head. She was tired, it was late in the afternoon and she still didn't have a place to stay. "Look, lady, I don't know what this is about, but I'm just trying to end a very long day, find an apartment and get ready to start school."

"So, you're about twenty-one?"

"Twenty-two."

"Going to Carlson?"

"Yes," Ronnie answered impatiently.

The woman whistled. "If you're going there, honey, you'll need money." She reached inside her purse and withdrew a business card. "My name's Nola. Nola Monroe. I'm a modeling agent. And you are . . ." she asked, clearly expecting Ronnie to fill in the blank.

At the word *modeling*, Ronnie lost all interest in the conversation. "I'm Ronnie Frost and I have absolutely no interest in being a model."

Nola smiled. "Have you ever *been* a model?"

"Not really, but the idea of parading around and having hundreds of people ogle me is totally unappealing." Ronnie glanced at her watch and over her shoulder, hoping to discern exactly where she was.

Nola craned her head to see both sides of Ronnie's face. "Your bone structure is incredible and your skin is flawless."

Ronnie rolled her eyes. Others had told her much the same, and her mother had badgered her for almost ten years to try modeling. She started the engine. "Not interested. Now, if you'll kindly remove your ass from the door of my car, I need to go find a place to stay."

Nola waved the business card at Ronnie. "Take this. You might change your mind after a few months as a starving student. With your looks, I can guarantee you at least a thousand for every booking." When Ronnie made no effort to take the card, Nola changed tack. "I also know someone who's looking for a roommate. Well, actually, he's not, but they've got this kind of dormitory thing going, and there's an empty bed. I'll write down the address. It's a house in West Hollywood."

She scribbled on the back of the card and extended it to Ronnie, who grudgingly accepted it, now that the woman had actually provided something that might be of value.

Nola started back for her car. "Think about my offer, Ronnie Frost. There aren't that many women who drive into L.A. and get handed an opportunity to make big money."

Ronnie watched Nola Monroe maneuver her clinging black dress back into the Jag and zoom away. She almost crumpled up the card, but Nola's last words rang in her ears. She had saved some money from bartending during the last year, but much of her graduate education would be financed through student loans. She knew money would be tight. Always somewhat cautious of missing opportunities, Ronnie committed the West Hollywood address to memory and stuck the card into her glove compartment.

She checked her map and realized she was only a mile from the university. It had been an interesting day with many surprises, but it was time to get serious.

3. The Inquisition

Instead of returning to the freeways, Ronnie traveled the surface roads to Carlson University, which was nestled in the heart
of a historic residential district. Mature trees lined every block,
their branches creating an umbrella of shade over the streets.
She marveled at the incredible homes, most of them large
Victorians with extensive, well-manicured lawns. Ronnie
remembered that the Carlson brochure had specifically stated
that many of the professors lived in the homes and invited students over for tea or lunch in an effort to build a personal rap-
port.

Each house seemed more unique and breathtaking than the
one before, as if the original owners had participated in a game
to outdo their neighbors. Large verandas, second-story balconies
and wraparound porches gave each house its distinct look. It was
truly a blending of architecture and art. The most exclusive

homes were out of view, their exteriors obscured by massive hedges and electronic gates.

At some point the meandering streets ventured into the university boundaries, the stately, scholarly buildings looking remarkably similar to the private homes with the exception of the large granite signs that sat in front of each entryway. Ronnie conducted a self-guided tour of the campus, stopping in front of the Grant Edwards Social Sciences Building, the place where she would spend most of her time for the next two years.

White columns and large square windows accented the four-story red brick building, which seemed immense. Ronnie took a deep breath, pride swelling inside her. During her initial visit a few months before, she'd known immediately that she belonged here. She loved this campus, its location and its warmth.

The afternoon was fading away and she realized she still didn't have a place to stay. She maneuvered her car into the nearly empty parking lot of the student union, all of the students away enjoying the Labor Day holiday no doubt, their last major break before the intense school year was to start.

The student union was the only building that seemed more modern and less traditional. Her footsteps echoed in the hallway and she saw no one until she walked past the study area and spotted one lone occupant engrossed in a large textbook. There wasn't anyone to help her, but she found the Student Communications Center rather easily. Spanning an entire wall, the communications center was really nothing more than a large bulletin board with a few hundred index cards, flyers and notices of various shapes, sizes and colors.

She smiled as she recognized a constant theme—liberal thinking. A marijuana leaf caught her eye, and Legalize Marijuana Now! invited her to attend their next meeting. The ACLU, Young Democrats and the NAACP all had flyers encouraging membership and participation. A rainbow flag adorned several announcements and Ronnie smiled when she counted five different gay groups. This was why she had come— to be around people who thought as she did. Also, the opportunity to work with some of the greatest minds in America was a clear draw. Carlson was expensive and prestigious.

Ronnie found the section devoted to housing and read through the inquiries for roommates. Nothing stuck out, and they all seemed to be saying the same thing: someone quiet, non-smoker without a pet, reliable with the rent. She sighed, horribly overwhelmed and not knowing where to begin. Of course, she could always stay at a cheap motel if nothing worked out. She scanned the index cards once more, looking for any clues to a good lead but unimpressed by the wordings of the ads. The only address that stuck in her mind was the one Nola Monroe had given her. She headed back to the Mustang and West Hollywood, not bothering to write down any other possibilities.

The For Rent sign leaned so far over that the corner stuck in the ground. Ronnie gazed up at the wood-framed house. The yard was well kept, flowers bloomed in pots on the porch, and a rainbow flag hung from a third-floor attic window. An old mini-van sat in the driveway, its backside plastered in anti-establishment stickers with phrases like "Question Authority" and "Peace Now," preaching to all of the drivers who motored behind the bus. Ronnie got out and looked around. The neighborhood didn't compare to the Carlson area, but it was charming, even if it was a little rundown.

She approached the yard and found a man sunbathing in the sunset, wearing nothing but a silver thong. His skin was pale as milk, and next to the silver thong, the only other noticeable color on his body was a tuft of fuchsia hair sitting on the top of his head. He wore sunglasses and lay prostrate on his lounge, oblivious to Ronnie's presence. Only when she cast a shadow over him did he raise his head.

"Holy crap! If this is a dream, honey, you're gorgeous, but you're definitely the wrong sex. I haven't had a dream with a girl in it since second grade and that was Wonder Woman."

Ronnie grinned. "I'm interested in the vacancy. Are you the one looking for a roommate?"

"Well, not this week. My boyfriend and I have gone six whole days without pitching each other's clothes out the window. You're looking for Vandella." The man rose from the lounger and removed his sunglasses. "I'm Richard," he said, extending his hand at a perfect forty-five-degree angle.

"Ronnie Frost." She noticed his hands were smoother and softer than her own.

"Very glad to meet you. Are you a student at the university?"

Ronnie nodded. "I'm starting my master's degree in sociology. What about you?"

"Me? In college?" Richard gave a hearty laugh and threw back his head. Ronnie could tell he had a flair for the dramatic. "I'd rather give Jerry Falwell a blowjob! That man could really use one." He took her arm and led her toward the house. "I'm a cameraman at Paramount, hoping to be a filmmaker. I even have the name of my future company," he quickly added.

"What is it?"

"Dick's Pix!"

"Interesting," Ronnie said with a nod, trying very hard to suppress a giggle.

"Obviously I'll specialize in gay films. It'll be the first time in my life that having the name Richard might actually work to my advantage." He opened the front door and motioned for her to enter.

She was instantly taken by the old home, its solid oak woodwork and vintage décor, all from different periods. In the middle of the room an overstuffed parlor sofa faced a large armoire that served as an entertainment center. Bookshelves lined one wall, filled with titles from Ludlum to Freud. Prominently displayed in the corner of the room by the staircase was a suit of armor. Someone had evidently raided every antiques store in L.A. to furnish the house.

"My only *true* boyfriend," Richard said, bouncing over to the knight and lifting his arm. "Van!" he shouted up the stairs.

"Yes, Richard." A large black woman descended from the second story. She wore a T-shirt that proclaimed, "Support Your Right to Arm Bears" and cutoff shorts. Despite her casual appearance, her movements were deliberate, each step graceful and purposeful. Her hand grazed the banister, but only as if to caress the fine old oak. It seemed to Ronnie that she floated down the staircase.

It was Richard who spoke. "Potential tenant, Ronnie Frost, please meet potential roommate, Vandella Mobundi. Ronnie's a grad student in sociology, Van."

The woman smiled slightly and her eyes bore into Ronnie's. "Excellent. You score a point there. I'm working on my bachelor's in women's studies."

"Shall I get the others for the inquisition?" Richard asked.

Ronnie looked startled. "The what?"

Vandella placed her hand lightly on Ronnie's arm. "It's not a big deal. We just need to ask you some questions."

Richard let out a laugh as he started up the stairs. "No big deal, right. The last person ran out of the room crying."

Twenty minutes later Ronnie was sitting in the dining room across from all four of the roommates at an immense table that could seat twelve. Ronnie had been shown to the chair at the head, while the roommates crowded around the other end.

Vandella, who sat in the position of authority, said, "Okay, everybody, this is Ronnie, and she's applying to be my roommate. Ronnie, this is Brody; he lives on the third floor." She pointed to a stout guy with a flattop who didn't smile. A NASCAR fan, Ronnie thought. "You've already met Richard, and this is Dave, Richard's lover."

"Hi." Dave waved from across the table. He was exactly the opposite of Richard. Whereas Richard was very thin and pale, Dave was muscular and tanned. Ronnie realized that as a couple they spanned the extremes of gay male stereotypes. No wonder they fought so much.

Vandella readied her pen and looked around the table at the others, who were studying index cards they each held. "Who has the first question?"

"I have the first question," Dave said. He turned dramatically and faced Ronnie. "Have you ever committed or been convicted of a felony?"

"Uh, no."

"Done drugs?" Vandella added.

"No."

"Not ever?" Brody asked, his tone clearly implying disbelief.

"Okay, a few joints in high school," Ronnie admitted.

"Do you smoke?"

Ronnie looked up but couldn't tell if Richard or Dave had asked the question. "Rarely, and only outside."

Van took the lead. "Where are you from?"

"I was born in Globe, Arizona."

Richard immediately stuck up his hand to ask an unplanned question. "Any pets? I'm really allergic to cats." He grimaced for added effect and held his hand over his heart.

"Nope."

"What's your sign?"

"I'm a Capricorn." Ronnie took a sip of water from the glass they had offered her. The questions were coming fast, but she was growing tired of the game.

"Where did you go to college?" Dave asked, reading from his card.

"I got my bachelor's degree from the University of Arizona."

"What do your parents do?"

"My mother's a librarian and my father's a baker."

19

"What kind of car do you drive?"

"'Sixty-six Mustang convertible."

"V-four or V-six?" Brody asked.

Ronnie narrowed her eyes and met his. "That's a trick question. There's no such thing as a V-four, and mine's a V-eight."

Brody nodded his approval. "Do you cook?"

"I love to cook, especially when I'm depressed."

Dave held up his last card. "Are you handy around the house?"

"I'm great with plumbing."

Richard took a deep breath and rubbed his chin. "What sports did you play to keep you in such great shape?"

"I was on my college softball team all four years."

"I say abortion. What do you say?" Vandella asked, pointing a finger at her.

"I say pro-choice, but I don't think I could have an abortion."

"Are you a Democrat or Republican?"

"Democrat, but I have a mind of my own."

Vandella folded her arms and leaned back. "The Religious Right."

"They're neither religious nor right."

"Are you homophobic?" Dave asked pointedly.

"I'm a lesbian," Ronnie retorted, growing impatient with the questions.

"Really?" Dave gasped.

Ronnie smirked. "Really."

Brody leaned toward her, reading carefully from his card. "Do you have any annoying siblings who want to visit Hollywood, stay for weeks and take every single bus tour around?"

"I'm an only child."

"What's your shoe size?" he persisted.

"Eight."

Richard clapped his hands. "Me too!"

"Where's Liberia?" Vandella asked, clearly testing her.

"Off the Western Coast of Africa, I think."

"If you could be a tree, which one would you be?"

"Richard!" Brody interjected. "That is the dumbest question."

"I happen to like that question. It says a lot about a person," Richard fired back.

Ronnie threw up her hands. "A pine tree?"

Richard nodded. "I say she's in."

"Me too," Dave agreed.

"Yes," Vandella said with a nod.

All eyes turned to Brody. He stared down, tapping his pen on the table. When he looked up at Ronnie, his eyes were filled with mischief. "Tell us about your last sexual experience."

Ronnie held his gaze and sat up straight in the chair. "Well, normally I don't kiss and tell. To detail the entire sixteen hours would take too long. I could focus on a specific aspect, like the hot fudge, the ropes or the six Kama Sutra positions that were used. Which would you like?"

Brody paused and smacked the table with his hand. "She's in."

Once Ronnie had passed the test and they ironed out the details of rent, everyone unloaded the Mustang, helping Ronnie carry her belongings up to the second-floor room that she would share with Vandella. The entire house was unbelievable, filled with antiques and Richard's props and costumes from many movie sets. As Ronnie turned a corner to her room, she almost plowed into a life-size mannequin of Dorothy from *The Wizard of Oz* that was stationed outside Richard and Dave's room. One thing was for sure—in this house of eccentrics, she would never be alone.

When the last of the suitcases and boxes was finally piled on Ronnie's side of the room, the men excused themselves, leaving

Ronnie to study her new surroundings. The room was spacious and airy, with three old windows and enough light to keep her from becoming claustrophobic. A window seat in the corner provided a view of the hills.

She stared at the poster of Martin Luther King, Jr. that hung on the door. More intriguing were the hundreds of slogan buttons and campaign pins that covered the wall above Vandella's bed. Every liberal presidential candidate for the last fifty years was represented, and most of the slogans promoted women's rights and social issues.

The door opened and Vandella entered carrying two glasses of iced tea. She offered one to Ronnie before lowering herself onto the settee at the foot of Ronnie's bed. "If there's a cause, I probably have a button for it," she said, pointing at the wall.

"So what happened to your previous roommate?" Ronnie asked.

"She graduated last spring. Brody, Dave and I still have two years to go, and I've already got senioritis, and I'm only a junior!" Van laughed, and Ronnie felt her warmth and depth of compassion. She had only known Van for an hour, but she knew they would be good friends. "I'd give you the tour, but it's pretty self-explanatory."

"It's great." Ronnie eyed the flowered wallpaper and beautiful white wainscoting that circled the room. "I love it here already."

"California can't be that much different from Arizona, can it?"

Ronnie joined Van on the settee and tucked her feet underneath her. "Globe, Arizona, is both sweltering and conservative. I spent four years in Tucson, which is great, but I want something bigger, something around water. So for me this is like finding heaven after riding out of hell."

Van nodded. "I hear you. California's got great weather and beaches, and it's about as liberal as a state can be. West Hollywood is the capital of free thought. As a lesbian, you'll have a much easier time."

"So you're not . . ." Ronnie started, unable to complete the sentence and embarrassed that she had even asked the question to someone she barely knew.

"No," Van answered with a smile and a shake of her head. "Many have tried to convert me, and I even kissed a woman once just to get my women's studies friends off my back, but the fact is, I need a man." They both laughed, and Van patted Ronnie on the leg. "Don't worry, Ronnie Frost, you'll meet plenty of lesbians in the sociology department. I'm the minority in more than one way. In fact, the best sociology professor is a lesbian, Dr. Diane Cole."

"She's my advisor."

"You're lucky. Most of the new students wind up with the department chair, and judging by your looks, I'm glad you're with Dr. Cole."

"Why? Is the chairman some sort of weirdo?" Ronnie asked.

"He's a letch," Van said emphatically. "And considering how incredibly beautiful you are, he'd spend the whole year trying to get in your pants."

Ronnie blushed at the compliment and thought to change the subject. "So, what was with all of the questions?"

"Please don't be offended. That's our way of checking you out. We had to see if you could handle a no-nonsense black woman, a redneck and a couple of true fairies. It takes a special person to take all of us together, and we're pretty tight."

"So, have you all lived here for a long time?" Ronnie asked.

"Since freshman year. Well, except when Richard sleeps around and Dave throws him out, or it happens the other way 'round. In the end they always make up and get back together. My last roommate was pretty cool, but Brody had this guy with him last winter who was a thief. Brody caught him stealing from Dave and beat the devil out of him. After that we decided to do interviews. You, my new friend, passed with flying colors."

23

Ronnie opened her mouth to comment, just as a wave of obscenities penetrated the walls. Feet pounded up the stairs and Brody burst into the room. "Van, you've got to do something about Richard."

Van sighed. "What's going on now?"

Brody's face was bright red. "There's a . . . a . . ." he stammered. "Just get down there," he pleaded.

Van rose and she and Ronnie followed Brody down the stairs. All the while he kept swearing under his breath. He led them to the kitchen where Richard was hovering over a plate on the counter.

Only when Ronnie was inches from the object did she realize it was a large, gelatin penis standing on end. "I'm not sure it's hard enough," Richard said, gently moving the plate back and forth while the red penis wavered slightly. "What do you think, Van?"

Van closed her eyes momentarily and took a cleansing breath. "Richard, when you asked if we had any Jell-O this morning, I didn't realize—"

"This is what I see when I open the fridge to get a beer," Brody interrupted.

"What is it?" Van asked. "No, let me rephrase that. I know *what* it is. I guess I want to know *why* it is."

"It's my friend Nico's abstract art project. I'm keeping it for him. Don't you think he did a good job?" Richard beamed with admiration until he met Brody's glare.

Brody leaned closer to him. "If you don't get that thing out of my refrigerator right now, I'm going to circumcise it."

"I can't take it out yet," Richard whined. "It's not hard enough."

"It looks hard enough to me, Richard," Van said.

Richard stamped his foot and picked up the plate. "All right, I'll call my friend Tara and see if she has any room in her fridge. You people have no appreciation of art."

4. Forty

Diane wore only a French bikini in the dream. The waves lapped at her feet and the shock of the icy seawater against her toes made her gasp.

Her father laughed. "C'mon in, Diane, honey. It's only cold for a few minutes."

She watched him fall back against an incoming wave, his arms outstretched and a huge smile on his face. His flat belly and a full head of hair made his chronological age impossible to gauge. Diane stood at the shoreline, hugging herself against the wind, feeling her nipples harden against the small patches of cloth that barely covered her breasts.

Suddenly she was very conscious of her appearance. She would never wear a French bikini—not at her age, and certainly not in front of her father. She turned toward the beach to see hundreds of strangers pointing and laughing at her. She looked down at her body, the target of their ridicule. A bloated paunch hung over the waistband of her tiny suit, and her breasts drooped toward her stomach. The inside of her thighs touched, the fat rolls on her legs kissing one another.

This couldn't be her body. She twisted her torso to see her backside, and she was horrified to discover enormous buttocks that nearly wrapped around to her front. The roar of the crowd increased. Diane turned to her father, the protector who would defend her. He had swum to the shore and emerged from the ocean, and he was holding out his arms toward her. Tears blinded her eyes as she entered his embrace. He held her and the crowd was silenced. When he pulled away, he patted her rear end. "That's quite a load you got back there, sweetheart!" he shouted.

The crowd laughed heartily at his cruel joke.

"Happy Birthday, Diane!" he cried as his face morphed into an obscene caricature and his head ballooned to three times the size of his body.

Diane Cole jolted up in bed, her breathing ragged and her nightshirt soaked. The bedside clock read three thirty. It had only been a dream. She wasn't wearing a bikini, and as far as she knew, her overly critical father was still twenty-five years older with a beer gut and male-pattern baldness.

All of it was fiction—except for the fact that it was indeed her fortieth birthday.

The ringing of the phone woke her again at eight. She made no effort to reach for it, honoring her first rule of birthdays: no phone calls. Diane hated her birthday. She refused to really celebrate or acknowledge it, and for the most part her family and friends respected that wish.

The ancient answering machine clicked into action and Diane heard her friendly voice followed by the beep. "Diane, it's Mom. Dad and I just want to wish you a happy fortieth, dear."

Diane cringed at hearing the number actually verbalized, and she doubted her father even remembered it was her birthday, let alone her age. She clenched her teeth at her mother's insistence on including her father, but it had always been that way. Her father worked and golfed while her mother took care of everything else. Like many of her Beverly Hills friends, Diane grew up with an absentee father, one who only made appearances at events and weddings. Since she'd already graduated from school several times, and there would never be a wedding as long as the Republicans controlled any part of government, Diane assumed he had fulfilled his parental obligation. Of course if she wanted to see her father more often, she could take up golf, but she had no desire to learn the difference between a five-iron and a nine-iron.

Her mother prattled on about their social engagements and her father's job as the head of a financial corporation. She was sorry they couldn't get together, but they were attending a conference in New York. "So, I hope you have a happy fortieth, sweetie. This is the beginning of the best time of your life. I mean that in all sincerity, honey. Bye-bye."

The *best* time of her life. Diane sighed and stared out at the ocean, suddenly feeling extraordinarily guilty for thinking such ill thoughts about her father, the man who had given her a Malibu bungalow. Few people could boast that they woke up each morning to the sights and sounds of the Pacific Ocean. Malibu was paradise and her father had signed over the family beach house to her when she turned twenty-five. A beautiful view and no mortgage. Her age shouldn't matter. She gazed at the waves from her bed for another half-hour, listening as the answering machine screened three more calls from friends who cared.

She dragged herself to the bathroom and stared at her forty-year-old face. Her short, curly black hair remained unruly, but still free of gray. She didn't wear much makeup and she didn't need to hide many lines. Only a few crow's feet were etched around her brown eyes, and if her genetics proved true, she wouldn't need any plastic surgery.

"Thanks, Mom," she said aloud.

The rest of her body had also remained loyal. She'd stayed in shape and hadn't left the single-digit pant sizes. If a list of romantic conquests could provide a scorecard to attractiveness, she would fare well. She'd had her share of liaisons and relationships, and her ego was continually inflated by numerous flirtations and propositions from students. Still, every time she looked in the mirror, she felt her age. Her twenties were long gone and middle age was tapping her on the shoulder.

She shook her head. "Why do I care?" She stared at the mirror, perturbed. Grasping both sides of the sink, she leaned toward her reflection. "You are a brilliant woman whose education cost more than the gross national product of several countries. You own an exceptional home that most people would kill to have. You owe no money to anyone, you are not disfigured by a horrible accident or disease, and you want for nothing. You dine at fine restaurants and have never tasted a TV dinner or spoken into some clown's head at a fast-food joint. People desire your company, and your friends would readily give you a kidney or other vital organ should you need a transplant. In fact, one or two of them might actually lay down their lives for you in a moment of crisis. You are indeed one of the most fortunate souls on the planet, and you need to get your pathetic, sorry attitude into check, or you will permanently screw up your karma."

5. Happy Birthday, Diane

Within two weeks of arriving in L.A. Ronnie decided things were falling into place. She loved her roommates, all of whom made her laugh and welcomed her into their little group. They included her in their weekly game nights and encouraged her to cook—all the time. Ronnie had treated her friends to four exquisite meals and allowed each one to choose the fare. Only Richard surprised her when he said he wanted a dinner of beans—and only beans. Ronnie served him sixteen different bean dishes, and the evening turned into a smelly and loud farting contest between the three guys, which was Richard's intention all along. Surprisingly, Ronnie warmed to Brody, a guy she was sure had no respect for gay people. He proved her wrong when he offered to help her land a job at Simply Understated, a hot new restaurant and the place where he worked as a bartender.

A local newspaper had described Simply Understated as "a

bistro that lives up to its name and relies on good food and excellent service. No gimmicks distract from the central message of eating and drinking well." Ronnie had not read that review, but she knew she liked the place from the moment she walked in. Simply Understated's décor was just that—except for the bar. An antique oak behemoth from the turn of the last century, it sat in the center of the restaurant. Brody told her it had cost the owner a fortune to move it from an old saloon, an investment that was anything but simple or understated. Ronnie considered it an honor to work behind such a bar with so much character and history.

Obtaining the job had been relatively painless. Ronnie appeared one afternoon with Brody and had a casual interview with Randy, the owner. An African-American man in his late thirties, Randy's bulging muscles nearly ripped the seams of his T-shirt. Owning Simply Understated had been the culmination of a lifelong dream for Randy, whose father left him an enormous inheritance, one rumored to include a yacht and a small island.

He hired her on the spot after she proved she could make the most obscure of cocktails and answer a few standard questions.

"Have you ever been fired?" he asked.

"No," she answered honestly.

"Will you be on time every day?"

"Absolutely. I've never been late to work a day in my life."

He pointed a finger at her, his expression sobering. "Do you want to work here?"

Ronnie realized this was a man of few words and great integrity. "Yes," she said emphatically. "Very much."

He smiled, his white teeth in stark contrast to his dark chocolate brown skin. "If Brody says you're okay, then I like you too. You're hired."

That had been a week ago.

Now, on a hectic Friday night, Ronnie quickly pulled the

glasses from the shelves and poured the alcohol. She covered one end of the bar with Brody at the other. They worked as a team, developing a rhythm that kept the drinks flowing and the customers happy. Her life had settled much the same way, in a comfortable pattern, and all that remained was school. The fall trimester would start in a week, and Ronnie found herself a little anxious about life as a graduate student. For now she was content to milk the rest of summer, earning some great tips, becoming a bona fide California girl with the help of her roommates and pleasuring several Southern California women, including Officer Jenny.

"Look who's here." Brody's gaze flicked toward the doorway.

Officer Jenny assumed her regular stool and stared at Ronnie. Although Jenny's presence was part of Ronnie's routine, Jenny's deepening interest in commitment made Ronnie uneasy. She merely wanted some fun, not a gay wedding, rings or a joint checking account. What she wanted was hot sex, and Officer Jenny certainly accommodated, as evidenced by the bruises on Ronnie's wrists. Ronnie winced as she lifted the full bottle of vodka, the price for a night of bondage with Jenny handcuffing her to the bed. It had been a new experience for Ronnie, who had found herself tethered to the headboard while the good officer did everything imaginable to her.

Jenny had excited Ronnie immensely because she was a risk taker and knew no boundaries, compared to Ronnie's other liaisons. Their first sexual encounter had occurred in a bathroom stall at Jenny's precinct, with Jenny's unsuspecting sergeant right outside, talking on her cell phone and primping at the vanity mirror. While Ronnie hovered over Jenny's mouth enjoying the officer's talented tongue all over her wetness, she simultaneously learned of the sergeant's impending divorce and scheming husband. The orgasm exploded into silence and the sergeant left as Ronnie fell into a heap on top of Jenny.

Each liaison was either daring or unconventional. If they

weren't testing the limits of decency in public, such as fingering each other under the table during dinner at a restaurant, Jenny was exposing Ronnie to sex games and toys she'd only seen in adult shops. Jenny's collection of bondage paraphernalia was vast, but Ronnie sidestepped her constant pleas to try total submission. The night before, Jenny had worn down Ronnie's defenses, and Ronnie allowed herself to be shackled to the headboard. Wearing only leather chaps and a leather bra, Jenny crawled between Ronnie's legs, a sly grin covering her face. She pinned Ronnie's thighs open with her knees and pulled a set of nipple clamps seemingly from nowhere.

Ronnie's jaw dropped, as she watched Jenny pinch the clamps over her breasts. Jenny's tongue flicked across each nipple, and Ronnie was amazed at her body's instantaneous anticipation. Her breathing was ragged and she cried out. She strained against the handcuffs, unable to move, helpless. Jenny's knees kept Ronnie's thighs parted, and the officer set her sights on Ronnie's throbbing clitoris.

Her tongue trailed down Ronnie's stomach and disappeared between Ronnie's legs. Ronnie gasped as her whole body reacted to a single touch. She pulled her body forward, but the handcuffs held her in place and all she could do was wait for ecstasy. Jenny's whole mouth sucked greedily on Ronnie's center, and Ronnie's moans increased.

"Jenny, please . . ." were the only words that escaped Ronnie's lips before the explosions rocked her body. Jenny pulled herself on top of Ronnie, grinding against Ronnie's pelvis.

They came together twice, and when she was finally spent, Jenny slowly detached the clamps and uncuffed Ronnie's wrists. Jenny gently kissed the bruises on Ronnie's wrists and breasts, and she even planted her lips on Ronnie's fragile mound before falling asleep.

It had been exciting and fulfilling. And terrifying. It had been enough.

Ronnie had tried to break it off tactfully on the phone that morning, suggesting they take a break from each other, and Jenny seemed to accept the outcome. Her presence at the restaurant surprised Ronnie.

"Hi," Ronnie said, placing a house draft in front of her.

Jenny's stare could have melted ice. Without saying a word, the patrolwoman grabbed the beer and tossed it in Ronnie's face. Ronnie reached for a towel while Jenny exited and the other nearby patrons sat stunned.

"Should we do that instead of a tip?" someone asked.

Ronnie wiped the beer out of her eyes and turned to the voice. She found herself staring at an attractive brunette with curly hair and deep brown eyes. She searched for words, wanting to deliver an equally witty retort, but her brain stalled. "Drinks in my face are reserved for special customers," she mumbled. Not witty at all.

The woman ran her hand through her curls and laughed at the weak response. Ronnie smiled and wondered if she was drunk.

"Look," the woman said, "I'm caught in this nightmare called my surprise birthday party." She motioned to the back room, and Ronnie realized this was the guest of honor from the lesbian birthday party. The group had already ordered forty drinks and showed no signs of slowing down. "Anyway," she continued, "my friends have promised that they'll let me go home after this round, if I would come out here and ask you a question."

Ronnie realized the woman was not drunk, just terribly embarrassed as she shifted her weight from one foot to the other. "What's your question?"

The woman sighed and looked at the bar. She inhaled and whispered, "My friends want to know if you're gay or straight."

"What's your name?"

"Diane."

Ronnie looked toward the back room. Ten lesbians were lined

up against the glass wall in various states of inebriation. When they saw Ronnie watching them, some waved, others blew kisses, and one mouthed, *I want you.*

"Listen, do you really want to get out of here?"

Diane raised her head, her gorgeous brown eyes pleading for help. "Yes."

Without another word Ronnie leaned across the bar and kissed her squarely on the lips. "Happy Birthday, Diane."

6. A Surprise for Diane

Something was wrong. Daylight bathed the entire bungalow. Diane's mind quickly registered that it was the first day of school, and she was late. She sat straight up in bed and stared at her clock, which read seven forty-five. Her alarm had not gone off at six thirty, most likely because her very fat, belligerent tabby, Claude, was perched on top of the clock radio, his large rear end depressing the alarm buzzer.

"Damn it, Claude," Diane muttered. She showered and dressed at warp speed. Fortunately she'd already chosen her outfit for the first day, a power suit that would command the respect of her students and accentuate the parts of her figure that were still somewhat attractive. By the time she parked the BMW in front of the Social Sciences building, she had ten minutes to rush to her office and gather her materials for class.

The hallways were filled with lost freshmen and returning

students engaging in mini-reunions, recounting tales of the summer. Several students called to her, but she could only wave and continue her dash up the four flights of stairs.

"Shit," she exclaimed when she saw that her office door was already open. Only one person had the ability and, to some slight extent, the right to enter her office. At the sight of Elliott Michaelson, her department chairman, sitting at her desk and talking on his cell phone, Diane slammed her briefcase down in front of him. "May I help you, Elliott?"

Michaelson hurried a good-bye and slipped the phone into his jacket pocket. "Diane, I apologize for the intrusion, but I thought you would be here a little earlier." He checked his watch disapprovingly. "It is, after all, the first day of classes."

Diane seethed and busied herself by opening her briefcase to hide her anger. "I'm well aware of what day it is, Elliott. And what could I have possibly done in the last two minutes to warrant your presence in my office, and *in my chair*?"

Michaelson slowly rose, ascending to his full six-feet and four inches. It was his attempt at intimidation. "I just wanted to give you the courtesy of telling you that Stacy Armbruster has agreed to be my teaching assistant."

Diane shook her head. "No, that's wrong. Stacy agreed to work with me this semester."

"Well, apparently, she changed her mind," he said, folding his arms across his chest. The matter was evidently concluded, and he'd won.

"What the hell is going on, Elliot?" Diane snapped. Several students slowed their pace in front of the office.

Michaelson held up his hand for silence. "I only offered her a job, Diane. I had no idea she had already agreed to work for you. Ms. Armbruster certainly didn't mention it."

"Bullshit! Did you shovel any of your homophobic crap on her, Elliot? Maybe suggest that I would make a pass at her during a long work night? Try to run away with her to San

Francisco?" Diane could only picture the preppie Stacy Armbruster, gasping and blushing all the way from the pinpoints of her Oxford cloth shirt to the bottoms of her penny loafers while Michaelson disparaged Diane's name.

Michaelson's face turned beet red and a vein in his neck enlarged. Diane knew she'd gone too far, but she continued to meet his stare. "I'm only here as a courtesy, Dr. Cole. You'll need to find a new teaching assistant." He stormed toward the door, then turned to add, "And I suggest you show a little more respect for your department chairman."

"Damn it," Diane muttered. It was only the first day of the term and already she'd pissed off the man who wrote her evaluation and controlled much of her professional livelihood. On top of that, she had lost her TA and research assistant. In other words, Elliot Michaelson had just cut off her right arm. As she walked to her class, she practiced some breathing techniques her friend Judy had taught her. The day would surely get better, and she was starting the semester with the graduate seminar, comprised of the students she advised, the students who loved her and valued what she said. These were the students who wanted to be sociologists; she'd known many of them since their undergraduate days. It was like a small family, somewhat dysfunctional at times, but usually cohesive and always supportive of her. They would be a welcome sight after the morning's beginnings.

"Good morning, everyone," she said as she entered the room.

The twelve master's and doctoral students greeted her, and it was only when she turned around completely, to face the class and introduce the four new students into "the family," that her eyes locked on the tall blonde in the second row.

The woman was the most beautiful person she'd ever seen, and indeed, she had seen her before. In fact, they had kissed on Diane's fortieth birthday. At the sight of the bartender Diane gave up hope for the first day of school. She realized nothing could salvage it, not even her power suit.

7. Ronnie Confides in the Gang

"I can't believe this question!" Brody exclaimed, holding up the game card. "Name Howdy Doody's human partner."

"Buffalo Bob," Ronnie replied.

Dave moaned. "You get all the easy questions, Ronnie."

"Now, that's not true," Vandella disagreed. "She knew the Australian airline was Qantas. None of you white boys knew that."

Ronnie rolled the dice while her roommates watched her advance to the center for the win.

"All right, folks, what should we give her?" Richard asked.

"Give her geography," Brody suggested.

Van shook her head. "No, give her science. She sucks at science."

Richard, Brody and Dave nodded their assent, and Brody pulled the next card, scanning the question. "Unbelievable," he said. "What is the common name for deoxyribonucleic acid?"

Ronnie took a deep breath and tapped her finger to her forehead. "Hmm. Let me see. Would that be DNA?"

Everybody groaned and Richard stood up, collecting beer bottles. "Who wants another one?" All four hands shot up in the air. "Why did I ask?" He sighed.

Brody grabbed the card box and started flicking cards on the table. "That does it. I'm getting rid of all the easy questions," he snapped.

"It won't matter," Ronnie said. "My superior intellect will prevail."

Brody snorted. "Damn grad students all think they're so smart."

"Speaking of school," Van said, "Ronnie, how are your classes?"

"They're great," Ronnie replied, her mind automatically focusing on her graduate seminar. After completing a month's worth of classes, Ronnie gauged Carlson would be highly challenging, but clearly it would be Dr. Cole's class that would require the most work.

As if Van could read her mind, she asked, "How's Dr. Cole? Don't you just think she's terrific?"

At the mention of the professor, Ronnie felt heat on the back of her neck. She couldn't explain the emotional reaction that occurred whenever she saw Diane Cole or thought about her, but it was evident.

Brody looked up from the card box. "Wait. Is this the same professor you macked lips with at the restaurant? The one who almost got you fired?"

Ronnie looked down, trying to suppress a grin.

"Excuse me?" Vandella raised an eyebrow.

Brody laughed. "Not only did Ronnie lock lips with this dyke professor, but Officer Jenny threw a drink in her face."

"Who's throwing drinks?" Richard asked as he placed a tray

of beers on the dining table. "I hope I'm not missing any drama."

Vandella crossed her arms and glared at Ronnie. "You're not missing any more than I am, Richard."

"I'm lost too," Dave whined. "What happened with Officer Jenny? I liked her. It was comforting to have a law enforcement presence in the house. Did your breakup have anything to do with the professor?"

"Stop! All of you," Ronnie pleaded. "It wasn't that big of a deal."

"Yeah, right," Brody retorted. "Randy got so pissed about the commotion at the bar that he threatened to fire you." Ronnie just shook her head and rolled her eyes. Brody turned to the other roommates. "First, Jenny was all upset because Ronnie dumped her—"

"You dumped Jenny?" Dave interrupted.

Ronnie smiled at him. Dave was always the hopeless romantic, and even though he and Richard cheated on each other shamelessly, they always came back together and probably always would.

"May I continue?" Brody asked. "So this dyke professor sees it and says something to Ronnie. Her friends are all trashed in the back room, daring her to talk to Ronnie. Ronnie kisses her, and the whole restaurant goes wild. You should have heard all those dykes cheering for Ronnie."

"Would you stop using the word *dyke*?" Ronnie said.

"Why?" Brody was puzzled.

Vandella answered for her. "It is offensive, Brody."

"So what the hell else do you call women who suck off other women?"

"You call them lesbians," Richard said.

Brody sighed. "Anyway, the les-bi-an almost got Ronnie fired."

"It doesn't sound to me that the lesbian professor was to blame," Vandella observed. The room went quiet as Ronnie met

Vandella's gaze. "Out," she commanded to the others, pointing to the living room.

The three men complied and headed for other parts of the house.

Vandella took a deep breath and fingered the beaded African necklace she wore around her neck. "Let me address my emotions first. Why didn't you tell me about any of this? I thought I was your new best friend here in the City of Angels. Who is teaching you to be a true Angelino? I am hurt, Ronnie."

Ronnie hung her head. "I'm sorry, Van. I think I felt a little ashamed to tell you. I know that you're close to Dr. Cole, and she's your advisor . . ." Ronnie didn't know what else to say.

"When did this happen?"

"A week before the term began."

Van processed the series of events thoughtfully while Ronnie waited for her to speak. Eventually she asked, "Why did you kiss her?"

Ronnie's throat went dry, and she shrugged. She had no answer. "I don't know. I had no idea who she was, though."

"How was it?"

Ronnie smiled and blushed, remembering that night several weeks ago and Diane's soft lips. Diane had seemed startled momentarily, but instead of pulling away, she had leaned farther into Ronnie, clearly enjoying it.

When their lips parted, Diane's eyes were closed. The bar was as quiet as it was when it was empty, and only when Diane opened her eyes and whispered something Ronnie couldn't understand did Ronnie hear the deafening roar of the patrons around her.

"So where do you stand with her now?" Van asked, pulling her away from the memory. "If neither of you knew the other, then it must have been a shock on the first day of classes." She laughed.

Ronnie joined in Van's laughter. "It was really funny to me, but I don't think Dr. Cole felt the same way. She took one look at me and never looked my way again. She went around and asked everyone to introduce themselves, and she made me go last. For everybody else, she offered these wonderful heartfelt welcomes, and then she glossed over me like I was nothing."

"That doesn't sound at all like Dr. Cole," Van said. "She's the epitome of compassion and good manners. I would guess she was embarrassed and probably a little worried that you would bring it up."

"All I know is that the other students were asked every acceptable personal question and all she asked me was my name. It was really obvious that she was uncomfortable."

"Have things improved? You've been in her class for a month now. Is it still so awkward?"

"Yeah, it's a little better. I think she realizes I'm not going to go to the campus newspaper and report that one of the sociology professors is an excellent kisser."

Van still looked troubled. "I'm not sure this is a good situation for you. If she can't get past this and give you what you need from an advisor, then maybe you should switch. Camille Eberhardt is a close friend of Dr. Cole's and a very good professor."

The thought of changing advisors had already crossed Ronnie's mind, but she enjoyed seeing Dr. Cole twice a week. "I don't want to do that. You were right. She's a great instructor, and I'm learning so much."

"And she's easy on the eyes," Van added, gauging Ronnie's reaction.

"Yes, that's true." Ronnie laughed. "I'm just hoping we'll have a breakthrough soon. I think she'll be really impressed with the paper I just turned in. It's a precursor to choosing our topic for our thesis. I'm studying phallocentric smog."

Van's eyes widened. "What?"

"Well, it has to do with barriers to women as they climb the corporate ladder or make progress in society. Anyway, it's just an idea I'm exploring, but I've poured my heart into this paper."

Van tapped her index finger on the table. "I'm not comfortable with any of this, Ronnie. I hope you don't destroy your education, your personal life or both."

8. The Confrontation

Diane checked her watch and realized she still had ten more minutes before class. Perfect. She could organize her notes for the day's seminar and do the filing that was growing into a mountain on the corner of her desk. She sighed. It was six weeks into the term and she still didn't have a teaching assistant. Losing Stacy Armbruster to Elliot proved a blessing. The girl was a subpar student, and she wouldn't have met Diane's expectations. Now, Diane was determined to hold out for the right person. Although many of her grad students had inquired, she was very particular. As she stared at the stack of files, a symbol of the disorder that had invaded her life, she reminded herself that an unqualified TA would only make her life miserable.

She checked her watch again. She now had nine minutes. Just as she was about to pick up the files and address the task, a knock sounded on the door. She closed her eyes and took a breath before turning to the student who was inevitably going to swallow what little time she had left to herself. Such was the downside of being highly accessible to students, even though it paid massive dividends in her yearly student evaluations. She was surprised to see Ronnie Frost at her door, and even more surprised to realize that her mouth had gone dry.

"Dr. Cole, do you have a moment?"

"Of course, Ronnie. Please come in," she said, motioning to a chair. Diane savored Ronnie's tanned legs as she sat down. An eclectic dresser, today Ronnie wore a muted Hawaiian shirt and khaki shorts, although it was just as likely that she could appear in class wearing leather pants (Diane's personal favorite) or a flowing gauze skirt with a white peasant blouse. There was nothing usual or predictable about this woman and Diane was fascinated by her, not to mention the fact that she was an incredible kisser, and as much as she tried, Diane couldn't put that memory out of her mind.

She watched Ronnie pull some papers from her backpack, and Diane's face fell when she realized why Ronnie was in her office.

"You wrote on my paper that you wanted to see me," Ronnie said. She set the document in front of Diane and folded her hands in her lap. "Since *See Me* was the only thing you wrote, can I assume there's a problem?"

Diane took a swallow of her coffee. She hated these conversations. "I have concerns about it."

"Concerns? What kind of concerns?"

Diane ran her hand through her thick hair. "There were several problems. First, your grammar and use of language was impeccable. Your use of vocabulary was exceptional, probably the best I've seen in years."

Ronnie shook her head and said somewhat defensively, "So? I'm a great editor with a passion for the English language."

"Still, such perfection is highly unusual for a report of this

45

length."

"I'm an unusual student, Professor," Ronnie said with a smile.

Diane looked down, avoiding Ronnie's eyes. "What really surprises me is the depth. I can't believe a new grad student is capable of research at this level. I know doctoral candidates who don't research this thoroughly. And some of your sources, well, I've never even heard of them."

"It sounds like you're praising my work."

"If it is your work," she said softly.

Ronnie's smile evaporated. "Are you accusing me of plagiarism?"

"Let's just say that I question whether or not you wrote this." She held up Ronnie's report.

Ronnie grabbed her paper and stood. "Dr. Cole, that's my work. I wrote it. If it's not cited or it doesn't have quotation marks around it, then it's mine. Good or bad, it's mine."

Skeptically, Diane leaned back in her chair, running her fingers through her curls. "Can you prove it?"

"How?"

"Show me your notes. Let me see your working outline."

Ronnie's cheeks reddened and she looked away. "Um, that's not going to be possible. My notes had an unfortunate accident with a bottle of Merlot."

"Then we have a problem," Diane said flatly.

Ronnie slumped back into the chair and stared out a window.

"You could rewrite the paper," Diane suggested.

"Excuse me?" Ronnie snapped. "Why should I do that? I already wrote it!" She dropped the paper in front of Diane in a gesture of defiance.

Diane held up a hand, knowing it wouldn't address the real issue. She flipped through the report again, scanning the bibliography page. "There is one other way."

9. Diane Makes a Proposal

Three days later on a Saturday morning, Ronnie stood outside the Carlson library finishing her coffee and cigarette. Although she had smoked only twice since arriving at grad school, the idea of meeting Dr. Cole alone had made her nervous—and excited. She sat down on a bench outside and waited for the professor. When her mother's ring tone chimed, she jumped.

"Hi, Mom."

"Hey, Ronnie, it's Dad. I hope I didn't wake you up."

Ronnie's face brightened at the sound of her father's voice. He didn't call often, and it was a pleasant surprise when he did. "No, I can only talk for a sec. I'm meeting someone at the library to work. How's everything going?"

"Oh, it's okay."

Ronnie could hear the hesitation in his voice. Something was wrong. "Dad, what's going on? You don't sound normal."

"Well, Ronnie, your mother took a little spill and broke her hip yesterday. It's nothing to be too worried about. She'll be fine, but she'll need some time to heal."

"That's awful. Do you need me to come home?"

"No, no. I've got it under control. All of our friends and your mother's coworkers at the library have been very helpful. You stay at school, and we'll see you at Christmas."

"Are you sure? Thanksgiving's next week, and I could come home then."

"No, no. We're good. Really."

Ronnie listened carefully, trying to read between the lines. Her father was the master of understatement. To him the Titanic was a little boating accident. She pictured her mother lying in a hospital bed and was just about to insist that she come home for the holiday, when her father spoke again.

"Okay, honey. I'll call you tomorrow. Stay well."

He hung up before she could say anything else, and Ronnie slowly holstered her cell phone.

"Hey," someone called.

She turned to see Dr. Cole approaching. Dressed in jeans and a white T-shirt, the professor looked like one of the other students. A shiver went up Ronnie's back at the sight of her and suddenly she didn't mind giving up a Saturday. "Hi."

Diane frowned and touched Ronnie's arm. "Is everything okay?"

"My dad just called and told me that my mom broke her hip."

"Oh, no. Is she going to be all right?"

Ronnie nodded. "Yeah, it was just surprising."

Diane motioned to the library. "Are you okay to do this now?"

"Yeah, I'm fine." Ronnie drowned her cig in the last few drops of coffee and tossed the cup into a garbage can at the entrance. They headed to the third-floor reference section and found an empty table. Using the bibliography as a guide, Ronnie pulled the sources and showed Diane the actual raw data. It was like doing the research again only at light speed. Ronnie was determined to do in a morning what had taken her two weeks to do for the real report.

Ronnie showed Diane the specific passages she could remember and Diane checked the footnotes against the sources cited. By the time they had exhausted the sources around them, it was clear that a role reversal had occurred. Ronnie was the teacher and the professor was the student, experiencing the library for the first time from an entirely new perspective.

"The rest is up on the fifth floor," Ronnie directed. She stood up but Diane motioned for her to sit down again. Ronnie watched as Diane thumbed through the paper.

When Diane finally looked at her it was with kind eyes. "There's no doubt in my mind now that you wrote this report. Just watching your behavior this morning was enough to convince me of that. You're an excellent researcher, it's a wonderful paper and I'm sorry I ever doubted you."

Ronnie's face flushed and her heart pounded. "That's all right."

"I feel bad that you wasted your Saturday morning."

"That was my own fault. I should have been more careful."

Diane grinned. "You've learned not to drink wine while you work."

Ronnie's cheeks reddened. "Something like that."

The story was much more embarrassing, involving some unexpected sex in her living room with the UPS delivery woman. No one was home when the wiry brunette drove up to drop off a care package for Ronnie from her mother. They wound up naked on the sofa, and it was only after they pleasured each other fully that Ronnie noticed the overturned wine bottle and the puddle on her notes. Fortunately Ronnie had already saved her paper to the computer.

"It's too bad you lost those notes. You could probably use them again. I'll tell you, when the work piled high and I'd run out of time, I often recycled a report. It saved my butt."

Ronnie grimaced. "I wouldn't do that. Then I'd miss out on this part," she said, glancing around the reference section.

Diane looked at her like she was an idiot. "You really love research, don't you?"

Ronnie brightened. "It's just so incredible to think about all that we don't know, but it's right here." She paused, embarrassed. "Well, I think it's pretty incredible."

Diane smiled. "Listen, Ronnie, let me buy you a cup of coffee."

They wandered down Pine Street to a coffeehouse nestled on a cliff overlooking the ocean. The view from their balcony table was incredible. They talked freely about school, education, society and politics. Ronnie felt a connection, and when Diane's knees occasionally brushed against her own, she sensed the professor felt it, too. Several students stopped by to talk to Diane, interrupting the conversation, but Diane was always cordial and welcoming.

As a trio of undergrads wandered away from their table, Ronnie said, "I can understand why you're so popular with your students."

Diane shook her head. "You're fooling yourself. Those girls came over here to stare at you. The one on the far left? The only reason she passed was because my Christmas spirit got the best of me."

Ronnie stirred her coffee and met Diane's gaze. She could stare at her all afternoon, losing herself in the professor's deep brown eyes. Diane didn't seem to mind, and in fact, Ronnie realized, Diane was staring right back. They sat in silence for far longer than seemed polite, looking at each other. The appearance of another one of Diane's grad students broke the spell.

"Hello, Dr. Cole," Stacy Armbruster announced.

Diane acknowledged Stacy with a nod. Stacy was a true preppie, with an upper-crust background. Her wardrobe was entirely comprised of designer labels and she dropped names of stores and couture that Ronnie had never heard of. Her family was apparently well known back East and had made their fortune in steel—old money, which Ronnie knew meant super rich.

Ronnie disliked Stacy, not because of her wealth, but because she was so shallow. During class, Stacy was ready to offer up opinions on everything, but she could never probe beneath the surface. Ronnie had noticed the large red D on Stacy's paper and heard the heated temper tantrum between Stacy and the professor.

As she stood in front of them, all smiles, the incident was forgotten and the brownnosing was in full operation. "I wanted to know if you'd seen this recent article in *Ms.*, the one about lesbians and power." Stacy's head bobbed when she spoke, or maybe it was just her pageboy haircut.

"No, I haven't seen it," Diane said as she took the magazine. "Thanks. How's everything going with Dr. Michaelson?"

At the mention of the department chair, Stacy's face reddened. "Oh, it's fine. He's got me doing some very important research."

"I'm sure," Diane replied.

"Hi, Ronnie," Stacy said, finally acknowledging that Diane was with someone.

"Hi, Stacy."

Stacy returned her attention to Diane, clearly having fulfilled her quota of pleasantries with Ronnie. Ronnie watched the waves crashing against the rocks, ignoring the conversation that followed and focusing on the breeze that washed over her like silk. She tuned out Stacy's blabbering and didn't even notice when her pageboy had bobbed away.

"Ronnie," Diane said, her hand grazing Ronnie's arm. "Where were you?"

"Anywhere that doesn't involve Stacy," Ronnie replied mildly.

"I don't get that luxury," Diane whispered conspiratorially. Almost as an afterthought she added, "I'd advise you to watch your back with Stacy."

Ronnie shrugged. "Why?"

Diane looked out at the sea. "You don't fit her image of a lesbian. She's liable to see you as an enemy."

"I don't understand," Ronnie said, puzzled.

"Stacy is straight as an arrow, and you, well, in her eyes, you should be straight, too."

Ronnie let out a laugh. "Why me? Does she want the whole world to be straight?"

Diane picked up her coffee cup and held it between her hands. "Stacy doesn't have issues with people who are different as long as they fit her mold. And you certainly don't."

"What does that mean?"

"You don't look like a lesbian," Diane said plainly. "Now," she said, clearing her throat and sitting up straight, "Ronnie, I have a proposition for you."

"Oh, really?"

Diane's face turned red. "Let me rephrase that. I have a *business* proposition for you. I'm compiling an enormous amount of data for a book on homosexuality in the American public school setting. I'm going to need a fabulous research and teaching assistant. One with the patience of a saint, the writing ability of Kate Millett and the mind of Margaret Mead."

"And here I am."

"Yes. Here you are. There is one problem. I usually don't hire students I've known for less than a year. That gives me ample opportunity to apprise myself of their work ethic, their research capabilities and, frankly, how compatible I would be with that person, considering we spend a lot of time together."

"You don't think we'd be compatible," Ronnie said.

Diane laughed and ran a hand through her curls. "What I

meant was, well . . . I'm not sure about you."

"Why not?"

Diane took a sip of coffee before she looked at Ronnie. "I'm thinking of that night in the bar. Why did you do it?"

Ronnie responded with a shrug. "Why not? It just came to me at the moment." She decided not to mention that the shape of the professor's lips and the smell of her perfume drove her into action.

"That *moment*, as you call it, could have been disastrous for both of us," Diane said seriously.

"But it wasn't."

"But it could have been."

Ronnie focused on the dark eyes. "*Could* and *did* are two different things, Professor. Life's too short to always worry about what might happen. Spontaneity makes life exciting but I don't imagine you agree."

"You just see things differently when you're older, I suppose." Diane tousled her hair and finished her coffee.

Ronnie bristled at her patronizing attitude, but she could tell she'd struck a nerve. "I have a question for you. What did you whisper after we kissed?"

Diane slowly set her cup down, as if she were placing a rare antique on a shelf. "I don't know what you're talking about," she said, her eyes never leaving the cup.

"Yes, you do," Ronnie insisted.

Diane shook her head a little too vehemently to be believable. "I didn't say anything, Ronnie. I was too shocked."

Ronnie decided to let it drop and changed the subject. "I think you should hire me."

"Why?" Diane folded her arms across her chest.

"You should hire me because I'm a fabulous researcher and I make a mean pan of chicken enchiladas."

"Hmm. I do like chicken enchiladas." She tapped her finger on the table in thought. "This project could take two years to complete. Do you think you could put up with me for that long?"

"Honestly, I'm not sure. I've never been with anyone for two years."

Diane flushed and ran her hand through her hair again, restoring her businesslike demeanor. "How are you going to handle working for me, taking classes and tending bar?"

"It can be done," Ronnie said, sure she could do it. She also realized it would probably be the end of dating, since she had most likely just committed the remainder of her non-sleeping hours. After classes, work, her own research and now Diane's job, there would only be a few hours a day to sleep—and not with anyone else. Yet as she stared across the table at the attractive older woman whose curly hair fluttered in the light breeze, she found herself eager to spend time with the professor.

Suddenly Dr. Cole pulled her briefcase to the table. "All right, Ronnie, I'll give you a chance." She withdrew a thick file folder and set it on the table between them. "Here is everything I have so far. At this point much of the research has been compiled and now the data must be analyzed. Also included are my early notes and a peripheral glance at the topic of homophobia in public school settings. What I'm attempting to do is to explain how the public school system promotes homophobia through the culture it creates."

Ronnie cocked her head. "How so?"

"When you think about the textbooks and resources that are chosen for schools, the social norms that are established and the general attitudes of teachers toward homosexuality, you can see that a climate of intolerance is created. I want to get specific about what is happening and how it is happening. We're spending a lot of energy now talking about gay support groups in high schools and teaching tolerance, but I want to go back a step and see how we got to this point in the first place. How do schools contribute to homophobia and how can this be changed. What do you think?"

"It sounds fascinating. My mother's the librarian at Globe Junior High, and I remember her complaining that there weren't any books about alternative lifestyles in the library. She thought that was wrong."

Diane smiled and nodded. "I take it you're out to your parents?"

"Oh, yeah." Ronnie picked up the file folder. "Okay, what do you want me to do first?"

"What I need is for you to start analyzing the data. There's a huge amount of research here. Also, we'll need to start working on a bibliography of sources for the outline. This includes abstracts, theses, articles, anything related to the topic."

Ronnie inhaled and raised her eyebrows. "This is a rather broad topic. When do you want this bibliography, Dr. Cole?"

"Please," she said, "now that you're my research assistant, call me Diane. And I'd like it by Monday."

Ronnie blinked in surprise.

"Is there a problem?"

"No. None whatsoever."

"Good. I'll see you on Monday." She stood, ready to leave. "So, do you have any questions for me?"

Later Ronnie realized she should have asked how much it paid, exactly what the job description was and a multitude of other things, but all she could think about was the two of them sipping Coronas and eating chicken enchiladas.

"Is there anything else I can do for you? Maybe pick up your dry cleaning?" Ronnie asked.

A wry smile crept onto Diane's face. "Only after I know you better."

10. The Happiest Place on Earth

Sunday traffic on I-5 moved swiftly at seven thirty in the morning. Vandella's minivan whipped in and out of lanes, passing all of the slow drivers who couldn't or wouldn't do eighty. She shook her head in frustration at a tiny sedan doing fifty-five in the fast lane. "Damn drivers need to stay out of my lane, especially those tourists from Arizona. Zonies are the absolute worst!"

"No kidding," Brody agreed from the back.

"I don't know," Dave said. "I think the old drivers from the Midwest are slower."

"Well, I wish they would all get the hell out of my way," Van shouted, pressing on her horn for the Chevy Malibu with Arizona plates to move over.

Ronnie, riding shotgun, pressed her feet against the floorboard and tried to activate an imaginary brake. "Speaking as a

Zonie, I'd just like to remind you that people from Arizona have guns and lots of road rage," she said.

Van shook her head and honked the horn again. Finally the Malibu moved over to the right. "See. They don't want to mess with a black woman on a mission. And that's what we've got here. A mission to see the Mouse."

"Yes," Richard added. "We are going to the happiest place on earth, so I think we should all be focusing on beautiful, wonderful thoughts, not talk of road rage, guns, hostility or anger."

"Jesus, Richard," Brody mumbled.

"Actually, Jesus would probably be a good subject for Sunday morning," Richard said. Everyone laughed and both the traffic and the mood lightened. Ronnie's heart stopped pounding, and Vandella stopped driving as though she were at the Indy 500.

Ronnie leaned back in the passenger's seat and smiled. When Van had learned that Ronnie had never been to Disneyland, despite living only one state away, she insisted they all indoctrinate the virgin with a pilgrimage to see the Mouse. It would be a perfect finale to her month off from school. Half of it had been spent at home in Arizona, visiting her parents and spending time with her friends. She'd driven into Phoenix five times to hang out at the bars, and she'd made up for lost time by dating several different women. She'd also worked on her thesis outline and finished the winter break reading, but she felt a little guilty for not studying as much as she should. Each day she thought of Diane, and she wondered if the professor was enjoying her vacation in Hawaii with her parents. Diane had sounded only mildly enthusiastic, and Ronnie realized that she and Diane shared a common feeling about parents: they were best enjoyed in small doses.

Diane had phoned once to ask a question about the research, which she was working on in Hawaii. Ronnie answered her question, but they had chatted for over an hour. It had been a highlight of the vacation. Now, with classes looming, Ronnie was determined to have one last day of fun. So instead of studying or indexing Diane's research, Ronnie was spending the day at an amusement park.

Once they arrived Ronnie was pulled in different directions as her roommates urged her to see their own favorite attractions. She was floored by the spectacle that was Pirates of the Caribbean, awed when Abraham Lincoln stood up after reading one of his speeches and totally annoyed by the end of It's a Small World, a ride Richard insisted that everyone must experience once. Her first clue should have been that no one else would go on the ride with them. Instead, Van, Dave and Brody had laughed hilariously as Richard and Ronnie's little gondola disappeared into the tunnel. Ronnie had been entertained not by the spinning dolls, but by Richard, who sang the ride's theme song at full volume and clapped his hands at all the cute boy dolls.

After six hours of rides, eating and shopping, Ronnie was exhausted and everyone was ready to call it a day.

"But wait!" Richard cried. "Ronnie can't leave until she's had her picture taken with a character."

"Richard, she's had pictures taken with you. You're enough of a character," Brody teased.

"No, Richard's right," Van said. Whenever Van spoke everyone knew better than to argue. They wandered over to Main Street, where most of the characters congregated. Ronnie really could have cared less but she wanted to please her friends.

Eeyore and Cinderella were posing with tourists. Given the choice of an ass or a beautiful woman with an incredible figure, Ronnie opted for the princess, much to Van's dismay.

"Don't you understand she represents every stereotype we sisters have fought against for a century or more?" Van asked, grabbing Ronnie by the arm. "All she wanted was her man, someone to take care of her, because she couldn't do it herself."

"Van, I really don't want to be photographed with Eeyore," Ronnie whined.

"What's wrong with Eeyore? Yes, he's got some self-esteem issues, but he's the symbol of the Democratic Party."

Ronnie pulled away from her and smiled. "I'll always be a Democrat, don't worry."

"I don't believe this!" Van pouted.

"Oh, Van," Richard exclaimed. "It's Cinderella! She's got incredible fashion taste, a wonderful work ethic and very dainty feet. What a woman!"

"Besides," Dave added, "she's been staring at Ronnie every since we came over here."

Ronnie needed no further prompting and pulled Richard with his camera over to Cinderella.

"Hi, Cindy!" Richard announced. "My friend Ronnie here has never been to Disneyland."

She stared at Ronnie. "So you're a virgin?"

"At least in one way," Ronnie replied seductively.

Ronnie stepped next to Cinderella, who let one gloved hand caress Ronnie's back and drop into the waistband of her shorts.

"Say cheese!" Richard prompted.

Ronnie smiled, feeling a growing wetness between her legs.

Cinderella turned and whispered, "I'm done in ten minutes. Why don't you let me show you my favorite sites in Disneyland? It will be a goodwill tour."

"I'd love to, but my friends drove me here from L.A."

"Not a problem. I live in L.A. too. I'd be happy to take you home."

The innuendo of Cinderella's words was not lost on Ronnie, who nodded. "Great. So you get off in ten, right?"

Cinderella licked her lips. "No, I'm done working in ten minutes. To get me off, you'll need at least twenty."

After a hasty farewell to her roommates, including a furious Vandella, who didn't mind being dumped nearly as much as she minded Ronnie dating a subservient fairy princess, Ronnie waited outside the characters' entrance.

She didn't recognize the tall brunette with the butch haircut as Cinderella. "I look a little different?" she said, shaking out her short, wet hair.

"Yeah. What happened to the big blonde in the prom dress?"

"I lent the whole outfit to one of my drag queen friends for the evening," she joked.

Ronnie noticed she had a great figure, which included a large bosom. Somehow she'd masked that attribute from the tourist families who stood next to her all day.

"What's your name?" the woman asked.

"Ronnie. And yours?"

"Just call me Cindy."

"Ah," Ronnie said. "I take it we're not going to develop some sort of lasting relationship, huh?"

"Nah, I'm married to Snow White already. Had a big wedding in San Francisco. All the dwarfs came, but that Grumpy sure was a downer. Talk about a homophobic ass."

"Hey, it's okay. No strings. At midnight you turn into a pumpkin."

"Something like that," Cinderella said, clearly pleased that Ronnie understood the situation. "C'mon. I want this evening to be special for you."

Ronnie soon learned Cinderella had connections. They were both starving, and as luck would have it, the manager at the Blue Bayou, Disneyland's nicest eatery, was more than happy to serve an early dinner. Afterward, they wandered through the various lands, Ronnie learning more Disney trivia than she ever wanted to know. They went behind the scenes at several rides, including Richard's beloved It's a Small World. They explored the various secret passages used by security, and before Ronnie knew it, nightfall had come.

"This way," Cindy directed. "I have one more place to show

you."

They walked over the moat of Sleeping Beauty's castle into the interior. They leaned against the wall waiting for a family of five to pass through. When they were alone, Cindy withdrew a key and opened a door Ronnie hadn't even noticed. They silently ascended the stairs to a tower, and Cinderella led her into an alcove that overlooked the entire park.

"This is amazing," Ronnie said. The millions of lights illuminated throughout the park were breathtaking.

Cinderella ignored the view, her arms slipping around Ronnie's waist, her lips kissing Ronnie's ear and her fingers lightly stroking the bare skin between Ronnie's shorts and crop top. She deftly unsnapped Ronnie's shorts and parted the zipper, exploring the curves of Ronnie's buttocks and pushing her thong down between her thighs. Ronnie lolled her head back against Cindy's shoulder only to find the princess's lips and teeth hungrily at her neck. Ronnie winced, knowing the bites would leave a mark.

"We're so naughty," Cindy whispered.

Ronnie understood the nuance of Cindy's statement as she gazed down at the unsuspecting families enjoying the wonder that was Disneyland, while she and Cindy basked in the darkness of anonymity afforded them by the tower window. Ronnie gasped as Cindy's fingers entered her from the front and the back simultaneously.

Ronnie closed her eyes, allowing the princess to work her magic. Ronnie pulled off her shirt and freed her breasts. The breeze kissed her skin, and her nipples hardened immediately. She could feel her knees giving out with Cindy's every stroke and thrust. Cindy was amazingly strong, a fact that would please Vandella, and she refused to let Ronnie sink to the tower floor.

"Oh, no, you don't," Cindy chastised. "We're going to stay right here in front of this window, and I want you to scream as loud as you can when you come."

"What?" She gasped, fighting for breath between the quiet moans that left her lips. Cindy rocked her back and forth, alternating pressure that boiled toward explosion.

"Don't worry. No one will ever hear you above the thirty thousand people who are already talking, laughing and screaming. Disneyland may be the happiest place on earth, but it's also the noisiest," Cindy assured her.

Ronnie hovered near the edge of exhilaration, her gaze fixed on the top of the nearby Matterhorn. Cars whipped in and out of the top tunnel every thirty seconds or so. She knew she was close and she knew she couldn't hold back any longer. As the white metal bullet shot through the tunnel with its passengers, Ronnie screamed in rapture with them. Only after Cindy coaxed three more orgasms from her did she finally allow her to rest on a blanket she kept conveniently stored in the corner. Ronnie watched Cinderella disrobe, and she doubted that the Disney people would approve of the colorful tattoo that covered Cindy's lower backside. Ronnie could give as good as she got, a fact she proved to Cinderella, whose orgasm was undoubtedly heard in Sacramento.

Once spent, they remained in an embrace, lightly caressing each other's arms and backs.

"You are incredibly beautiful," Cindy said. "You *are* Cinderella."

Ronnie started to disagree just as the melodic voice of the Disneyland announcer informed them that the park was closing. "Do we need to go?" she asked.

Cinderella cupped Ronnie's face and kissed her deeply. "Not yet. We've got at least a half-hour." She pushed Ronnie down on the blanket, while her lips worked their way down Ronnie's abdomen. Just as she was about to enter Ronnie's personal "Happiest Place on Earth," she brought her head back up. Using a voice and a smile that only a Disney employee could possess, she said, "I hope you've enjoyed your stay at Disneyland. It's been a pleasure to service you. Please come again."

11. Point/Counterpoint

"All right, Diane, I think I found them," Ronnie called from a stack of papers on the floor.

"My notes?" Diane asked from a corner of the room.

"No, the Lilliputians. They're demanding better housing."

"Very funny, Ronnie. Keep looking. I've only got ten more minutes!"

Ronnie stood up and surveyed the mess in Diane's office. As January turned into February, they were amassing many resources, studying the possibilities for what would become the focus of Diane's book. Books and papers were set out everywhere in a form of organized chaos. Somehow, amid all of the references and articles, Diane had misplaced her notes for her Courtship and Marriage class.

"Well, they're not in that corner," Ronnie announced.

"God," Diane said in exasperation. "How did the office get

this bad?" Ronnie opened her mouth, but Diane pointed at her and barked, "Don't say anything. Keep looking."

Mondays were always extraordinarily hectic. Diane had the graduate seminar first thing in the morning, with only a fifteen-minute break until her Courtship and Marriage class. The two were polar opposites—the graduate seminar an intimate setting filled with students who had made a commitment to sociology, and C&M, which any undergraduate could take to fulfill his or her social science credit.

C&M met every Monday, Wednesday and Friday at Peck Lecture Hall. Ronnie often attended just for the opportunity to watch Diane teach, and sometimes as Diane's TA, she gave the lecture in Diane's absence, when Dr. Cole needed to be at an oral defense or in a meeting. She loved the students and they all knew her. During this class Diane would attempt to get personal with eighty-five apathetic students, usually sophomores and juniors who had taken the course hoping to find romance or at least to develop a better understanding of it.

Ronnie knew Diane loved teaching the class after the first week, once she had weeded out the students who thought it would be easy. "I have this speech," Diane had told her, "that usually scares the shit out of some of them."

"What do you say?"

"I walk in, drop my stuff on the podium and look out at them. Then I say, 'Okay, people, listen up. Before we look over the hell I'm about to put you through, let's get one thing straight. There is no Prince or Princess Charming. If you've come to this course with the idea that you will find the person of your dreams, then you will be very disappointed. Also, if any of you already are couples, you may want to think twice about being here together. This is not marriage counseling. They're not paying me enough for that. And finally, if you think this is going to be an easy, blow-off class, you're sorely mistaken. For that you'll need to go to the philosophy department.' That little speech tends to eliminate the worst students," she said.

"What happened to hello, my name is Dr. Cole?" Ronnie laughed.

"Oh, that part comes later," Diane assured her.

Now that the term was half over, it was obvious that Diane had taken a huge class and made it interesting and intimate for the remaining eighty-five attendees, an impressive success, Ronnie thought, even if she didn't always agree with Diane's viewpoints.

"I'm giving up," Diane announced, plopping into a chair. She reached into the minifridge and found a bottle of water.

"They're around here somewhere," Ronnie insisted, bending over another stack. She hunted through several papers, focused on her task.

Only when she heard Diane say, "Elliott, are you coming in, or are you going to leer at my TA all morning?" did she think to stand up, realizing her rear end and tight jeans had been facing the open door.

His face flushed, Elliott Michaelson stood in the doorway. Ronnie was afraid to look at any other part of his body other than his pointy head, for fear she would see an enormous erection protruding from his pants.

Michaelson ignored Diane's comment and held out a list to her. "Diane, I cannot order all of these additional books that you want. There just isn't enough money."

Diane scanned the pages, her anger clearly growing. "I see. But there's enough money to order everything Doug wanted, and you're getting all of your materials."

Michaelson snatched the papers from her and glared at her. "I am the department chairman. I have needs."

"Damn it, Elliot. So do I. I can't exactly pilot a new class without resources. You've cut out every single request I made for my Women in World War Two class except the text."

"Yes, and frankly I have trouble seeing how we can justify

more than one book for that course, let alone the course."

The veiled threat hung in the air and Michaelson's eyes never left Diane's face. Of course she knew who made the decisions, Ronnie thought, and he could easily kill her new class with one red line through the schedule of Offerings.

"Fine, I'll take what I can get," she said dejectedly.

"Good choice," he hissed as he stomped out.

Diane returned to her chair and sipped her water. Ronnie leaned against her desk, watching her fume. "Why do you take that crap from him?" she asked gently.

"Because I have to. He's my boss and he's out to get me. He hates me because I'm a liberal and a lesbian. The only reason I'm here is because the year I applied, he was on leave at some rehab center drying out. When he came back and found out the interim department chair had hired me, he was furious. Of course, this was after he tried to seduce me and realized he couldn't have me or change me. The bottom line is, if I do anything questionable, he'll have me in front of the faculty review board."

Ronnie checked her watch. "C'mon, it's time for class."

Diane threw up her hands. "Great. I have no notes. What the hell am I going to do?"

Ronnie rubbed her chin. "I think we should have a debate."

"On what?"

Ronnie smiled slyly. "Well, there is one particular topic on which you and I so strongly disagree—"

"And that is?" Diane interrupted.

"Love."

Diane chuckled. "So, you want us to publicly debate our differing views on falling in love. Is that it?"

Ronnie grinned. "Yes. I think it's time that you see how skewed your opinion really is."

During a lecture the week before, Diane had postulated on the science of love, and Ronnie listened, too stunned to interject to Diane's views. Today would be an opportunity to balance the class's perspective and maybe help the good professor think with her heart.

Diane arched her eyebrows and gazed out the window for a moment. She stood up and faced Ronnie. "Fine. Bring it on."

The students filed in, their conversations echoing throughout the large lecture hall. By now all of them had favorite seats, and small cliques had formed in various pockets. The stadium seating allowed Diane and Ronnie to see everyone, and it was amusing to note where different types of students camped. Diane's "groupies," as Ronnie called them, tended to sit right in the front row center. The group of women hung on every word she said, probably hoping that one day she would go wild and strip off her shirt, hurling it into the audience. They were clearly family, clad in jeans or athletic wear, their short haircuts telegraphing their sexuality.

The more serious students tended to flock toward the middle center just as they would at a movie. They wanted a good seat and didn't want to miss anything, but they also didn't want to be too close. They always arrived first and had their pens poised from the moment Diane began to speak. They often made thoughtful comments and had the highest grades. Ironically, during the regular class periods they tended to be loners, but on test days, people jockeyed for the seats next to them.

"Are you sure you're up for this?" Diane murmured as they approached the podium.

"Absolutely." Ronnie winked as she handed the professor a microphone. She parked herself to the side and waited for Diane to begin. A few of the groupies were practically drooling at Diane's tailored white shirt and black dress pants. Actually she couldn't blame them. They had good taste.

"Okay, people. Let's settle down." Diane glanced again at Ronnie, who nodded. "Today we're going to talk about love in

American culture, which is, of course, an important part of courtship to our society. In fact, it is the driving force of courtship in the twenty-first century. This is, of course, not the case in all cultures. For example, Eastern culture and many religions place greater emphasis on the wishes of family, particularly the patriarch, in arranging marriages. How the intended man and woman may feel about each other is of little consequence. But in our society, it's quite the opposite. Now, before you get married, you supposedly fall in love, and most people believe this happens during the courtship period. So you fall in love and then get married. Right?"

Ronnie watched many heads nod.

"Wrong," Diane declared, her voice booming throughout the hall.

The crowd mumbled at her emphatic response and Ronnie repressed a grin. Hector Ramirez, one of the serious students, raised his hand and Diane pointed to him.

"So, Dr. Cole, are you saying there's no such thing as love?"

"No, Hector, what I'm saying is that love is a much more logical and time-consuming process than what we, Hollywood or the media would like it to be. And actual love is something that doesn't occur until a great amount of time has passed."

Ever polite, Hector raised his hand again before speaking. "I don't know, Dr. Cole. I just got married last summer, and I'm here to tell you it's *primo*—the best. And it's certainly love."

A roar of applause rushed through the room, most of the students siding with Hector. One of the groupies, Destiny, stood and faced Hector. Diane's faithful fans would never allow the class to gang up on her. "I think what Dr. Cole is trying to say is that we confuse love with something else, like infatuation or lust."

Diane beamed at her. "That's it exactly. Love is like an onion, and when we peel away the outer layers, the lust, infatuation and romance, we're left with reality. And that reality is daily life. Can I live with this person on a day-to-day basis? Can I wake up with this person every single day?"

"I sure can," Hector piped up. "You should see my wife."

Ronnie broke into uncontrollable laughter along with the class. Hector was a great guy, and if she were straight, and he were single, he'd definitely get her attention. Diane turned to Ronnie, apparently ready to share the spotlight. Ronnie knew she felt unprepared and vulnerable without her notes.

"I think I'd like to know what Miss Frost has to say about this subject. Ronnie?"

From the look on her face, Ronnie knew Diane was not making a request. She cleared her throat and joined Diane at the front of the stage. "While I agree with Dr. Cole that love can grow over time, I don't agree with her analysis, and it's her desire to analyze the whole concept of love that is creating her faulty conclusions."

A shocked murmur rolled through the class, and Ronnie thought one of the groupies might have passed out. She looked at Diane to gauge her reaction.

The professor narrowed her eyes and gave a slight, amused smile. "I think you need to expand your argument, Miss Frost."

"I just don't think love is an onion, or any other fruit or vegetable for that matter. Love just *is*."

"Oh, that's deep, Ronnie," Destiny the groupie called out.

The class chuckled and Ronnie turned to face them. "You can laugh, but love is a mystery. It's confounded and confused human beings for all of time. Think about it. Poets, artists, musicians and *especially* sociologists spend most of their life trying to understand love. But until you've been in the kind of love where you can't eat or sleep, and work is just out of the question, you can't know." Ronnie stepped toward the groupies and looked at Destiny. "I'm talking about the kind of love that consumes you, makes you feel like the person gives you the air you breathe. When you're truly in love, you'll do things you never thought possible—like go over to your lover's house at three in the morning, just to tell him or her how you feel." Destiny avoided look-

69

ing at Ronnie, who noticed most of the other groupies' mouths had fallen open.

"Have you ever done that, Ronnie?" Hector asked.

Ronnie looked up at him and flashed a wide smile. "Only once," she said playfully. The class cheered and Ronnie stepped back toward Diane, who was looking at her thoughtfully.

Diane raised a hand for silence. "Hold on. I think I should get a chance to respond to this. Are you sure you're not confusing love with lust, Miss Frost?"

"Not necessarily. You can have those feelings for someone and never have slept with them. Love isn't always sexual. Sometimes it involves no physical contact whatsoever. People fall in love through letters or the Internet. It's a connection, one that can happen the moment you see someone."

Diane gasped deliberately into her microphone. "Surely you're not talking about love at first sight?"

"Of course. It's a highly unlikely phenomenon, but for some people, it's really happened."

Diane started to laugh and shook her head, only strengthening Ronnie's desire to prove her opinion.

"Hey, you guys, I don't think Dr. Cole believes me. Raise your hand if you think you've ever fallen in love the moment you met someone." A few hands went up and Ronnie turned to Diane. "There you are, professor, testimonials to love at first sight."

Diane looked at those students and back at Ronnie. "Of those who raised their hands, I'd like to know how many of you are still involved with the object of your affection." When no hands returned to the air, she nodded. "So does that mean you fell out of love with the person, or were you ever really in love?" She paused and when no one responded, she added, "Only time really tells if you're in love with someone. That's why some people have such long engagement periods. Why don't they just run off and get married? And of course some do, and we know what usually happens to those quickie marriages." She was back in full professorial mode. "Remember this: the kind of love necessary to build a relationship is not immediate. There are so many factors—"

"Whoa, hold on, Dr. Cole," Ronnie interrupted. "Factors? Love isn't a math problem. It's irrational. And more than likely, judging from divorce rates, time will hurt a relationship, not help it. We start off with something pure and beautiful and then we corrupt it, and sometimes we kill it. Sure, you meet someone, and over time you get to know the person better, and it might strengthen the love you first felt. But more than likely you weaken it with your words, your analysis and your paranoia. You leave the beauty of your heart for the safety of your mind, thinking you'll only improve the love you feel. But, pretty soon, you're just going through the motions because of daily life. You fight about money, and who's going to pick up the dry cleaning, and who's going to cook, and your jobs. All that stuff gets in the way and the love dies." She looked over at Diane, petrified that she had crossed a line, but Diane gazed at her with admiration, and Ronnie felt her heart start beating again.

"So what's the answer, Ronnie? How do we keep from ruining love?" Diane asked.

Ronnie shook her head. "I'm not sure." She looked at the students. "I can't tell you, and by the end of the semester, I don't think Dr. Cole will be able to tell you either, but you'll have your three credits." She approached the groupies, who looked at her with pure disdain for contradicting their hero. "What I do know is that if you focus on how much you love a person and keep that at the center of your being, then your relationship will follow. It won't always work the other way. Relationships can rarely save love, but love can save relationships."

Several students started applauding and Hector stood up. When the applause had died, he fell on one knee and shouted, "Hey, Ronnie, if my wife doesn't mind, will you marry me?"

12. Diane's Saturday Night

George Winston's piano music filled the bungalow. Diane poured a glass of Chardonnay, found the novel she was reading and settled out on her deck in a redwood lounger. Even though she couldn't see the waves in the black night, she could hear them. Their repetitious sound was soothing and comforting and washed away the loneliness she always felt on Valentine's Day. She detested the contrived holiday, which honored nothing and only supported the chocolate and condom industries. Her thoughts drifted back a week to her debate with Ronnie during C&M. She chuckled, doubting that Ronnie would share her dislike of Valentine's Day, and she frowned when she thought of Ronnie spending the evening with some blonde coed. She reflected and realized she was jealous and basking in self-pity. "How astute of you, Diane," she murmured. Claude jumped in her lap, and she stroked the purring cat. "You love me, don't you,

Claude?"

She focused on positive things. Her classes were going well, her research was on schedule and Ronnie was a godsend. She marveled at Ronnie every day, the way her memory worked, cataloguing information, indexing and cross-indexing. Ronnie was working to assemble the data pieces that Diane would need. She kept an accurate bibliography and had created a skeletal outline for the book that matched Diane's vision. Sometimes she found herself watching Ronnie as the young woman sat immersed in the readings, marking passages or taking notes. When she typed her hands flew across the keyboard, her eyes glued to the screen. She was a workaholic, a driven researcher whose mind never rested, and she reminded Diane of herself.

The phone rang and Diane let the machine pick up. "Diane, it's Ronnie. I know you're there. Pick up."

Diane reached for the phone. "How did you know I was here? Maybe I was out."

"You? Out on a Saturday night? I'm willing to bet that you are sitting on your deck and listening to jazz. Maybe having some wine . . . perhaps a Merlot—no, I think a Chardonnay."

Diane could feel her defenses rising. "So what if I am? What's wrong with spending a Saturday night at home? Not that you would ever do it. But it can be quite enjoyable and relaxing—"

"Hey," Ronnie said, "I was just teasing you a little. Besides, I wasn't guessing that you were home, I *know* you're home. Look out at the beach."

Diane peered at the shore. "I don't see anything."

"What about now?"

Diane watched as a sparkler suddenly illuminated the beach. Ronnie was holding it out and waving it.

She had to laugh. "Ronnie, what are you doing? Fireworks are illegal! What if my neighbors see you?"

"Calm down. It's no big deal. They're just harmless sparklers."

"They're still illegal."

"Do you ever do anything against the rules, Dr. Cole?" Ronnie asked.

"Rarely."

"What about blurring the edges or coloring outside the lines?"

"I really don't know what you're talking about."

"Diane, do you ever park in a red zone if you're only going to be in a store for sixty seconds?"

"Of course not. How do you know you'll really be just a minute? What if it turns into five or six? What if there's a fire?"

"Oh, God." Ronnie sighed.

Suddenly the sparkler was extinguished and the phone line went dead. Diane watched her approach, lit by her deck lights, her blond hair falling loosely around her shoulders. Ronnie looked like any other California girl, wearing board shorts and a large blue cable-knit sweater over her T-shirt. Suddenly the age difference between them seemed to grow to Grand Canyon-size proportions, Ronnie in her beach clothes and Diane in her pressed jeans and button-down shirt. Ronnie, though, didn't seem to notice the difference in their attire, and in fact, Diane may have imagined it, but she thought she caught Ronnie's gaze roaming up and down her body.

"What are you doing here?" she asked as Ronnie ascended the deck stairs. "It's after nine thirty. Shouldn't you be at work?"

"I got the night off since I spent the entire afternoon working a wedding for Randy. I let Sammy have my shift. He can deal with all of those happy couples on their Valentine dates. Also, I wanted to give you the rest of the outline." She took a stack of papers out of her backpack.

Diane quickly scanned them. "You didn't have to do this. I was going to take care of it tomorrow."

Ronnie shrugged. "I had the time and I knew where you were going with it."

"You certainly did," Diane agreed, pleased. The fact that Ronnie could practically read her mind was uncanny and somewhat unnerving. "Would you like some wine?" She motioned with her glass and went inside. "I think I have some cheesecake, too."

Ronnie followed her, gazing at the bungalow's interior while Diane watched her carefully. Ronnie had never actually been inside Diane's house. Their work was always done at school, a policy Diane had adopted only after hiring Ronnie. In the past, she had worked at home with her other teaching and research assistants, but for some reason, she had never suggested they work together on weekends, and she had kept Ronnie separate from her private life. Why this had happened, she couldn't explain.

She watched Ronnie take in the entire space, which was really only one great room divided into areas by furniture groupings and décor, the Pacific Ocean serving as her backyard. Uninhibited by the lack of walls, Diane wasn't afraid to mix styles. Her contemporary living room fronted a country kitchen, which faced the Queen Anne bedroom furniture hidden by some sheer screens that provided a notion of privacy. Her office covered the entire back portion of the house, an attempt to camouflage work from her personal space. In most cases such an assortment of styles would be offensive to the eye, she knew, but the bungalow proved to be an exception.

"This is some place," Ronnie said.

Diane brought the wine and cheesecake to the sofa. "I can't take much credit. My grandfather built it and my father gave it to me. I just picked out the furniture."

"It's incredible," Ronnie murmured. Her gaze settled on Diane's bed. She rose from the sofa and headed to the far side of the room.

As Ronnie peered between the screens, Diane watched her, more than a little uncomfortable at Ronnie's proximity to the queen-sized mattress. She knew she was being entirely irrational, but if Ronnie actually sat down on the comforter, Diane knew she would lose the ability to speak. Instead, Ronnie squatted and gazed through the enormous picture window, giving herself an idea of what Diane saw at the beginning and end of each day.

"If I had this view," Ronnie said, still staring intently at the ocean, "I don't think I'd ever get up."

"That's tempting sometimes."

Ronnie returned to the living area and plopped down next to Diane, putting an appropriate distance between them.

"If tonight is your night off, why are you here? I would have thought with it being Valentine's Day and Saturday night that you'd be out hitting the clubs, dancing the night away," Diane said.

Ronnie swirled the remaining wine in her glass and swallowed it quickly. "Contrary to popular belief, Professor, I do not have a bevy of honeys who keep me warm every night, or a calendar that's full of dates until Christmas. The fact is that I do not have a valentine."

Diane raised an eyebrow. "So all of those stories I've heard aren't true?"

Ronnie gave her a crooked grin. "Well, some of them are true, but much of it is just talk."

"There's a lot of gossip about you floating around the campus, not that I believe any of it. I just want you to be careful," Diane said, concerned.

"I know. I've heard it, and I know dear little Stacy Armbruster is responsible for most of it."

Diane pointed at Ronnie. "Don't underestimate that girl. She'll ruin your reputation."

Ronnie waved off the warning. "That doesn't concern me. I'm not an angel, Diane. I love to have a good time, and I've done quite a bit of dating, but I do what I want to do when I want to do it, and not because I have an image to protect. If I'm here

76

right now it's because it's where I want to be."

Diane felt the air go out of her lungs. "I guess I'm just surprised."

"Why? That I would want to spend time with you? What? Aren't you any fun?"

Diane laughed. "Well, I think so, but I doubt you would."

"Maybe, maybe not. Try me."

"Well, this is fun for me," she said, gesturing to the open room. "I enjoy just sitting and listening to music."

Ronnie nodded in agreement. "What else?"

Diane wracked her brain for something to say, something that would impress Ronnie. "I go out with my friends."

"Would those friends be the same out-of-control group from your birthday party? Now, *they* look like fun."

Diane's face burned at the mention of the evening.

"Don't worry, Professor. I wasn't going to mention the you-know-what," Ronnie added, reaching for the wine and filling both her glass and Diane's. She eyed the bit of Diane's cheesecake remaining on her plate. "Why didn't you finish your dessert?"

Diane shrugged and took a sip of wine. "I never do."

"Why not? That's great cheesecake."

"It is. I just choose not to finish it."

Ronnie leaned back on the sofa and eyed her shrewdly. "Even if you're still hungry? What if you really want that last little bit?"

"I don't. First, my body doesn't need the calories, but also it's a test of willpower. I'm proving to myself that I can control my desires."

"That sounds a little warped. It's cheesecake. It's not like you're trying to control homicidal impulses."

Diane searched for an easy way to explain; she was becoming quite uncomfortable with the conversation. "I just like to be in control of myself at all times."

"Do you ever get drunk? Or smoke weed?"

"I drink," Diane admitted. "But that's different. Alcohol is my one vice. Everything else I do, I do in moderation. I'll try a lot of things but I'll never go overboard. I never lose control under any circumstances. It's just not in my character."

"That explains a lot," Ronnie said, nodding.

"What do you mean?"

"That's why you think you can control love, right?"

Diane chose her words carefully. "To some extent, yes. If you give love to someone a little at a time, and don't go too fast, then you're more likely to have a successful relationship."

"Love in tablespoons, huh?"

Diane squirmed. "Well, maybe a little more than that."

"What about sex? Do you hold back then, too?"

Diane's mouth went dry. Suddenly the room became quite warm and she could feel perspiration on her back. "I've had an orgasm, Ronnie."

"That's not what I'm talking about. I'm talking about pure hedonistic fun for you and your partner, with pleasure to the nth degree. Tell me, Professor, do you ever make love with total abandon?"

Diane was speechless. She watched Ronnie scoop up the cheesecake with the tip of her index finger. She held it out in front of Diane before feeding it to herself. Diane stared as Ronnie pulled her finger from her mouth slowly.

"You ought to try it," Ronnie said.

When she was breathing again, Diane looked up, having regained her composure, safe in her professorial mode. "I was more unpredictable when I was your age."

"Oh," Ronnie said. "So you gave it all up and became mature."

"I wouldn't put it quite that way. You get older and things change."

"You become boring," Ronnie concluded.

"I'm not boring!" Diane snapped.

"Prove it."

Diane noticed that Ronnie was now very close to her, and she wasn't sure whether the wine was affecting her, but if the young woman leaned three inches closer, they would be kissing a second time.

Would that be such a bad thing?

Her heart started to pound, and she found herself wishing Ronnie would kiss her. Of course, she couldn't initiate it. Ronnie was the unpredictable one. Ronnie was the risk taker. That was Diane's past and now she really was boring. She took a deep breath and inhaled Ronnie's cologne. It was intoxicating and made her tingle. What the hell? She could reach back in her mind and remember . . .

Ronnie held up a firecracker, and Diane's resolve withered. "Prove to me you're capable of having some unexpected and slightly illegal fun." Ronnie flashed a killer smile that was only matched by the deep blue twinkle of her eyes.

Diane grabbed the firecracker and headed out to the beach, Ronnie trailing behind. They reached the shoreline and Diane glanced around until she was certain they were alone. She motioned to Ronnie for the lighter and set off the firecracker. It let out a loud pop, which scared Diane so much that she fell backward. Ronnie caught her and brought her back to her feet. They both laughed hysterically, tears streaming down their faces.

"Shit!" Diane pointed to the next bungalow. Her neighbor's porch light had come on, and a silhouette moved past the window toward the door.

Ronnie grabbed Diane's hand and they ran back inside, shutting the curtains and turning out the lights. Ronnie stayed long enough to finish the bottle of wine, assuring Diane she was sober enough to drive home and that Diane's neighbor had not called the police.

Much later Diane replayed the evening as she lay in bed—

Ronnie staring out at the ocean from her bedside, their lips just inches apart and, most of all, Ronnie's strong arms wrapped around her for those few seconds when she lost her balance. She fell asleep imagining they were still intertwined, caught in the comfort of Ronnie's secure embrace, their bodies pressed together.

13. Confrontations

Simply Understated was packed with the regular Wednesday night crowd, and Ronnie and Brody could barely keep up with the drink orders. Ronnie smiled when she realized she had probably cleared two hundred dollars in tips. There would be one more profitable hour left, but by eleven, all of the academics and students would clear out, hastening to get home, knowing that another day of learning was in front of them. Ronnie thought of the two hours of reading that waited in her backpack, and she doubted she would get to bed before three. It seemed that all of the professors were piling on the work, recognizing that spring break was only a few weeks away.

"Hello, Miss Frost," a familiar voice said from over the bar. Ronnie looked up and into the eyes of Elliot Michaelson. He had seated himself on a stool right in front of her and was grinning like a man who had seen something he shouldn't have. Ronnie glanced down, realizing that she was responsible for Michaelson's happiness, the front of her white shirt exposing some significant cleavage.

"What can I get for you, Professor Michaelson?" she asked curtly.

"I'll take a Scotch and soda, but I also hoped we could chat for a moment," he added quickly.

Ronnie glanced around the bar, amazed at his self-centeredness. "I'm rather busy right now."

"I'll speak while you prepare my drink. I'm doing a study on college students and I'm in the process of selecting a few intellectual coeds to be my subjects. I thought you'd be perfect."

Ronnie nodded and mixed the drink, already plotting a diplomatic way to say no to the department chairman.

"Over the course of three evenings you would answer two hundred written and oral questions about college life. For example, your expectations as a graduate student versus life as an underclassman, things like that." He waited for a response but Ronnie just stared. "Of course, you would be paid."

"How much?" she asked, placing the drink before him.

"Five hundred dollars."

Ronnie blinked in surprise. She quickly recognized that there had to be a catch. Her mother had always told her if it sounded too good to be true, it probably was. "Tell me a little more about the logistics."

"Well, it would be for three nights, starting at seven and ending at ten. You'd come to my home—"

"Your house?"

"Yes," the professor said, hesitating. "I've found that my subjects are more relaxed in a less threatening environment. School laboratories can be so cold."

So can the sheets on your bed, Professor, Ronnie thought. She shook her head and said, "I appreciate you thinking of me, Dr. Michaelson, but I really don't have any extra time with school, my job with Dr. Cole and working here at the restaurant. It just isn't feasible." She started to back away from the bar, hoping Michaelson would take the hint that the conversation was over.

"Are you sure, Ronnie? Five hundred dollars is a lot of money."

Michaelson stared at her and she felt dirty. "I know, but my responsibilities to my jobs and my studies need to come first. I'm sure you understand."

He nodded. "Yes, of course. Well, if you change your mind, let me know."

Ronnie busied herself with other patrons, and when she looked up at Michaelson's seat, he was gone, a one-hundred-dollar bill left for her tip.

Brody whizzed by and whispered in her ear, "I think your friend the professor just sat down at table three."

Ronnie looked up to see Diane, dressed in a beautiful navy blue cocktail dress, chatting with two women, one older and one about Diane's age. The older woman had long gray hair and a round face. She was portly and wore a baggy shirt. A dream-catcher necklace rested on her large bosom, and when she spoke, her face came alive, full of animation. The other woman was more butch, dressed in khakis and a button-down shirt. The butch was a stranger, but she knew the older woman was Camille Eberhardt, Diane's best friend and fellow sociology professor.

It only took a second for Diane to scan the bar and find Ronnie, who smiled and nodded her approval at Diane's dress.

Diane had hesitated when Camille and Judy had suggested they get a nightcap at Simply Understated. She reminded them of the birthday debacle, but they argued that the Wednesday crowd would be a different group, and as they found a table, Diane did not notice anyone pointing or gasping. She did, though, notice Ronnie standing behind the bar staring at her.

She smiled at her TA, a fact not lost on either Camille or Judy. "I can't believe that woman is your assistant now," Judy marveled. "Who would have thought?"

"Honey, don't tease Diane," Camille reprimanded her partner. "Apparently she has her hands full with Ronnie." She turned back to Diane. "I heard you had quite the lecture during Courtship and Marriage last month. Tell me, how do you feel about being contradicted by your TA?"

Diane chuckled, remembering Ronnie's passion about the subject of love. "I really didn't mind. We definitely don't agree. She made some good points, though, and she had me thinking."

Judy snorted. "You, the great rationalizer and love destroyer? You considered using your heart to deal with your emotions? My God! Where's a historian when you need one?"

Even Diane had to laugh. When she glanced over at the bar again, Ronnie was smiling at her.

"Now that's very interesting," Camille remarked.

Diane's mind returned to her friend. "What?"

"You looked at her and she gave you a sex smile."

"A what?"

"She smiled at you in a seductive and sensuous manner. That was not a friendly smile. That smile said, *I want you.*"

"Camille, what are you talking about?" Diane asked, her face burning. The waitress brought their drinks, and Diane took a hearty slug of her brandy alexander.

Judy attempted to clarify. "She's talking about you and the coed goddess naked on the bed, rocking back and forth until you have orgasms that blow your brains out."

Diane was aghast. "Are you crazy? She's a student and my TA. Michaelson would have my job in about ten seconds." She drained her drink and motioned to the waitress. "Not to mention the fact that she's only twenty-two."

Camille swirled her wine and looked toward the bar. "That's not what you're really afraid of, my friend, and we both know it.

You've always dated older women and you've never given all of yourself. You worried about your career and made them deal with the relationship. They carried you through it."

Diane opened her mouth to protest, but Judy interjected, "It's true, Diane."

Diane just shook her head. "You are both way out of line."

"What about Nancy? And Susan, and Norene, and of course Alex," Camille put in.

At the mention of Alex's name, Diane winced. Alex was the one ex she truly regretted hurting. "You've both read this all wrong. Ronnie and I have an excellent professional relationship. End of story." She hoped she didn't sound too disappointed at her own summarization of their relationship. "Besides," she added, "Ronnie has several girlfriends."

"And I'll bet she'd give them all up for you," Camille said.

Diane waved off Camille's comment, but her gaze drifted back to Ronnie, who was engrossed in pouring a martini.

"Think about what I'm saying, Di. I've never regretted being with Judy. I know you're worried about the age difference, and the fact that she's still a student. But don't throw away something that could last a lifetime just because it's hard right now." Camille looked at Judy and kissed her on the cheek. "I know I don't have any regrets."

Diane took her second drink from the waitress and glared at her friends. "I'm ending this discussion. I'm not going after some baby dyke student. I'm not interested."

Camille laughed and patted Diane's hand. "Calm down. You've been staring at her since we got here. And she's done the exact same thing."

"That's not true!" Diane spat. "I have been entirely engrossed in our conversation."

"I'll bet you five bucks that you can't stop looking at her."

Diane's eyes widened. "That's going to be rather difficult, considering she's coming over here."

85

The three of them turned to greet Ronnie, who sat down on the fourth chair next to Diane. "Well, you are definitely the best-dressed patron here tonight."

Diane was mortified and Camille and Judy both repressed a laugh. "We just came back from the symphony," Diane explained. She found her manners and introduced everyone. "Ronnie Frost, please meet my friends Camille and Judy. You've probably seen Camille in the sociology department, and Judy is a rape counselor at the women's center."

"I hear you've been quite the participant in the Courtship and Marriage class, Ronnie," Camille said.

"Well, Diane's been nice enough to let me share my opinion."

Camille nodded pleasantly. "Yes, I've heard there have been some fireworks. People who aren't even enrolled in the class are showing up."

Diane continued to smile as the conversation progressed, but she had no idea what was being said, since her entire focus was on the heat that was coursing through her body. Ronnie sat very close to her, their hands almost touching, Ronnie's cologne invading her personal space. If Diane leaned back just a few inches, Ronnie would undoubtedly engulf her in another embrace, and Diane couldn't be responsible for her actions.

"I've got to get back." Ronnie stood up and shook hands with Camille and Judy. When she turned to Diane, her gaze slowly wandered up and down the length of the dress. She kissed Diane on the cheek. "You look absolutely beautiful," she whispered into her ear.

The three of them watched her depart, and Diane shot daggers at a smiling Camille and Judy. "Don't say anything," she warned.

They both raised their hands in submission and ordered another drink. Diane joined them, grateful that they didn't want to leave yet. She needed at least another twenty minutes before her knees would permit her to stand.

By the time Brody and Ronnie had closed the bar and sent the last regular home, it was nearly one thirty. All that remained was the short walk to the Mustang, and then a quick jaunt down the 101. It had been a lucrative evening, counting the lecherous Doctor Michaelson's extravagant tip.

Brody escorted Ronnie down the side street, his arm linked through hers. "Saw you spend your break with the good professor," he said. "You like her, don't you?"

"Can you blame me? God, she looked hot." Ronnie was visualizing the blue dress clinging to Diane's shapely body. She had tried not to stare at her chest, but all she wanted to do was kiss the creamy slopes of her cleavage. "Don't you think she's hot?"

"I'm really not one to judge women," Brody said quietly.

As the weight of Brody's words hit her, Ronnie stopped. "Brody, are you—"

"I'm not anything," he said. "Certainly not a fag."

Ronnie froze and Brody continued ahead. When he reached the next streetlight, Ronnie watched him take a deep breath and rest his back against the pole. He fished a cigarette and a match from his jacket pocket. He stood there smoking, deep plumes of black and blue swirling above his head in the glare of the incandescent light.

Ronnie slowly approached him, hesitant and cautious. She didn't know what to say so she leaned against the pole and gestured for the cigarette. They passed it between them silently until only the filter remained.

"You know I'm your friend, right?"

Brody dropped the butt and squashed it with the toe of his boot. When his eyes finally met Ronnie's, he nodded slightly.

"No one cares, you know?" she said. "We all just need to be happy."

He opened his mouth, as if desperately wanting to talk but unable to speak. He pulled his gaze away from hers and stared at the street.

"We're all your friends," she whispered. "You can be yourself around us."

"I am," he suddenly spat, pulling his large frame away from the streetlight and lumbering down the street. "C'mon," he called. "No more bullshit."

14. The Graduate Seminar

Ninety-five percent of the students in Diane Cole's graduate seminar were women, and ninety percent of that ninety-five percent were lesbians. Ronnie calculated that this equated to two heterosexual women—Stacy Armbruster and a cool lady named Jill, as well as a guy named Hank, who thankfully seemed secure with his own sexuality and all the lesbians' sexuality as well. Ronnie was sure that he visualized himself in a threesome with every woman in the class, including Diane. Of course he never would have verbalized his fantasies for fear of being castrated.

While the purpose of the seminar was to provide a forum for the students to discuss their master's or doctoral theses, more often than not the discussion shifted to general feminist topics, which suited everyone just fine as far as Ronnie could tell. Even Hank didn't seem to mind, although Ronnie wondered when they would find the time to discuss Hank's topic, the emaciated male of the 21st century. Actually, she thought, the seminar itself was probably proving to be the best source of confirmation he could find.

"I just don't understand why matriarchal societies are not more prominent," Cassie Bell whined. Ronnie closed her eyes. There were only two people in the seminar who drove her nuts—Cassie Bell and Stacy Armbruster.

"It's because men create the societies and women fulfill an established role," Stacy explained.

Perfect, Ronnie thought. Stacy and Cassie had both spoken. Her day was complete.

"I mean, just look at what we value in women in our society," Stacy continued, not caring that she had totally abandoned Cassie's topic. "Hank, as a heterosexual male, has the most value. He's white, good-looking and has a decent intellect." Hank beamed at the compliment. "Jill and I would be the next people on the hierarchy. Although we're not males, we are white and we are heterosexual. As lesbians, everyone else in this room would be beneath us, and no offense to Claire, but she would be in the lowest position, because she's a lesbian *and* an African-American female." Claire nodded in agreement. "The only person who could possibly escape her place on the hierarchy is Ronnie."

At the mention of her name, Ronnie's thoughts shifted from picturing Diane in a bikini to Stacy. "What?" she said.

"I'm just saying, Ronnie, that your looks are the key."

Flabbergasted, Ronnie's jaw dropped.

"It doesn't really matter whether you're gay or straight if you look like a runway model," Stacy finished.

Ronnie turned on Stacy. "Are you saying my looks are the most important part of me?"

"Only if you are," Stacy said pointedly.

"What the hell are you talking about?" Ronnie shouted.

Diane interceded, literally stepping into the middle of the room. "Hold it. Stacy, you've made some very broad generalizations that you need to explain."

Stacy nodded and began. "Look, we all know that our society overemphasizes physical beauty. Good looks are a key to success and people with beauty have influence. Let's face it. If Ronnie gets stopped for speeding and I get stopped, which one of us is more likely to get out of the ticket?"

The room was quiet and Ronnie was momentarily stunned, thinking of Officer Jenny.

"Have you ever gotten out of a ticket?" Stacy pushed.

"Yes," Ronnie answered, losing a point but keeping her integrity.

"See? Ronnie, you've been blessed with great genes or a great plastic surgeon, I don't know which."

"That's it!" Ronnie exploded. She jumped out of her seat and headed for Stacy. It took both Diane and Hank to keep them from attacking each other.

When Ronnie had finally returned to her seat, a furious Diane turned to Stacy. "I think we've heard plenty from you, Miss Armbruster. Your point is noted. Physical beauty can open doors and create opportunities. I think, though, Ronnie deserves a chance to respond."

Ronnie glared at the self-righteous little bitch. She knew Stacy Armbruster was behind several of the cruel rumors surrounding her sexual exploits, but why Stacy hated her so much was a mystery. She stood up, knowing she always thought better on her feet. "I don't disagree with your basic premise that physical beauty can be helpful, and yes, it may work to my advantage, and I might have gotten out of some speeding tickets, but I'll bet others in here have as well."

Ronnie's gaze fell to Stacy. She was so smug, so sure that her moral and ethical footing was sound. She glanced at the Polo logo on Stacy's shirt.

"In fact," Ronnie said, "there is definitely something that trumps beauty—and that's money." Stacy pursed her lips and folded her arms across her chest. "People who have money are people with power, and it doesn't matter how beautiful you are."

"That's true," Jill agreed. "Warren Buffet isn't very attractive, but I'll bet he never waits for a table at a restaurant or has trouble finding a place to park his plane."

Ronnie sat on the edge of Stacy's desk. "What do you think of my theory, Stacy? I know you understand the wealthy. Has your family ever bought their way out of a problem? Daddy ever used his money to influence people, maybe an admissions board at a prestigious college?"

"How dare you imply that I couldn't get into this school on my own," Stacy hissed.

"I didn't say you couldn't. I'm sure you're extremely bright."

"I am. How high were your admission test scores?"

"I'm sure your scores were higher," Ronnie acknowledged, and Stacy looked surprised. "Stacy, I'm sure your test scores were higher than mine, your grades superior, and although I've had many fine teachers, your education was better, too. Because money can buy it. Money can buy admittance to prep schools, special classes to prepare for exams and opportunities that I could only dream of having." She paused. "You see, unless I sell my body like a hooker, I doubt I'll ever have your life. How many times have you been to Europe, Stacy? Did you summer at the shore, or do winter break in Switzerland? Have you been to the Louvre, the Met, the Vatican? I'd really like to know, Stacy, what's it like to ride in first class on an airplane?" She took a breath and continued. "I'll agree with you that my looks give me certain potential advantages, but yours are guaranteed. For the right price you can hire people to meet your every little whim twenty-four hours a day. If you want someone to literally kiss your ass, for enough money, your backside can be covered in lipstick. Whoever said money couldn't buy happiness was a poor, jealous asshole—or was he?"

Stacy looked away, toward the window. Ronnie almost felt

sorry for her, but she felt compelled to finish the argument. Maybe Stacy would finally leave her alone.

"You assume I have such an easy life because of my looks, but can I make the same assumption about you?"

A tear rolled down Stacy's cheek, but Ronnie wasn't done.

"I'll make you a bet, Stacy. I'll bet you that you've paid a higher price along the way. My mother is a real piece of work, convinced as you are that my looks are my ticket, but at least she was there when I was a kid. How well do you know your family, Stacy? When you count the memorable days in your childhood, do your nannies and housekeepers come to mind? How many Christmas presents were disappointing because your parents had no idea what to buy for you? Who saw your first steps? Did both of them attend your high school graduation? Tell me, Stacy, do your parents have any idea who you *really* are?"

Cassie leaned over and put an arm around Stacy, whose head was buried in her hands. "That's enough, Ronnie."

"I agree," Diane said softly. "You made your point. Class is over."

The other students filed out silently, but Ronnie remained, hovering over Stacy. Cassie continued to whisper in Stacy's ear, and when Stacy finally looked up at Ronnie, her eyes were filled with hatred.

Ronnie retreated to Diane's office couch. A raging headache had developed behind her left eye, and she needed to relax. A few minutes of deep breathing and focused concentration would help the pain subside.

"Hey, sleepy. Wake up."

Ronnie opened her eyes to see Diane's beautiful face leaning over her. "I must have taken a nap." She yawned.

She sat up next to Diane, who gently smoothed her hair back and put a reassuring arm around her. "Do you want to talk about what happened in class?"

"You were there. She is just such a self-serving bitch. I've never met anyone so devoid of understanding of the world, of other people."

"You, my friend, have obviously never spent much time with the wealthiest part of society."

Ronnie shook her head. "No, I spent too much time with them."

Diane seemed surprised. "I just never pictured high society in Globe, Arizona."

"Well, I doubt too many of them were old money like your family, but I spent most of my childhood touring the beauty pageant circuit, and those families were rich, and the ones who didn't have much spent most of their time trying to act like they did."

"You were in beauty pageants?" Diane's brow shot up. "I had no idea."

"Surprised? My mother started entering my photo in contests when I was six months old, and by the time I was two, we were on the circuit, I was posing for magazines, and my mother was sending me on TV and movie auditions. Her whole life was focused on making her daughter a star. During the week, after working at the library, she would come home and sew costumes for me, because we certainly couldn't afford to buy them, and then the weekends were spent driving to Phoenix or Tucson in our beat-up Honda. The other contestants came in expensive, big cars with an entire wardrobe closet. The mothers would have huge makeup cases that looked like a department store beauty counter. We'd pull up in that junk heap with my one outfit on a wire hanger and my mom's small makeup pouch." She sighed. "That's what I remember most about my childhood, sitting in that Honda. I read a lot. I don't think any kid read more than I did. Even at the pageants during the breaks the other girls would be off playing together, and my mother and I would be in a corner, our noses stuck in books."

"Why didn't you socialize with the other girls?"

Ronnie felt a lump in her throat and her eyes filled with tears. She looked away from Diane. "I was an outcast and so was my mom. The pageant circuit is very small. It was always the same girls week after week. They all got tired of losing to the kid in the homemade dress and the mother who drove a piece-of-shit car."

Diane took Ronnie's hand. "They were jealous of you. It's understandable."

"Not when you're seven," Ronnie whispered. "All I wanted was to have friends, play ball in the park, and instead I got evening gowns, tiaras and runways. Endless runways. And no friends. I didn't understand why the girls hated me so. It's not like I ever wanted to be there, and I couldn't help the way I looked." She shook her head. "I spent most of my childhood crying, dreading the weekends. And summers were worse, because that's when we could really go places. We drove over here to L.A. at least twice each summer, but we never had time to do anything that I thought was fun, like go to Disneyland or Sea World. No, I had to work. I'd do commercials, print ads, and I even did a film. I loved my mom, and for the longest time I believed her when she told me I had a beauty to share with the world. That ended when I was twelve. I told my mother I was done. By that time my father saw how unhappy I was, and so he sided with me."

"How did your mom take it?"

"Just as you would expect. Not well. She told me I was giving up the most important thing in my life, an opportunity to write my future, make millions and be famous. She said the kids at home would be just as cruel as the pageant girls, and in fact she was right. Some were vicious, especially the pretty girls like the Stacy Armbrusters of the world. They would spread gossip, so I learned to let it roll off my back. That was when I started playing

95

softball, and I did make a few good friends, and there were always some boys who would let me hang out with them," she added with a chuckle. "That's why I'm not worried about people like Stacy. I've been dealing with them my whole life."

Ronnie glanced down. Diane had clasped her hand, and their fingers lay intertwined on the couch between them. Ronnie gently stroked the top of Diane's thumb with her own, refusing to look up into her face, afraid that her touch would seem repulsive. They sat there in silence, allowing the tender caress to connect them, oblivious to the bustling sounds outside the door.

Diane took a deep breath and squeezed Ronnie's hand. "I wanted to ask if you were going home for spring break or if you were going on some outrageous vacation involving debauchery and X-rated fun."

Ronnie laughed and looked at Diane, whose grin spread across her face. "No, I'll go back to Globe for a few days in June, and I don't have the time or money to play. I thought I'd just stay here and work, if that's okay with you."

Diane nodded and seemed pleased. "That would be great. Maybe we could go to Disneyland someday during the break, you know, just for a little comic relief."

Ronnie nodded and decided not to share her previous experience at the Magic Kingdom with Diane. "I'd love that."

Ronnie checked her watch, gave Diane's hand a squeeze and stood to go.

"Ronnie, can I ask you something else?"

"Sure."

"How many pageants did you win?"

Ronnie shrugged. "A lot."

"How many did you lose?"

"None."

15. Détente

"Happy Birthday, Van!" everyone cried in unison. Vandella blew out the single candle that floated in her Scotch on the rocks.

"How did you do that, Richard?" Van marveled at the candle, frozen into an ice cube.

"Oh, just a little Martha Stewart magic," he said.

"To great friends and the end of spring break. Drink up, 'cause on Monday we're all going back to class!" Van raised her glass in salute, and Ronnie downed her third shooter of tequila. She was turning numb and feeling a little claustrophobic.

Dusty's Bar, a weekday hangout for all of Carlson University, was packed. The bar had no décor, very few booths and a back room that Ronnie had already seen horizontally with Nancy the bartender, Dusty's wife. Nancy was also responsible for Ronnie's present inebriation, since one of the pleasant benefits from their night of passion a few months ago were free drinks any time Ronnie came into the bar. Dusty apparently didn't mind that his wife bedded many of the attractive female customers. He no doubt knew he was her only man.

Ronnie nodded at Nancy, who prepared another shooter immediately. Ronnie flashed a smile and Nancy licked her lips.

"I'm out of here in ten minutes. Are you free?" Nancy asked with a wink.

Ronnie thought Nancy's personality was as fiery as her red hair, and she was a lot of fun. She had been crowned Miss Texas years ago and was probably pushing fifty, although when they had wandered into the back room, Ronnie thought she was much younger. Yet Ronnie had no interest in returning to bed with Nancy.

"I can't. We're having a birthday party," Ronnie hedged, pointing to Vandella.

Nancy handed her two shooters. "Some other time. Here's an extra for the road." Ronnie took the drinks, suddenly remembering Stacy's accusations. So what if she was right?

Ronnie rejoined the group, the tequila clearly in control. As if her thoughts of Stacy could conjure her presence, Ronnie looked across the room as Stacy Armbruster and her entourage found a booth. Within seconds Stacy's gaze settled on Ronnie, and all the little preppies began pointing and whispering in her direction. Ronnie glared back as Stacy gave her the finger.

How mature. Ronnie shook her head and smiled, unable to comprehend Stacy's behavior.

"Is that who I think it is?" Van asked.

"Yup," Ronnie replied.

Brody stood up and stared. "Oh, so that's little Miss Snooty Bitch," he bellowed, loud enough for the entire bar to hear. Several people turned around, and Ronnie grabbed him by the arm and sat him back down. When she looked at Stacy's table, all of the girls were talking to one another, no doubt calculating the level of their response to this public humiliation.

"Great, Brody." Ronnie sighed. "You've challenged them. Thanks."

Brody gaped at her. "Why are you mad at me? That bitch has been spreading all kinds of rumors about you."

"It's true," Richard agreed. "I don't even go to Carlson, and I've heard stuff about you. And the talk about you and the farm animals is really gross," he added.

Ronnie rolled her eyes. "I didn't realize I was such a topic of interest."

"Some of it is deserved," Van said quietly.

They all looked at Van, who remained stoic. Ronnie had to hand it to her. She was always honest, even when it hurt. And now Ronnie just wanted to go home. She kissed Van good-bye, making her way to the exit and avoiding Stacy's icy glare.

She'd had to park the Mustang down the road, her punishment for arriving late. She'd been determined to finish some typing for Diane, who was spending the evening at a charity benefit with Camille. She'd stayed to type while Diane had showered and prepared for the benefit. When Diane had emerged from the bathroom in a gorgeous emerald dress, asking Ronnie to zip her up, it took all of Ronnie's willpower to pull up the zipper and imprison Diane in the dress, rather than run her hands underneath the sleeves and rip the velvet in the opposite direction.

Ronnie was spending more and more time at Diane's bungalow, and their relationship was clearly crossing some lines. She smiled when she thought of the past week. She and Diane had spent most of the days compiling some of Diane's data, and Diane had answered several of Ronnie's questions about her thesis outline, but they had also managed to squeeze in an afternoon at the Getty Museum, the promised adventure to

Disneyland and nightly walks on the beach. While Ronnie had enjoyed the museum and a return trip to the Magic Kingdom, Ronnie found herself anticipating their evening walks along the shore. They strolled for a few miles, and Ronnie noticed they traveled farther each night, which meant they spent a little longer together, discussing family, hobbies and world events. It was the best spring break Ronnie could ever remember.

"And now it's over," she said into the night. She walked along the shoulder of the road, the Mustang in sight. She longed for a shower and bed, the tequila relaxing all of her muscles. Her mind returned to the image of Diane in her dress just as she felt the first push. In her tipsy state, it was enough to send her into the dirt. She sat up, but there was no pain, at least not yet. Stacy and her three friends stood over her, doing their best to look dangerous in their pullover sweaters and designer khakis.

"Jesus, Stacy," Ronnie muttered. "What the hell are you doing?"

She stood up and faced them, four petite blondes with variations of the same pageboy haircut. Collectively they probably weighed one-fifty, she thought, and when she confronted them, she towered above them. They instinctively took a step back.

"Don't you think that was very unladylike?" A full six inches taller, Ronnie leaned over into Stacy's face.

Stacy winced, probably assuming Ronnie was about to deck her. In fact, they were lucky she had been drinking, and she found herself slightly amused to be bullied by rich preppies.

"Did they teach you this in charm school?" Ronnie teased.

Stacy glowered. "Ronnie Frost, you are an absolute bitch! Aaaargggh!" She let out a primal scream and delivered a quick kick to Ronnie's shin while her tiny fists pelted Ronnie's shoulders. Ronnie's reflexes were dulled, giving Stacy a clear advantage. While the physical assault was unpleasant, Stacy's deafening scream forced Ronnie to clamp her hands over her ears, leaving her susceptible to more of Stacy's wimpy version of catfighting.

The other girls cheered Stacy on, careful not to become too involved. When Stacy's vocal chords collapsed, Ronnie quickly grabbed both her wrists and brought them over her head.

"I hate you, Ronnie!" she cried, recognizing she was now pinned into one position.

Ronnie turned to the other three, who stood frozen, apparently unsure of what to do. "I want you all out of here now, or the first cosmetic surgery you'll need will be nose jobs—tomorrow!" The girls started to back away in horror, Stacy pleading with her friends to stay. Self-preservation won out, and Ronnie was soon left standing on the side of the road with a whimpering Stacy.

"What are you going to do to me?"

Ronnie saw that Stacy was genuinely afraid. Her eyes were blotchy from crying, her face was beet red from the screaming, and she was covered in dirt. Ronnie didn't think Stacy's mother would recognize her cotillion daughter turned bar fighter.

"If I let you go, do you promise to keep your hands to yourself?"

Stacy nodded.

"Promise?"

Stacy nodded again, and Ronnie released her wrists. What Ronnie wasn't expecting was for Stacy to charge forward, sending Ronnie off the shoulder and into the ditch, Stacy flailing on top of her. It wasn't until Stacy hit her in the jaw that Ronnie's anger took full control.

"Damn it, Stacy!" she screamed.

Ronnie easily flipped her over, pinned her arms to the ground and rested her knees against Stacy's thighs.

"You're hurting me, Ronnie!" Stacy moaned.

"Too fucking bad!" Ronnie hissed. "What the hell are you doing? Are you five years old?" She sat over Stacy, catching her breath, dizzy and suddenly nauseous.

Stacy snarled and tried to break free, only angering Ronnie further.

"What do you want from me?" she screamed into Stacy's face. "Why are you doing this to me?" She squeezed Stacy's wrists together until Stacy cried out in pain.

"Please, Ronnie!"

"Tell. Me. Why."

Stacy sobbed and shook her head.

Unable to hold herself up over Stacy any longer, Ronnie let her body slide down on top of her, careful to keep her grip on Stacy's wrists. "I'm not letting you up until you give me some answers. All that crying isn't going to get you anywhere, so you'd better start talking. It's going to get awfully chilly lying in this ditch for much longer."

Stacy squeezed her eyes shut and took a deep breath. "I don't know," she whined, tears streaming down her face.

"What do you mean, you don't know?"

"I can't explain it. You're so sure of yourself and so gorgeous. At first I thought you were just stuck up, and then there were some stories about you, people who had seen you with some police officer."

"And what business is this of yours? Why do you care?"

"I don't care." Stacy's voice broke and Ronnie thought she would cry again, but instead, she tried to free herself by shifting her lower body. Her hips ground against Ronnie's pelvis and their breasts collided. "I don't care about you at all."

"Just talk to me," Ronnie whispered. A look of uncertainty replaced Stacy's panicked expression, and she responded by relaxing her entire body. Ronnie remained motionless, resolved and unwilling to trust Stacy. "Tell me why you hate me so much."

"I don't hate you," she said, resentment in her voice. Stacy wrapped her legs around Ronnie's calves and undulated against her. "I don't hate you at all."

The physical contact awakened Ronnie's senses. She moved with Stacy, who started to smile.

"Yes, Ronnie. Don't stop. Kiss me, please." Her voice was a haggard whisper.

Ronnie hovered over her, her mind trying to fight the fatigue and the growing desire between her legs. This was Stacy, the self-serving little rich bitch who thought of nothing but herself at whatever cost. She wasn't even gay.

Ronnie blinked, released Stacy's wrists and rolled off of her. She lay in the ditch, her head spinning and her energy drained. Stacy stood up, hovering over her, and Ronnie was sure Stacy would press the heel of her boot into Ronnie's chest, collapsing her lungs and killing her.

"You are so incredibly beautiful," Stacy said as she unbuttoned her shirt. "I'm not really gay, but I want to be with you. I had never thought about being with a woman until I met you."

"It's all genetic," Ronnie mumbled.

Stacy laughed and discarded her bra. She let her fingers slide over her nipples and down her abdomen.

"Jesus, Stacy, what are you doing?"

Stacy stepped out of her jeans and knelt before Ronnie. "It's your choice, Ronnie. We can spend an hour psychoanalyzing my obviously confused sense of sexuality, or we can fuck."

Ronnie started to laugh and sat up.

"I don't think this is funny, Ronnie. I'm throwing myself at you."

"I wasn't laughing at you, Stacy, or your very generous offer. It's just unbelievable to hear you say *fuck*. It's like imagining the Queen of England saying *shit*. This whole scene is totally surreal, and totally not you."

Stacy's expression soured. "What do you mean? I can be a slut like you!"

"Ouch."

"I didn't mean it in a bad way. Sluttiness is in. It's very *Sex and the City*. You're just acting on your impulses, and I actually admire that." Stacy pushed herself on top of Ronnie and started kissing her neck. "Please, Ronnie. I want you." Her hands were everywhere, unbuttoning Ronnie's jeans, groping her breasts, as she pressed her mouth against Ronnie's. As much as Ronnie tried to push Stacy away from her, she had a feeling she might be raped by this undersexed preppie. "God, Ronnie, you wear a thong. That is such a turn-on!" she cried, her hand sliding between Ronnie's legs.

Ronnie stood up suddenly, while Stacy tumbled farther into the ditch. "I can't believe this is happening." She rebuttoned her fly and realized that three of the buttons on her shirt were missing, exposing her red, lacy bra. *Terrific*, she thought.

Stacy remained in a heap at the bottom of the ditch. Ronnie stepped carefully down the side.

"Stacy, are you okay?" Muffled cries and a head shake were the answer. Ronnie didn't dare touch Stacy's naked body, but she moved closer to her. "Look, you need to understand something about me. I'm really not what you think I am. I don't have sex with just anyone and I certainly don't go to bed with straight women. Bi-women, yes, but you're straight. There is no way I'm going to have sex with you. It would be cruel because you're really not gay. And more importantly, it would mean that what you said in class about me was true, and that I would use my good looks to get whatever I wanted, even to humiliate someone I don't like."

Stacy looked up at Ronnie, and her face crumbled. "You don't like me?"

Ronnie could only shake her head. "It's pretty hard to like someone who makes your life hell, telling lies about you and spreading gossip."

Stacy bit her lip. "I'm sorry about that. I guess I just wanted your attention."

"You could have just introduced yourself. That would have worked for me."

"Could we still be friends? Could you forgive me?"

Ronnie attempted a smile. The pain from Stacy's punches and kicks and the throbbing headache in her temple were all she could think about. She felt sorry for her in so many ways. She nodded in agreement and pulled Stacy up. Stacy dressed and they climbed out of the ditch, both of them covered in dirt and smelling rancid. Ronnie gave Stacy a ride back to her car, her friends long gone.

Stacy paused before she got out of the Mustang. "Ronnie?"

"Yeah?"

"I'm sorry about tonight. I can't believe I attacked you. It must have been the three kamikazes that I drank in ten minutes."

Ronnie shook her head in disbelief. "Stacy, you shouldn't drink. You're a mean drunk. And an immature one, too."

"You know, you're right. And I'm really not gay. In fact, I'm seeing someone."

"Really?" Ronnie asked mildly. All she wanted was a shower and her bed.

"He's older and well . . ."

"Stacy, I'm not going to say a word about tonight. Our story will be that we had a long talk and worked it out. Okay?"

Stacy sighed, clearly relieved. "Good night, Ronnie."

Ronnie waited until Stacy was in her car and had driven away. She was about to put the Mustang in gear when the bar's back-door opened and Brody staggered out. Just as Ronnie was about to call to him, another man appeared behind Brody and gave him a hard shove. Ronnie started to search for a weapon, something with which to defend her friend. She found a heavy flashlight on the floor and reached for the door handle, prepared to stop a hate crime.

She glanced out the windshield and dropped the flashlight onto the passenger's seat at the sight of Brody, pressed against the wall, his companion kneeling in front of him and unzipping his fly.

16. Diane's Evaluation

Oak leaves covered the beach, which was black as coal. She looked around, unable to locate the shedding tree, for where would an oak tree be on the beach? As the tide rolled in and out, the leaves remained, unmoved and unaffected by the wind. The sky was gray and a storm was imminent. She hugged herself and bowed her head as a gust of wind whipped by, the cold penetrating her body. Dressed only in a sheer negligee, she knew she would freeze. Suddenly warm arms embraced her, shielding her from the wind. Ronnie kissed her neck and nibbled on her earlobe.

"I want to make love to you," she whispered.

"Yes." Diane moaned.

Ronnie pulled her into the sand and opened her negligee. Diane closed her eyes, pleasure rippling through her body. Ronnie kissed her everywhere, caressed her body. It was ecstasy.

She opened her eyes and brought Ronnie's face to her own. They shared a long kiss, but when they parted, Diane was no longer staring at Ronnie's twinkling blue eyes, but at Elliot Michaelson.

"Hello, Diane." He leered. "My, you are fetching!" She tried to sit up, but Michaelson pushed her deeper into the sand. "First, I'm going to fuck you, and then I'm going to fire you." He gave a quick tug on his zipper.

"No!"

Diane bolted up in bed, her heart pounding. She took deep breaths to steady herself, focusing on the sound of the ocean that surrounded her. "Gee, what should I make of that dream?" she asked herself sarcastically. The clock read four thirty, so there was no point in going back to bed. She got up and headed to the kitchen, glancing down at the memo, which she had deliberately placed on the dining room table as a reminder. As if she really needed one.

Dr. Cole: Please see me on Friday at two for your yearly evaluation. We will meet in my office, and I expect that you will be prompt.

Dr. Michaelson

Before she left for work, Diane checked her liquor cabinet, noting that she had half a bottle of whiskey left.

She carefully planned her day on the way to work, relying on her established routines to avoid conflict or chaos. She only had to teach two large classes, and Ronnie could easily handle those for her. All she wanted to do was isolate herself inside the safety of her office until the meeting with Michaelson and maybe have some lunch with Ronnie. Her plan quickly fell apart when she reached the office and checked her messages.

"Diane. Listen, I didn't get in until three. We had some problems at the bar. I'll catch up with you this afternoon, probably around one. Talk to you later."

Diane seethed quietly. How could Ronnie be so irresponsible? She pulled the notes for the classes, downed a strong cup of coffee and did her best to put the meeting with Michaelson at the back of her mind.

By noon she was a raw nerve, full of anxiety and anger. The classes had gone poorly, very flat and dry. She was now feeling she deserved the poor evaluation she would receive. She checked the clock for the fourth time in ten minutes. It was 1:05. Where was Ronnie?

She reread a disjointed essay for the third time, still not comprehending the student's point. She threw the paper on her desk, determined not to give the writer a bad mark because of her foul mood.

"Hey," Ronnie said, entering her office with a big smile. "I feel *much* better," she added. When she saw Diane glaring at her, the smile faded. "What's wrong?"

"What's wrong?" Diane repeated. "How about, where were you?"

"I called you. I left a message. An entire shelving unit collapsed at the bar. Randy, Brody and I were there for two hours cleaning up every kind of red wine you can imagine. I was dead tired."

Diane stood and approached Ronnie. "You have responsibilities here. When I hired you, I asked you if working two jobs was going to be too much. I'm beginning to think it is." She crossed her arms and turned to the window. Her anger was building into rage while a warning signal flashed in her mind. She ignored it.

Ronnie went and closed the door before facing Diane. "What is going on? Did something happen? I've been late before. *You've* been late before. This isn't about that."

"I needed you today," Diane said sharply. "I needed your help and you weren't here. If you didn't have this other job, you would be available. It's that simple."

Ronnie shook her head, clearly frustrated. "It's not simple!

Life isn't simple. I had an emergency that I couldn't control. You can't understand that?"

"I think we need to reevaluate this relationship," Diane said sternly. "The quality of your work is also a factor."

Ronnie winced at the criticism and her eyes welled up with tears. She swallowed hard and picked up her backpack. "Consider it reevaluated."

Diane jumped when the door slammed shut.

Diane tossed the evaluation in her briefcase, resisting the urge to throw it in the trash. "You know I'll appeal."

"That's certainly your prerogative. However, I assure you there is nothing inaccurate in that review. Your classes are unorthodox in nature, you're biased toward females, and you display a lack of sensitivity toward your male students."

"In other words, I'm a man-hating dyke."

Michaelson raised a hand in defense. "Those are your words, not mine."

"Bullshit."

"I beg your pardon?"

"I said this is bullshit. Elliot, you've used your position to attack my character. This review is not about my teaching. It's about my lesbianism. I'm an excellent instructor and you know it."

Michaelson stood and moved to the door, giving Diane her cue to leave. "Dr. Cole, I will not enter into a shouting match with you. Consider yourself on probation. According to the faculty guidelines, you have one calendar year to correct the areas I deem insufficient. Failure to improve will result in an academic review and possible dismissal. Do you have any questions?"

Diane turned to him, fire in her belly. "I don't think I can improve on my lack of heterosexuality."

She stormed out of the building, jumped in her car and raced down the highway, only stopping long enough to hit a drive-through liquor store. One bottle of whiskey would not be enough. Only when she'd shed her work clothes, downed two shots and retreated to her deck did she finally unravel. The tears came and she sobbed, partly at the confrontation with Michaelson, but mainly because she had been so cruel to Ronnie.

The phone rang and Camille's concerned voice floated through the room. "Diane, pick up the phone, now."

Diane sniffled, wiped away the tears and found the handset. "Hi."

"I take it from the shouting I heard this afternoon that your review did not go well. It was your review, wasn't it?"

"Yes."

Camille sighed. "I'm sorry, honey. He's such a bastard. But you knew it was coming. You just have to get over it. Your job is not in any jeopardy, because the faculty review board would never side with him. Everyone hates him, not you."

"I know."

"Are you okay? You don't sound like yourself."

Diane rubbed her temples. Camille was so damn perceptive. "Um, I've had a really bad day. It started with this horrible dream where Elliot was going to rape me, then later I fired Ronnie, and then I got put on academic probation."

"Hold on. You fired Ronnie? Your TA?" Camille's voice cracked in disbelief.

Tears streamed down Diane's face and she couldn't control her emotions. "I don't know what happened. I needed her today, and she left a message saying she would be late. And I just got so angry. I needed her, and when she finally showed up, I just—"

"You exploded," Camille said, finishing her sentence. "Um, well, Diane, this is a mess. And it's significant on several levels. Do you realize that?"

Diane reached for a tissue and blew her nose. "What do you mean?"

"Well, first of all, from a strictly academic perspective, you've made a horrible mistake, firing a woman who is probably the best teaching assistant I've ever seen. But more importantly, you've shown yourself how you really feel about her. Why did you get angry?" Camille asked gently.

"Because she wasn't there. I needed her help," Diane said again.

"No, honey. You were upset because you *wanted* her there. You were going through a terrible day, and you wanted the person you care the most about in the world to stand by you and support you. Now, I want you to hang up and call her. Better yet, go see her. Find her, Diane."

Diane thought the room would spin out of control. She stretched out on the deck chair and downed another shot of whiskey. She clicked off the phone, the connection already dead. It would be so easy to let it go. She had pushed Ronnie out of her life and saved herself potential misery since, with each passing day, it was becoming clear to Diane that they were attaching themselves to each other, emotionally and psychologically. It would only be a matter of time before it became physical, and the idea of touching Ronnie both thrilled and terrified her. God, she hated it when Camille was right, which was all the time.

She pulled herself out of the deck chair and went inside to change.

17. The Ride

"What smells so incredible?" Van called from the stairs. When she entered the dining room, her mouth fell open. "Good God." The entire seven-foot length of the dining room table was covered with bowls, dishes and plates filled with food.

Dave came in from the kitchen, carrying another soup tureen just as Ronnie was setting hers on the table.

"What's going on?" Van asked.

"Dinner," Dave answered.

"For who? The Osmonds?"

Dave went over to Ronnie, who was trying not to cry. "Ronnie's had a bad day, and so she cooked for us. Wasn't that nice?"

Van hugged her. "What happened? This has something to do with Diane, doesn't it?" Ronnie could only nod and sit down.

"Remember how Ronnie said she cooked when she got

depressed?" Dave said to Van. "Well, apparently she cooks a lot and she's into themes. Tonight's Chinese, and tomorrow we're having a luau."

"Ah," Van said. "I see."

The front door slammed and Richard entered wearing only a toga. "Well, is it me? Could I have been a Roman emperor?" He sashayed in front of the three of them, holding his crown of leaves in place.

"You look great, honey." Dave applauded.

Richard took another twirl in his toga, which got caught in his sandal. The fabric ripped at the shoulders and dropped to the floor. True to the Roman tradition, Richard was naked underneath.

Ronnie and Van gasped while Dave cheered. "Hey, hey, baby!" he shouted. "You really are glad to see your man!" Dave took him in his arms just as Brody appeared from the kitchen.

"Holy crap! What the fuck is going on?" he bellowed. "Did I walk into some kind of homo porno flick?"

Everyone laughed and settled down at the table. Ronnie told them about being fired and only cried a little.

"I think it's all for the best," Dave offered. "I can't believe she was that mean to you." The others agreed and busied themselves with the many offerings, including sizzling rice soup, sweet and sour chicken and crab puffs.

The revving of a motorcycle engine broke the quiet. The sound repeated, growing deafening.

Brody threw his napkin on the table and went to the window. "Holy shit!" He motioned to the others to join him.

They crowded around the window and saw that an antique motorcycle was responsible for the noise. The silver bumpers glistened in the twilight and the bike shone as if it were brand new. The rider was attired completely in black—leather jacket, chaps and boots, even a black helmet.

"That is the most fuckin' awesome bike I have ever seen,"

Brody said. He looked closer, and then turned to Ronnie. "Is that who I think it is?"

"Yes," Ronnie replied coolly, trying desperately to control her desire.

The revving continued, and Van pointed at her. "All I know, girl, is you better get out there and deal with this before our neighbors call the cops."

"Van . . ."

"Now, Ronnie." Van opened the door and gestured for her to go.

She strolled down the walk, unable to believe the sight in front of her, while the others followed at an appropriate distance. At last Diane cut the engine and removed her helmet, her black curls settling around her face. Her eyes were masked by lightly tinted sunglasses, but she had taken the time to apply makeup. Ronnie eyed the blood-red lipstick and swallowed hard, speechless.

"Surprised?" Diane asked, smiling.

Ronnie nodded, but she didn't smile back. Diane shifted on the bike, and Ronnie realized in the fading light of day that the only thing Diane wore under her leather jacket was a low-cut leather vest fastened by a single, small button. Much of Diane's cleavage was exposed, as well as a butterfly tattoo above her left breast.

Ronnie attempted to hide her shock, but Diane's amused grin told her she wasn't succeeding.

"Come for a ride with me," Diane said, still grinning.

Her entire demeanor was unusual, Ronnie thought, the way she slouched back on the bike, her voice exuding a seductive dreamy quality, her cockiness. She'd yet to mention what happened that afternoon, and she seemed entirely too pleased with herself, a fact that annoyed and hurt Ronnie even more.

"Take off your sunglasses," Ronnie said.

Diane removed her shades, confirming at least one of Ronnie's suspicions. Diane had indeed been drinking. She'd also been crying, and her eyes were puffy and red.

"I'll need five minutes." Ronnie went back into the house, leaving her roommates out on the lawn and Brody fawning over the motorcycle.

Ronnie sifted through her drawers, debating what to wear. The frumpy extra-large T-shirt and baggy shorts she had on wouldn't do for motorcycle riding, nor would they convey the appropriate image. If Diane wanted to play the hot biker chick game, she'd met her match.

When Ronnie descended the front porch steps, all eyes turned to her. Her tight, low-riding jeans granted everyone a view of her pierced belly button and the waistband of her thong. She wore a thick leather jacket, but underneath was nothing except a thin cotton tank top that left little to the imagination. Her boot heels clicked on the concrete walkway and her hair flowed freely in the light breeze. She'd hastily applied some makeup, which Ronnie knew in her case meant the difference between beautiful and stunning. Her roommates retreated back to the house, undoubtedly to watch from the window.

She straddled the front wheel of the bike and leaned over the handlebars toward Diane. Whatever confidence or daring that initially had possessed Diane seemed to vanish. She sat up on the seat, avoiding Ronnie's gaze and, much to Ronnie's dismay, she zipped up her jacket. Ronnie had bested Diane and shamed her in the process.

Diane glanced up, her eyes swimming with tears. "You look incredible."

"So do you."

Diane shook her head and stared at the ground. "This was so foolish of me, Ronnie. I don't know what I was thinking. I just want to go home and forget this whole day ever happened. Maybe we can talk tomorrow." She reached for the key to start the ignition, but Ronnie caught her hand.

"What about our ride?" Now it was Ronnie's turn to grin.

"Please, Ronnie. I just want to go home," Diane said softly.

Ronnie caressed Diane's hand. "In the first place, you've been drinking, and I'm amazed you got over here in one piece. You're not driving anywhere. Second, if you think that I'm going to let you leave before we've taken this incredible machine out for a spin, you're crazy." Ronnie leaned closer to Diane, their foreheads touching. "And finally, most important of all, I want to see that tattoo again."

Diane cracked a crooked smiled. "Which one?"

Ronnie's jaw dropped. "There's more than one?"

"Yeah," Diane teased, sliding to the back of the bike so Ronnie could climb on and take command. She tossed Ronnie a helmet from the saddlebag and slowly unzipped her jacket. Ronnie could only stare.

Ronnie started the motorcycle, revved the engine and felt the power of the machine. Diane wrapped her arms around Ronnie's waist, her fingers lingering on the thong and driving Ronnie crazy. They headed out of the city up the coast, following the full moon over the sea. The tension of the day and the anger between them subsided, the hum of the motor freeing her to concentrate on the open road. She lost track of time, her senses filled with the smell and sound of the ocean, the feel of the cool breeze against her skin and, most of all, Diane's body pressed against her.

When they were somewhere north of Santa Barbara, Diane motioned for Ronnie to slow down and gestured to a road ahead. They left the highway and ventured into the Santa Ynez Mountain range. With each turn they climbed higher, and the bike chugged as they slowly wandered down the dirt roads. Suddenly a wooden fence appeared in the headlights.

Ronnie stopped the bike and turned to Diane. "Do we go back?"

"No," Diane said, dismounting and approaching the fence, where she reached over and withdrew a metal pin. The fence proved to be a camouflaged gate, and Diane motioned for

Ronnie to ride through.

Diane repositioned the gate and hopped back on the bike, pointing to a grove of trees ahead. Uneasiness overtook Ronnie. She was clearly on private property and she had to drive very carefully, avoiding the natural obstacles, navigating around several tree trunks, dead limbs and large rocks. The full moon provided additional light, and Ronnie could see a clearing up ahead. She gunned the engine and burst through the tree line, suddenly surrounded by a vast field of green.

"Stop!" Diane yelled, and Ronnie immediately hit the brakes. She peered out into the distance, beyond the range of the headlights, and only saw darkness.

"What's out there?" she asked.

Diane dismounted, removing her helmet and jacket. She opened the saddlebag and withdrew a blanket. Ronnie walked out toward the center of the black night, shedding her jacket, suddenly rejuvenated when a gust of wind blew past her.

Ronnie nearly gasped when she saw into the darkness—nothing. They were on the edge of a cliff, the ocean in the distance and the grove behind them. She could only imagine how breathtaking this view was during the day.

She sat down next to Diane on a blanket. "This is unbelievable! Where are we?"

"You like it?" Diane asked, stretching out to look at the moon.

Ronnie squinted, craning to see beyond the precipice, listening to the ocean in the distance. "How far down is it?"

"Well, I've never fallen off, but I'd say it's about two hundred feet or so."

Ronnie rubbed her temples. "Did you bring me up here so I can test it?"

Diane sat up and touched Ronnie's shoulder gently. "If anyone should jump off a cliff, I think it should be me. I was horrible to you today, Ronnie, and it was wrong and undeserved. I didn't mean anything I said, and I hope you can forgive me."

"Why? What made you so upset?"

Diane pulled some papers from her back pocket and handed them to her. "I knew this was coming and I should have told you. Then you could have run for cover today. This is my yearly evaluation, which basically says I am unfit to teach chimpanzees, and I should use my PhD to wallpaper my bathroom."

Ronnie unfolded the sheets and saw the evaluator's name: Elliot Michaelson. *Oh God*. She skimmed through the pages, shaking her head, more furious with every paragraph. "This is such bullshit!"

Diane remained quiet and stared out into the distance. "You know, the scariest part is that I wonder if he's right. Maybe I really do . . ." She took the evaluation from Ronnie and squinted in the moonlight. "Maybe I do 'present historical information from a skewed perspective,' 'engage in questionable research,' and the best part, 'become too involved' with my students."

"And that's a bad thing? Diane, Michaelson's jealous of you. He'd give anything to have your talent and ability. He's just a vindictive bastard who's trying to rattle you. Don't let him. Just forget about it."

"If I forget about it, he'll have my job by next April."

"He's bluffing. You'd fight back and it would mean the whole college would learn the truth. That man is a coward. You could walk back into his office tomorrow and rip this up right in front of him and he wouldn't do a thing."

Diane laughed at the suggestion. "I wish I knew you were right."

Ronnie crumpled the pages into a ball and tossed them over her shoulder. She massaged Diane's shoulders and gently pulled her against her into an embrace. "I don't want to mention Elliot Michaelson's name again, but let me see if I understand. You were terribly worried about this evaluation, took out your anger on me, then attempted to make amends by plying me with your

118

hot bike and your even hotter attire, and now you've led me out into this field, where we'll probably be mauled by the owner's dogs or arrested for trespassing."

"No, that part won't happen." Diane shook her head. "There are no dogs."

"And how do you know that?"

"This is my parents' place."

"Your parents live here? I don't see a house anywhere."

"Oh, I think it's over there." Diane waved her arm to the north.

"How big is this place?"

"About a thousand acres."

Ronnie choked back a gasp. "Wow. Do they know you come up here?"

"No," Diane said adamantly. "One of the hired men showed me that gate years ago. My mother would be livid if she knew I came here and didn't see her."

"This must be an incredible view. Do you come up here often?"

"Not as much as I used to. When I rode my bike regularly, I used to bring friends and we'd have quite a time," Diane said vaguely.

"And what exactly would you do?"

Diane laughed and shook her head. "Oh, no. I'll never tell."

A pleasant silence fell between them. Diane rested her head against Ronnie's shoulder and they stared at the moon. "I really am sorry about today, Ronnie."

"I know. I want you to promise me that from now on, if something's bothering you, or if you need me, you'll tell me. All you had to do was call and I would have come in."

"But you were asleep—"

"Doesn't matter," Ronnie interjected. "I'll always be there for you if you need me," she whispered. She kissed the top of Diane's head and inhaled the lilac scent of her shampoo. "Tell me something. What did you say that night in the bar after I kissed you? And don't deny it."

Diane gave a short laugh and turned to face her. "I said, brilliant."

Ronnie was perplexed. "Why did you say that?"

"It was just the perfect description. The way you kissed me, and then when I looked in your eyes I got lost. And now that I know you, I can't think of a better way to describe you. You are brilliant, Ronnie Frost. I . . ." Her voice trailed off and she sighed heavily.

Their lips met. It was a sweet kiss, one that could easily promise another.

"I'm not ready to, well, to go to bed with you."

Ronnie traced circles on the back of Diane's leather vest. "I know you're not. That's not what I'm asking for, really. I don't want to push you. I'd just like a little hope that we're moving forward in some sort of positive direction."

Diane raised an eyebrow. "That's all you're after tonight?"

"Scout's honor," Ronnie promised.

"I truly doubt that you were ever a Girl Scout."

"I was a Boy Scout," Ronnie deadpanned.

Diane laughed and snuggled against Ronnie's chest. "You are so damned charming."

"And you're so beautiful. I don't know what possessed you to dress like this, but I approve."

"I wanted to show you that I have a wild side. I can be a risk taker."

"Hmm," Ronnie murmured. "You can take risks, huh?"

Diane hesitated for only a moment before she reached for Ronnie, whose whole body reacted to the connection. A shiver ran down her back. It was a long, passionate kiss, and Ronnie so wanted to reach up and pop that little button on Diane's vest, but she used all of her resistance to remain true to her word. She pulled away and caressed Diane's face. Diane's eyes were closed and she was smiling.

"Again," she whispered to Ronnie, who was happy to oblige.

They kissed and cuddled for an hour in the moonlight, Ronnie keenly aware of Diane's exposed cleavage and their entwined legs. Her mouth wandered to Diane's earlobes and neck, but she didn't dare kiss that bright, butterfly tattoo, which was only a tongue flick away from Diane's nipple.

It got to be too much. She pulled away and sat up, rubbing a hand across her face. "I need a break," she murmured.

Diane sighed. "Ronnie, why are you doing this?"

Ronnie turned to Diane and realized she was serious. "What do you mean?"

"Why did you agree to come here?"

"Why did you ask me?"

Diane reddened and took a breath. "I'm not sure. I know you have many girlfriends. Wouldn't you rather be feeling up some cute sophomore? I mean, practically every girl in the C and M class drools over you. You could have your pick, even of the straight ones. I don't understand why you would want to spend time with me. Don't you have some wild oats to sow?"

"Not anymore," Ronnie said. "That's what college was for." She cocked her head. "Well, actually that's what high school was for, too."

"I take it you were rather wild. Was that when you had your first girlfriend?"

"Eventually. First I went through a few boyfriends."

Diane's eyes widened. "You mean one wasn't enough to realize you were gay? Or are you bi?" she added suspiciously.

"I'm not bi. The first guy I ever slept with was so bad that I didn't know what to think, so I set my sights a little higher and went after the captain of the football team. He was supposed to be this incredible lay, at least that's what his girlfriend said. She was, sickeningly enough, the head cheerleader."

"So what happened?"

121

"His name was Bo, and he looked exactly as you might imagine, a huge, beefy guy with enormous biceps. So we're out in his car after a game and he's really ripe because he didn't shower for very long. I guess he thought he was going to get dirty again anyway from the sex, so what was the point? Well, he was pumping away on top of me, grunting like crazy, and I'm lying there, smelling his sweat and listening to him come. And it reminded me of a barnyard."

"A barnyard?" Diane asked incredulously.

"Yeah, I thought screwing him was like porking a pig." They both laughed. "That was the last of my male experiences. The next person I slept with was a female."

"Who was your first lesbian experience?"

"The guy's girlfriend—the cheerleader."

Diane roared and pulled Ronnie to her. They kissed and fell back on the blanket. "So was that your most colorful story?"

"Not even close. I went to a lot of raves in high school and did many things I probably shouldn't have. I learned about one-night stands and safe sex. And then there was college." She pointed her finger at Diane. "Don't ever let little sorority girls tell you they're virgins or they're straight. I probably bedded most of the Chi Omega house at Arizona State right underneath the nose of the housemother."

"Really?"

"Yeah. But then I decided I wanted a serious girlfriend. I was tired of shimmying down the drainpipe after sex. The next one wasn't much better, though. She was into threesomes."

"Hmm. What did you think?"

Ronnie grinned. "What did *you* think, Professor?"

"I thought it was too crowded," Diane said with a laugh.

"Me too." Ronnie chuckled.

"Have you been with any nice women? Stable women?"

Ronnie took Diane's hand and brought it to her lips. "Are you asking me if I've ever had a serious relationship, Dr. Cole? Yes.

I've had two and remained friends with both."

Diane let out a sigh. "Well, that's something."

Ronnie continued to stare at her, kissing each of her knuckles.

"Ronnie, how many women are you dating right now?"

"None."

Diane shook her head, as if unable to believe Ronnie's answer. She stood up and walked to the edge of the cliff. Her silhouette in the darkness outlined her vulnerability. She hugged herself and Ronnie recognized she was standing on a precipice in more than one way. Ronnie went up behind her and massaged her shoulders.

"You're the only one I want," she whispered in Diane's ear.

"I don't know if I can believe you."

"It's the truth. I haven't been with anyone in two months, ever since I saw you at the restaurant after the symphony. I knew then how much I wanted you and how little I wanted anyone else. I don't mind waiting. You're worth it."

Diane took Ronnie's face in her hands. She stared into her eyes, as if gauging her sincerity. Ronnie smiled, wondering if Diane could read her expression. Diane had to know that Ronnie had fallen in love with her. Diane said nothing. She simply kissed her on the lips and caressed her cheek.

"We need to go," Diane said. She returned to the motorcycle and folded up the blanket. Ronnie gazed out at the black night, savoring the taste of Diane's lips and the lingering scent of her perfume. Ronnie let Diane drive, her mind cleared of the alcohol she had imbibed earlier.

When they pulled up to Diane's bungalow, Diane quickly dismounted and turned to Ronnie. "You take it home for a while," she said with a grin.

"Are you sure?" Ronnie was delighted.

"Absolutely."

"Diane, I think you should know, well, I—"

Diane silenced her with a kiss and headed inside, leaving her with a lingering hope on her lips.

18. Girl Talk

The May afternoon was a perfect reminder of why sunny California was the most sought-after climate in the entire country. Although the pollution, crime and traffic could cause visitors and natives alike to gnash their teeth, when the weather hovered in the mid-seventies and a light breeze rustled through the trees, everyone was reminded why they lived on the West Coast. California was like a beautiful, desirable woman whose seductive nature overrode any of her obvious flaws.

Ronnie lathered her arms with more sunscreen. She checked the height of the surrounding bushes and removed her bikini top.

"Can someone please tell me why *I'm* doing this?" Vandella asked.

"Sunlight isn't just a physical presence, Van," Richard responded. "It's a state of mind."

Van sat up and found a bottle of water. "All I know is that I'm frying my ass off." She stood up and grabbed her towel. "We need an umbrella, Richard."

"You can't go," Richard protested. "We haven't had any good girl gossip."

"Yeah, Van," Ronnie agreed. "You need to stay."

Vandella sighed and returned to her lawn chair.

"Now," Richard began, "who wants to share?" No one said anything, so he recounted his latest story of a Hollywood idol in a homosexual encounter. "His pretend wife was apparently furious because he almost got caught," he concluded. "It seems the young man involved was for hire."

"I can't ever imagine sleeping with someone for money," Van said.

"The sociology department chair offered me five hundred to sleep with him," Ronnie said.

Van sat straight up. "You're kidding. Elliot Michaelson propositioned you?"

"Well, not directly, but the meaning was clear. We would *work* at his house for several evenings and he'd pay me."

"Are you going to do it?" Richard asked.

"Richard!" Van bellowed.

"What's the big deal? Prostitution is about two willing people engaging in a victimless crime. It's—"

Van got in his face, her finger pointed. "Don't you get started, Richard. I know what you're going to say. Even gay men don't realize that prostitution degrades *both* women and men."

Richard waved his hand in the air, speaking like Bette Davis. "Yes, dahling, yes. Okay, let it go, Van. I'm already bored. There's no room for philosophical arguments during tanning. Someone say something trivial, please."

Ronnie turned over and rested her chin on her hands. "So, what's Brody's story?"

Richard repositioned his tanning shield on his shoulders and

125

tilted his chin toward the sun. "I can sum him up in two words—homophobic homo. Brody's so deep in the closet that the door is locked from the inside and he's hiding behind the shoe rack."

"It seems like he has a lot of issues," Ronnie observed.

Van reached for the tanning lotion. "It has a lot to do with his background," she explained. "Brody's people are rednecks from Alabama."

"And the KKK," Richard added. "Brody left three years ago and has never gone back, not even to visit. Of course, he still hasn't come out, even to himself. He fluctuates between world-class asshole and a poster boy for self-hatred. Half the time I want to kill him and the rest of the time I want to stage a telethon for him."

"Even though he doesn't act like he needs it, we've all protected him to a certain extent," Van said. "He'll come out when he's ready."

"Enough about Brody," Richard said. "My love life is frustrating enough."

Van snorted. "Yours and mine, too. I have no life until I finish my independent project."

"Tell me about it," Richard whined. "Dave's finance class is all-consuming. Our sex life has been reduced to a quickie in my mind."

"So you made up?" Van asked.

Richard nodded. "I just needed to break some things. So, Ronnie, what about you? How's life with the professor?"

Ronnie's body tingled at the mention of Diane. "We've kissed," she simply said.

His eyes narrowed. "Kiss on the cheek, like, it's good to see you after your trip to Europe?"

"No. More like it's taking every bit of restraint I have not to pull you on top of me and swallow your tongue."

Richard threw his tanning shield over his head. "We have a winner! Start at the beginning, do not use your graduate-level vocabulary and remember, this may be the closest thing to sex Van and I get for the next month."

"Sorry to disappoint you, then. It's just been kissing. We hold hands and we snuggle sometimes, but I cannot get off first base." She sighed.

Richard patted her shoulder. "What's the problem? Are you in love, sweetie?"

Ronnie didn't answer, and her eyes filled with tears.

"You are, aren't you? You love her, but the object of your affections doesn't feel the same way."

"No, I think she's in love with me, but she won't get involved with a student. If we started sleeping together, I think she's afraid that her job would be in jeopardy."

"She's got a point," Van said. "I'm sure Elliott Michaelson would love to get rid of her."

"Besides," Ronnie continued, "she's eighteen years older than me."

Richard weaved his fingers together and rested them underneath his chin. "Ah, yes. A May-December romance."

"You know, that isn't that much," Van said. "It's only four Olympics."

"And only one complete decade," Richard added. "Hell, it's only three or four fashion trends, only one of which will be truly significant."

Van sat up, getting into the discussion. "And it's only a few fluctuations of the economy, three or four presidents at the most."

"All right," Ronnie said. "I get the idea. But that's not the point. She's having trouble because I'm a student. For her, kissing is really pushing the boundary. She can't sleep with a student."

"Can't or *won't?*" Richard asked pointedly.

Ronnie shook her head. "Richard, she's worked all of her adult life to become a respected academic. This isn't Hollywood, where everybody sleeps with everybody else."

"Twice," Richard said, waving two fingers for emphasis.

Ronnie ignored the joke, her mind reeling from all the thoughts she had kept to herself.

Van stood and kissed her on the head. "Ronnie, give it some time. She might be willing to go for it, if she really feels that way."

"Absolutely," Richard agreed, clapping his hands together. "Sex is much better in an illicit romance. All that sneaking around, doing it in public places. Living in the fear that you might get caught at any time." He looked dreamily to the sky. "God, Ronnie, I almost wish it were me."

19. Five Minutes

The twang of a steel guitar reverberated throughout the dance floor and the many patrons, most fashioning cowboy boots and hats, two-stepped to a Randy Travis tune. Ronnie suppressed a yawn and looked casually at her watch.

Two o'clock in the morning on a Tuesday, and instead of enjoying the comfort of her bed, she was sitting in a corner booth at the Trail Ride, watching Brody chug beer and do his best not to look gay. She gave a wry smile, thinking that the fact Brody had asked her to take him to a gay bar was amazing. She glanced sideways at her confused friend. His gaze flicked around the bar, as if he were terrified he'd see someone he knew but evidently fascinated by this new world. The likelihood of anyone recognizing him was slim. Ronnie had deliberately chosen a place on the outskirts of the San Fernando Valley, a place remote and far removed from West Hollywood.

"This is okay," Brody said. "Have you been here before?"

"A few times," she answered. She casually placed her hand on his knee, which was nervously jerking up and down under the table. "Hey, Brody. Take a deep breath."

He turned beet red and stared at his beer. "This is so weird. Why don't we just go?" He looked up at her with pleading eyes. It was an expression she hadn't believed he was capable of making.

She chuckled and kissed his cheek. "Oh, no. You wanted to come, and we've been here exactly twenty-two minutes. We're going to stay for at least an hour, or until you meet someone to take you home and make you his love slave."

"Huh?" Brody jerked his head up and Ronnie laughed harder. "Kidding!"

Brody stared at his Budweiser bottle and started to peel the label off. Ronnie knew he wasn't bored, and he was probably dying to get up and cruise, but it was too much.

She leaned back in the booth, remembering her first time in a gay bar. She'd been fourteen and a freshman. Still, no one cared about letting her in. Looking around, she realized how good it felt to be out. She loved bar-hopping, dancing, being with people. Gay bars had an energy, a feeling of camaraderie and, of course, the hope of sex, which many lesbians equated to love. Not her. She knew the only thing she ever found in a bar was a great lay.

And now that she had found the woman of her dreams, she couldn't get any to save her life.

Ronnie took a long pull on her beer and watched the amusing couples around her. She'd worked in enough bars to know that at two in the morning, all of the real couples had gone home to bed, and the only ones left now were the ones who had just connected, hoping to *couple*. Most were engaged in highly animated conversations with intense eye contact and surreptitious touching. They were selling themselves to each other and doing their best to hide their flaws—not speaking too loudly or saying the wrong thing. It was all about putting one's best foot forward, she thought. Of course, some couples were already making out, their bodies locked so tightly that tools would be necessary to pry them apart.

She smiled. How she would love to take Diane dancing and watch the people with her. Gay bars were a sociologist's heaven, but of course Diane would never consent. A double bonus would be dancing with her. She had a great ass, one that was meant for shaking. Ronnie imagined how amazing it would be to hold her tightly and sway to the beat, but it was highly unlikely they would ever be that close together in public. Diane could barely bring herself to be seen anywhere with Ronnie.

They had gone to the latest Jodie Foster movie the night before, their love for everything Jodie outweighing Diane's anxieties. When they arrived at the theater, the previews had already started, and Diane directed them to a corner of the back row.

When Ronnie attempted to take her hand, Diane gently kissed Ronnie's palm, then placed it back in her own lap. They sat like two friends for the rest of the movie, and when it ended, Diane bolted out of her seat before the credits even rolled, and then waited outside until Ronnie emerged.

"Are you sure you want us to get in the same car?" Ronnie asked sarcastically.

The hurt in Diane's eyes made her instantly regret the comment, and she had spent the rest of the night kicking herself for chastising Diane. She'd agreed to this arrangement, and Diane was certainly not going to make any progress if Ronnie berated her constantly.

She sighed and raised her beer to her lips, her eyes locking with those of a Latina beauty who'd sidled up to the booth.

"Your friend looks sad," she said to Brody.

"She is," he agreed with a glance at Ronnie. "Her girlfriend won't take her anywhere and she's stuck coming to gay bars with me."

The woman smiled seductively at Ronnie and leaned over the table. Her large breasts practically tumbled out of her sweater, and Ronnie's gaze was drawn to the large diamond that sat on the woman's ring finger.

"That's her loss," the Latina lady said. "Dance with me?"

Ronnie politely shook her head no and glanced at an approving Brody.

"It's only a dance," the woman pressed. "Your girlfriend controls you so much that you can't enjoy a simple dance?"

Ronnie's resistance melted at the logic. Diane wouldn't mind if Ronnie danced with someone. It was only a dance.

Brody swore under his breath as Ronnie left the table and wandered over to the dance floor. The Latina pulled her into an embrace, and as their bodies shifted from one position to another, Ronnie was conscious of where her hands drifted.

Her partner, though, wrapped her toned arms around Ronnie's waist and let her fingers explore. "You've got an incredible belly ring."

She had casually pulled up Ronnie's shirt while they danced, and although Ronnie made every effort to ignore the blood-red fingernails that trailed over her abdomen, she felt her entire body tingle.

The music drifted to a sad old ballad and their bodies collided fully. Ronnie mused that slow songs were really invented to be vertical foreplay. Ronnie looked into her eyes. A lot of makeup, she noted. Probably in her late forties. But she had a great body and knew exactly how to use it invitingly. Shorter by about five inches, she put her face between Ronnie's breasts and played with Ronnie's zipper.

"After this song, let's get out of here." She stroked the front of Ronnie's pants and Ronnie sighed.

She was in trouble.

"Excuse me. May I cut in?"

132

Ronnie looked up to see Brody, his muscular biceps crossed over his chest and a stern look on his face.

"I don't think your friend wants you to," the Latina replied. To make her point, she guided Ronnie's lips to her own while her hand slid between Ronnie's legs.

The woman's kiss was tantalizing, a sharp difference from Diane's sweet lips. These were the lips of sex.

And Ronnie missed sex.

The woman's tongue explored Ronnie's mouth fully and her thumb gently massaged Ronnie's wetness through her pants. Ronnie suddenly realized that at some point, her hands had drifted to the woman's buttocks and she was squeezing them gently.

"I know I can take you right here," she whispered into Ronnie's ear. Her free hand swept underneath Ronnie's shirt and the fingernails stroked Ronnie's nipple. "But," she continued, "it will be so much more fun in the back of my Lexus. Meet me in the parking lot in five minutes. I'm the red Lexus in the corner. Hurry. I have to get home in half an hour." She pulled away and headed toward the exit.

Brody stared at Ronnie in disgust. "So much for Diane," he snarled.

Watching him return to the table, Ronnie remained glued to the floor, too stunned to move. She couldn't believe what had just happened and her own reaction floored her. She had let a stranger dry hump her. That was nothing new, but she had declared herself to Diane.

What the hell was wrong with her?

She returned to the table where Brody stood. He finished his beer in three swallows, smacked the bottle on the table and wiped his lips on the back of his hand.

"Okay, I'm leaving." He dropped a few bills down and reached for his jacket.

"Brody, wait. I'm sorry about what happened."

"No, you're not. You wanted that woman to come on to you. All you think about is fucking women. It doesn't matter that you're involved with someone. Where I come from, we have a name for girls like you."

Ronnie's anger surged and she wanted to slap him across the face. "You think I'm a slut? How dare you judge me when you can't even look at yourself in the mirror! You're a homophobic asshole who wants everyone to think he's some macho stud, when really you're a pathetic coward. You're the worst kind of gay person, Brody, because of your prejudice. You say all those horrible things about gay people. You're one, too, buddy."

"Oh, yeah?" Brody yelled.

Ronnie got in Brody's face and poked him in the chest. "Yeah, you're a total ass."

"Slut!"

"Asshole!"

Brody glanced sideways and realization dawned that he and Ronnie were the main attraction at the bar. He pulled his jacket on. "If you want to be with that woman, then you can figure out how to get home. I'm not standing around watching you screw over Diane. I'm leaving in five minutes, too. You make your choice."

He left her in the bar. She sat down in the booth, not knowing what to do and not understanding her feelings at all. She nursed the tail end of her beer, losing all track of time. When she had arrived in L.A., she only wanted fun, but now she was in a complicated relationship with a woman who wouldn't return her affections.

She didn't know what to do, but as the time pushed three o'clock, she knew she wouldn't find the answers in a dive bar outside Van Nuys. She threw on her leather jacket and pulled out her cell phone. She'd need a cab for sure.

Once outside she scrolled through her phone book, knowing that at least two cab companies were listed amidst the many friends and lovers from her past and present. She never deleted anyone, and she was shocked by the number of women listed, women who no longer spoke to her or with whom she had any contact. Maybe Brody was right about her.

Huge headlights blinded her and Brody's enormous Ford truck stopped in front of her. He lowered the window and grinned. "Need a lift?"

"I thought you were leaving in five minutes."

"Well, when I watched the red Lexus peel out of here without you, I thought I'd give you a few more."

Ronnie smiled and the moment passed between them. She pulled herself into the cab and Brody steered the truck into traffic. He shifted in his seat and glanced at her, clearly wanting to say something.

"What?"

"Well, I'm not very good at this, but aren't we supposed to apologize to each other or something?"

She laughed and shook her head. "Was that your version?"

"Yup."

"Accepted. And I apologize, too."

"Great. I don't know about you, but I'm all warm and fuzzy now." Brody sighed and turned up the radio full blast as they sped down the interstate, heading for home.

20. Diane's Party

As was her tradition each year, Diane planned an end-of-the-year party. It was the one time she opened her home to most everyone she knew. Her friends came from all over the country, even her former lovers. The roots of the party stemmed from her upbringing and her mother's belief that every woman had a responsibility to be a good hostess and stage at least one event per year.

Mother would be pleased, Diane thought.

At ten o' clock in the morning the catering trucks began arriving with the food to be prepared and by noon the house smelled of salmon, various seasonings and freshly baked bread. The food alone was a gastronomic experience, since everything was prepared from scratch that day.

Tables filled her deck with china and crystal place settings, each table sporting an ornate centerpiece made of flowers and candles. By evening the view of the sunset was breathtaking, enjoyed by guests imbibing the finest wines and eating sensational food that any restaurant would envy.

Diane's well-stocked bar was complemented by a variety of extra glasses and goblets to serve her many guests. In the past, she'd always hired a bartender from Simply Understated, but when no one was available except Ronnie, it forced her to face an issue she had avoided for weeks—whether to invite Ronnie as a guest or to exclude her, since most of Diane's colleagues would attend, except for Elliot Michaelson, who'd wisely begged off. The bartending dilemma provided another option.

She had no idea how Ronnie would respond, and she didn't need Miss Manners to tell her that to invite a love interest to a party as an employee was poor form. Her mother would be appalled, but she could see no other way to handle the situation unless she banished Ronnie altogether, an idea that made her sick to her stomach.

"I need to tell you something—or rather, ask you something," she'd said over lunch one day. They were sitting in her office on the couch, splitting a chicken salad sandwich, as they always did on Thursdays. "Every year I have this large party to start the fall quarter. I invite a bunch of people from Carlson and my friends, too."

Ronnie nodded, listening and finishing her sandwich. When she didn't make any presumptions about being invited, Diane was hopeful she would understand.

"Anyway, I wasn't sure what to do this year, because on one hand, I really want you there, but on the other hand, I have to be careful since my colleagues are coming, including Dean Morgan."

"So what are you thinking?" Ronnie asked.

"I was hoping you would agree to tend bar."

Ronnie stopped eating and stared at Diane, who rushed to explain.

"That way, you could still be at the party, but no one would suspect anything."

"I see."

Diane watched for a change in her expression, but there was none. Ronnie could be very difficult to read at times, and this was frustrating. "What do you think, Ronnie?"

"Whatever you think is best," she had replied.

They had not spoken of it since, and Diane felt the issue was resolved, or at least she comforted herself by assuming it was fine. It wasn't until Ronnie appeared on the afternoon of the party dressed in her black-and-white attire that Diane became exceedingly anxious. After a quick embrace Ronnie assumed her professional demeanor, inventoried the bar and left for the liquor store to pick up Diane's order. Her air of detachment worried Diane only until one of the caterers needed her help in the kitchen with a crisis.

She checked her watch and went to shower and change. Ronnie still hadn't returned and Diane hoped nothing was wrong with the order. She reviewed the party plans while she dressed and put on makeup, confident that everything was ready. She gave herself a long glance in the full-length mirror, hoping Ronnie would be pleased. *No*, she thought with a smile. Actually she wanted to turn her on. She wanted to look hot and she certainly felt sexy. The backless gold lamé top tied at her neck and at her waist. Much of her midriff was showing, and the tight, black leather pants accentuated her shapely ass, defining every curve on her lower body. What no one could see was the black thong, the key to her real sexiness, she believed. She had invested in a bikini wax and some suggestive underwear on a whim one afternoon. It was the most impulsive thing she had done in ages, and she'd felt terribly embarrassed standing in Victoria's Secret holding the pieces of lace in her hand. Her embarrassment faded, though, when a saleslady offered to accompany her into the dressing room and model the underwear for her. Diane politely declined, but the sexual energy between them was intoxicating, and for the first time in a long time, Diane felt desirable.

She emerged from the bathroom and set her sights on Ronnie, who had returned and was busy arranging the bottles of liquor on the bar. Diane was halfway across the room when Ronnie glanced up and nearly dropped the Jack Daniels she was holding.

Diane smiled and turned around, giving Ronnie the full view of her outfit. "Well? What do you think?"

Ronnie stood there, her hand gripped around the neck of the bottle, her mouth slightly open. She blinked and nodded. "You look great."

Diane's smile faded at Ronnie's total lack of interest or enthusiasm. She watched Ronnie carefully place the Jack Daniels on the bar and return to the job of preparing the bar. She took a step forward and then thought better of it. She was afraid of what Ronnie was thinking, and the last thing she needed was a confrontation ten minutes before her guests arrived. Instead, she retreated to the kitchen to check on the caterers.

Within an hour the living room and deck were crowded, the academics choosing to enjoy the ocean view while the lesbians huddled in the living room, never straying too far from the alcohol. Having been trained by the best of all hostesses, her mother, Diane circulated among all of the guests, greeting each one and spending an appropriate amount of time making small talk but not allowing anyone to monopolize her. She glanced over at the bar and the multitude of women glomming on to Ronnie. Ronnie was leaning over the bar, looking at something Judy had in her hand. Diane instinctively moved in that direction, only to find her friends staring at a picture of her, topless, sitting on her Harley and holding a joint.

"Jesus, Judy! The dean is here." Diane grabbed the photo album and closed it.

"Hey, D. I just wanted Ronnie to see you in your prime."

Judy gave her a lopsided grin, forcing Diane to smile back. She turned to Ronnie and provided the history. "That picture was taken during our ride across America, back when we were lovers."

Ronnie blinked. "You and Diane?"

Diane rolled her eyes and ran her hand through her hair while Judy said, "Oh, yeah. You see, Ronnie, every lesbian in this room has slept with at least two others at some point. And there's still some residual anger or grief. Do you see Wendy at the end of the bar over there? She used to date Michelle, the dark-haired woman standing over in the corner. Their relationship ended really poorly . . . the cops, vandalism. That's why for the entire evening, neither of them will dare to go past the sofa in either direction. It's kind of like Switzerland. And there are at least ten other stories like that in this room."

"Including you?"

"Ah, we won't go there," Judy said. Camille advanced toward them and embraced Diane and Judy. With her was someone else from Diane's past.

"Hey, everyone," Camille gushed. "Ronnie, I'd like you to meet Dr. Susan Skaggs."

A tall blonde with a voluptuous figure, Susan reached for Ronnie's hand and brought it to her lips. "Hello, gorgeous. I'd like to know where Diane gets such incredibly beautiful help."

The comment stung Diane, and Diane forced a smile as Susan released Ronnie's hand and turned to her.

"How are you, darling?" she said, kissing Diane fully on the lips.

"Ronnie, what are you doing behind the bar?" Camille asked.

Diane grimaced, but before anyone could answer, she quickly led Camille away from the group.

"Do you want to tell me why your girlfriend is working and not standing at your side?" Camille prodded.

Hearing the situation voiced by someone else made Diane

keenly aware of the stupidity of her actions. She never should have asked Ronnie to the party. She shook her head, unable to explain.

"I'm shocked, Diane. I thought Ronnie meant more to you." She walked back toward the group of women by the bar, leaving Diane alone with her growing shame.

Diane continued to circulate among the guests, who were becoming more and more animated thanks to the alcohol that Ronnie poured nonstop. Diane herself had imbibed nothing, another expectation of the hostess. A roar came from the bar area, and Diane watched as Ronnie poured shots into the open mouths of ten women who lined up side by side, their cheeks pressed together. The women gulped the shots and sucked on limes, feeding them to one other. One woman stuck her lime in Ronnie's mouth, who willingly accepted it.

Not to be outdone, Susan Skaggs pushed her way to the bar.

"Ronnie"—she beckoned with her finger—"I need another cherry."

Ronnie grinned and the other women cheered. She walked over to the tall blonde, took a cherry from the bowl and dangled it over Susan's mouth. Susan leaned over the bar, exposing most of her cleavage, and licked the cherry while Ronnie held it in place. The barflies were mesmerized by the scene, Ronnie twirling the little red cherry over the woman's tongue.

Suddenly Susan's teeth appeared and she bit the cherry off the stem. The barflies screamed in glee. Ronnie took a napkin and gently dabbed the cherry juice from Susan's chin.

"Ronnie, that was the best cherry I ever had," Susan said, and the lesbians cheered louder.

Diane crumbled, and she knew she would cry. She made her way through the room and headed out the backdoor toward the beach.

"Diane!" Camille called, catching up with her. "I'm not sure what's going on, but you need to talk to Ronnie. This party is out of control, and we both know Ronnie is way out of her league with Susan. Unless you want your girlfriend to be seduced by your ex-lover, you'd better have a talk with her."

"Camille, if Ronnie wants to be with Susan, then that's her choice. I'm not going to stop her." Diane turned away and headed down the beach.

There was nothing like thirty lesbians falling all over you when you were depressed, Ronnie thought. Diane's friends had spent the entire evening flirting with her, making passes and suggestive comments, and one just wanted to go outside and fuck her. The most intriguing proposition had come from Diane's friend Susan, who asked her to take a moonlight swim with her in the ocean after the party was over. At this point all Ronnie wanted to do was go home. She had made a few hundred dollars in tips, because lesbians loved to tip other lesbians, and she needed to be away from Diane, gorgeous Diane.

Now the professor was nowhere to be found. The party was breaking up quickly, some guests taking their exit cues from others. No one wanted to be seen as the one who stayed beyond his or her welcome. All of the sociologists had departed, except for a few who found Diane's gay friends fascinating. Most of the lesbian couples were gone, the sober partners leading the drunk ones out to the cars. Judy and Camille were no exception, Camille supporting Judy on their way to the door.

"I'm not comfortable leaving you here with Susan," she said to Ronnie. "Diane's disappeared and you're too young to defend yourself."

Ronnie glanced at Susan, parked at the corner of the bar, smoking a cigarette, a vodka tonic in front of her. It was the first drink she'd had all night. "Do you really think she'll attack me?"

Judy put a hand on Ronnie's shoulder. "Just be careful," she warned. She slurred her words and reeked of tequila. "She's like a spider. She spins a web and waits. You're the prey. When you get anywhere close to her, wham! She pulls you in before you know it." She patted Ronnie's arm. "That's what happened to me. I speak from experience."

Ronnie looked at Camille. "Judy and Susan?"

Camille sighed. "It was a long time ago. A whole triangle thing between Judy, Diane and Susan. Don't ask." She hoisted Judy a little higher on her shoulder. "C'mon, Shakespeare, let's go home."

Ronnie watched them toddle outside and surveyed the remnants of the evening. She'd excused the waiters and caterers after they had with lightning speed dismantled their tables, washed all the china and packed up the leftovers. The last few lesbians were making plans to meet for brunch and didn't bother to say good-bye as they shut the front door.

It was then Diane appeared, climbing the steps from the beach, her shoes in her hand. She headed straight for the bar, retrieved a bottle of whiskey and a shot glass and planted herself next to Susan. Without a word Susan handed her the burning cigarette and fished another from the pack. She offered one to Ronnie, who declined and continued to clean the bar.

Susan fired up another cigarette. "Well, my love, I would say that was a hell of a party. It's too bad you missed most of it."

Diane downed her first shot and immediately refilled the glass. "An absent hostess is rarely missed when there's alcohol available."

"Is that straight from the Family Cole's *Guide to Party Planning*?" Susan joked.

Diane took a deep drag and ignored the stab. "My father was living proof. He never attended a single one of my mother's soirees for longer than twenty minutes. He just always made sure the bar was stocked and then he could retreat to the TV room."

Ronnie noticed the familiarity with which they spoke to each other, the easy way they read each other's actions.

143

"I thought you gave up smoking," Susan said.

"I basically have, except for once in a while. I'm a lot better than I was."

"I'll agree to that. Three packs a day was going to kill you."

Ronnie looked up from the glasses she was washing and raised her eyebrows. Diane met her gaze but looked away almost immediately. Ronnie worked faster, trying to finish quickly.

"Ronnie, you never answered me about my little proposition. What about our moonlight swim? We'd just peel off our clothes and let the waves wash over us. It would be fun."

"Jesus," Diane muttered.

"Did you say something, Diane?" Susan turned to her ex, an amused expression on her face.

"Do you have to hit on everyone?" Diane downed another shot. "Is there no time or place that isn't appropriate for sex?"

Susan looked up in thought. "Well, no. Sex is good anytime or anywhere. I know you don't agree, Diane, but I think Ronnie might."

"Bitch" was Diane's only reply.

Susan looked at Ronnie, a smug expression on her face. "Someone's had too much to drink, like that's unusual."

"Only when I'm around you, darling," Diane replied.

"Can you tell we were lovers? For a year and a half."

Diane smiled at Susan. "And that was probably two years too long."

Susan watched Ronnie's reaction. "I can tell you're surprised, Ronnie."

"You just don't seem compatible," Ronnie said, returning to her work. She couldn't look at Diane.

Susan stubbed her cigarette out and swirled her drink, which had barely been touched. "You're being kind. We're not anything alike. Polar opposites, night and day—you name it. Diane's a control freak and totally anal retentive. Everything has to be in order. She keeps her life and emotions in proper alignment at all times. Never allows herself to cut loose, except, of course, when she's drinking. That's the only time the professor lets her guard down, isn't it, darling?"

Diane glared at her. "Thank you, Doctor Skaggs, for yet another enlightening tour into my psyche. However, you're not telling Ronnie anything I haven't already told her." For the first time all evening, Diane actually spoke to Ronnie. "This was another reason we broke up. I couldn't live with a psychiatrist analyzing me all the time."

"Well, Diane, you are quite a case study." Susan eyed Ronnie and sucked in her breath. "Now, our lovely bartender here is quite the opposite. At the risk of becoming too personal, I think you're fascinating, Ronnie. I sense you have a wild side and very few inhibitions. I gather you've experimented with several taboos including illicit drugs and men. Your mother spent most of your childhood with white knuckles, praying you'd live through it. You were a rebel in school but you achieved good grades. You pulled a lot of pranks but rarely got caught, making you the idol of many." She paused and took a breath. "How am I doing?"

Ronnie chuckled. "Quite well." As an afterthought she said, "You're right. Diane and I are worlds apart, too."

Diane met Ronnie's gaze and held it. The two stared at each other long enough for Susan to say, "Oh, my. Well, what have we here? I would use my PhD to note some chemistry and issues between you two."

Diane ignored her and said to Ronnie, "Differences are not always a bad thing. They create a balance."

"Sometimes," Ronnie said, her eyes never leaving Diane's. "But opposites don't always attract." She threw down the rag. "I'm done." She picked up her purse and turned to Susan. "I'm not really up for that swim, but it was nice meeting you."

"Whoa! Whoa!" Susan jumped up to stop her. "If anyone's leaving, it's me. You need to stay." She led Ronnie to the couch and pushed her into a sitting position. "Now, you," she said, taking Diane's hand and shoving her down next to Ronnie. She stood over both of them, her arms crossed. "I'll leave you two with a little bit of sage psychiatric advice. There's enough sexual energy in this room right now to have a spontaneous orgasm. I suggest you talk, and remember, don't go to bed angry. But I would say that it's critical that you *do* go to bed." She kissed Diane on the cheek, then leaned over Ronnie. "If this woman doesn't treat you right, remember, I will."

Before Ronnie could react, Susan kissed her on the mouth and left.

"Is she always like that?" Ronnie asked when the front door had closed.

"Yes."

Ronnie shut her eyes, too tired to move. She sensed Diane had moved closer, the professor's perfume filling her head. Then Diane's lips were against hers in a gentle kiss. When Ronnie blinked, Diane was hovering over her on the couch, smiling.

"We need to talk, but I've wanted to do that all night."

Ronnie nodded and sat up.

Diane settled into the overstuffed chair and folded her hands in front of her. "I know you're furious and you have every right to be."

"That's a start," Ronnie said sarcastically. She had been holding her anger inside all night, but now it was ready to boil over. She took a deep breath and stood up. "This isn't just about tonight and what happened. I'm at the edge because this whole warped dance that we're doing, which certainly couldn't be called a relationship, is making me crazy on all sorts of levels. Sexually I am probably the most frustrated lesbian in all of America—well, maybe that's an exaggeration, but definitely California." She crossed her arms over her chest and nodded. "Yeah, I'd say that's fair. I'm to the point now where all I think about is *fucking* you, not even making love to you, because I'm beyond that. All I want is to rip your clothes off and take you, and I don't care where. And it only adds to my frustration when you parade around in these types of outfits in front of other people." She gestured to the tiny lamé top and leather pants and paced back and forth. Something dawned on her. "Stand up," she said, and when Diane obliged, Ronnie motioned for her to turn around. "Are you wearing underwear?"

Diane's voice was only a whisper. "I'm wearing a thong."

Ronnie grabbed the sides of her head and fell on the couch. She buried her face in one of the throw pillows and screamed. She slowly sat back up, breathing heavily.

"I'm okay," she told herself aloud. She went to the bar and downed a shot of whiskey before returning to face Diane. "Here's the hard part. I love you. It's that simple, Diane. I adore you. I think about you all the time. Every moment I'm with you is incredible. Whether we're working on the research, or taking a walk, or arguing about politics, it's all wonderful. There's absolutely no other place I'd rather be." She paused and got down on her knees in front of Diane's chair. "I would rather be fighting with you than vacationing in the Bahamas with anyone else. I'd rather be shopping at Ralph's and pricing tuna with you than sailing on a yacht in the Caribbean with Angelina Jolie."

Diane scoffed but Ronnie shook her head.

"No, it's true. And what's more amazing is that we haven't even made love!" She jumped up and stuck her hands in her pockets. "But what I'm not willing to do is sacrifice myself because you're ashamed of our relationship. You get all of me or you don't get any of me. I won't hide. I'm certainly not going to make out with you in a public place and jeopardize your career, but I expect to be seen with you—often. And if people start to whisper, or they think they've figured it out, then so what? I didn't leave one closet to go into another." She froze, trying to think if there was anything else. Satisfied, she nodded. "I'm done. That's all I wanted to say." She returned to the bar, picked up the bottle of whiskey and took a slug. She grabbed her purse and headed for the door.

"Ronnie, wait."

Ronnie stopped, her hand on the knob. Diane stood up and came to her. She stroked Ronnie's cheek with her hand, and Ronnie sank into Diane's dark, brown gaze. There was no way she could stay angry with this woman, not ever.

"Where are you going?" Diane asked.

"I was going to go home, give you some time to think."

Diane wrapped her arms around Ronnie's neck. "Well, you could do that or you could see my thong. Would you like to see my thong?"

"More than I want to breathe air," Ronnie replied, suddenly elated.

Diane laughed and kissed her. She took Ronnie's hands and guided them to the strings that held the lamé fabric in place. With two simple tugs, the sheath disappeared and Diane was half naked.

Ronnie saw the hesitation in her eyes and whispered, "You are incredibly sexy."

She pressed Diane against the door and let her mouth stray down Diane's jaw and into the hollow of her neck. She'd learned all the contours of Diane's incredible figure, and she was fascinated by the softness of her skin, which felt wonderful against her lips. Despite her overwhelming desire, she willed herself to move slowly, knowing Diane needed the reassurance of an unhurried, tender touch. Their lips met again, Diane's fingers buried in Ronnie's hair. The sweet taste of Diane's tongue immediately drove Ronnie into action and she explored the curves of Diane's breasts. She caressed them gently, almost reverently at first, gauging Diane's response to each stroke, wanting permission to continue.

Her thumbs found Diane's hardened nipples and the professor sighed. She increased the pressure of her touch, circling only

148

the nipples and nothing else.

"Kiss them," Diane pleaded, placing Ronnie's palms squarely over her chest. "Stop teasing me," she ordered.

Ronnie stared into the fiery brown eyes, boiling with desire. She fondled each breast roughly, no longer worried about Diane's intentions.

Ronnie tipped her head down and brought a nipple between her lips. Diane's moans echoing throughout the bungalow. When both aureoles shone red, Ronnie planted a kiss on the yellow butterfly.

"I want to see the rest of your tattoos," she said playfully.

"You'll have to go lower," Diane said, grabbing Ronnie's shoulders and pushing her down on her knees.

Ronnie whispered kisses down Diane's belly, savoring the feel of the skin against her cheek. She popped the button on the leather pants and lowered the zipper with her teeth, inhaling the sweet smell that was Diane's sex. Only when Diane stepped out of the pants did Ronnie notice the flying dolphin on Diane's hip and, more prominently, the bursting sun that covered most of her upper thigh.

"These are fabulous," Ronnie murmured, fingering the thong's waistband. The sheer black lace displayed Diane's freshly waxed mound. "Oh, God, you got a bikini wax," she said, her lips exploring the inside of Diane's thighs.

"We'll discuss body art and everything else later." Diane gasped. "As much as I hate to admit it, sometimes Susan is right, and I listen to what the good doctor prescribes."

Diane yanked the thong down and parted her legs for Ronnie, who didn't need a PhD to know what to do next.

21. The Morning After

The night had been full of surprises. Diane was shocked at her impulsive willingness to sleep with Ronnie after that impassioned speech. The sex had been incredible, and Diane was astounded that Ronnie was such a considerate and skilled lover. She didn't want to think about how many women Ronnie had bedded to become so adept, and while the sex had produced more orgasms than Diane had ever experienced in a single night, it was the way Ronnie held her tightly, kissed her shoulders and whispered tender words in her ear that motivated Diane to fight off the call for sleep.

When they did drift off into the afterglow, Diane rested securely in Ronnie's embrace, exactly as she had imagined in her dreams, with Ronnie's strong arms around her, both of them naked, sweaty and totally sexed. Diane couldn't remember the last time she had slept nude, but it seemed natural with Ronnie, an act that was both highly erotic and serenely beautiful.

Most surprising was her insatiable appetite that surfaced again around four o' clock in the morning. She woke to find herself curled up against Ronnie, her hand resting on Ronnie's breast, Ronnie's lips inches from hers and their legs entwined. Her arousal was immediate, and she slid over Ronnie's gorgeous body, tracing the outline of the labrys on Ronnie's shoulder with her finger and then massaging Ronnie's nipples. Ronnie stirred but remained asleep as Diane continued her descent, playing with the silver belly button ring and the wisps of hair between Ronnie's thighs. She gazed at her lover, awed by her breathtaking beauty and not fully believing that the encounter was real.

Only when Diane had nestled her tongue in Ronnie's center did the young woman awaken with a start. Diane looked up and Ronnie smiled and sighed. She pulled herself up to watch Diane make love to her and rocked her hips in unison with Diane's strokes. When the orgasm ripped through Ronnie's body, Diane started to cry, another surprising response that totally confounded her.

Ronnie had fallen back to sleep but Diane remained awake, and as the daylight hours crept upon the horizon, so did the doubt in her all-to-logical mind. The questions, analyses and rationalizations were forming, demanding answers and accountability for her unusual behavior the previous night. Now as she sat on her deck, having showered and wrapped herself in the plush terry cloth robe, sipping her morning coffee and staring into the harsh daylight, she began to have regrets.

The shower turned on and Diane knew Ronnie was up. They would need to talk. She was starting to formulate what she would say to Ronnie when the doorbell rang. Damn! She'd forgotten Sunday brunch with Camille.

Camille sailed through the front door, a brown paper sack in her hand. "I brought croissants today because Lou said they were fresh. And Jamaican coffee." She finally assessed Diane's apparel, her brow furrowed. "Why aren't you dressed?"

Diane smiled, certain that it would only take her good friend another two or three seconds to get the whole picture. She was right.

"Is that the shower I hear?" Camille pointed to the bathroom.

Diane blushed and nodded. Despite her growing anxieties, the imprint of the night before lingered, and she couldn't hide that from Camille.

Camille grabbed her by the shoulders. "Please tell me that you have a beautiful grad student using your shower."

Diane shrugged and Camille hugged her tightly, but Diane was hesitant to return the hug with as much enthusiasm.

"Oh, God. I'm too late! You're already in thinking mode." Camille suddenly broke the hug and stared at her. "You've already started analyzing the relationship, and I'm guessing you've formulated a list of why it won't work and convenient ways you can break up."

Diane smirked. "Stop! I am not. It was absolutely wonderful." As she said the words, every nerve ending in her body tingled.

Camille continued to stare, unconvinced. "But . . ."

Diane looked away and went to pour Camille a cup of non-Jamaican coffee. "No buts . . ." She stirred slowly and held up her spoon. "Except—"

"I knew it. I knew there would be a but, a however or an except. There's always some sort of subordinate clause with you."

"I can't help how I think!" Diane blurted.

"And you already regret it?"

Diane sighed, handed Camille the coffee and sat down next to her. She ran her fingers through her hair, trying to make sense of her feelings. "The logical side of me is having trouble."

"I see. Then forget the logical side. Sex isn't logical. Orgasms aren't logical."

"Camille, don't patronize me. I teach this class, okay?"

152

Camille raised a hand in surrender. "Tell me what's bothering you, honey."

"I don't regret being with Ronnie. It was the most passion I've ever felt with anyone. But I'm a professor and she's a student. You know the rules, Camille. And on top of it, I've got Michaelson to contend with. This would be all the fodder he needs to hang me. If he finds out I'm sleeping with my TA, my career will be over."

Camille remained silent. They both knew there was truth to Diane's concern.

"Besides," Diane continued, "she's from a totally different generation. We have different ways of looking at the world."

Camille shook a finger at her. "Nope. Not going to buy it. You should have stuck to your first argument. It was far more compelling. You're talking to the wrong person if you think I'll believe that age has any factor in love."

Judy was indeed fifteen years younger than Camille.

"It's just that she's so young. At least Judy's my age. We're all more mature," she argued.

Camille laughed and sipped her coffee. "God, Diane, you make it sound like you're eighty and she's twelve. Ronnie's a vibrant woman, or was that fact lost on you last night?"

They both had to chuckle at that.

"I just don't know if it's worth the risk," Diane said.

Camille took Diane's hand and patted it. "Anything special is always worth the risk. So you'll be careful."

The bathroom door opened and Ronnie appeared wearing only a skimpy T-shirt that came down to her navel and drying her hair with a towel. "Baby, do you have any boxers I could wear?" She pulled the towel off her head and gave a start at seeing a visitor. "Camille! Hi." Ronnie wrapped the towel around her middle. "Sorry for the peep show."

"Don't be. I very much enjoy gazing at a beautiful woman. Judy will be sorry she missed it."

153

Ronnie blushed and went to Diane. She leaned over and slowly let her lips touch Diane's until they sunk together for a full kiss.

"I may have an old pair in the top dresser drawer," Diane said after a moment.

Ronnie smiled and whispered, "You planned last night. You wanted it to happen. Remember that."

Diane closed her eyes and gave a slight nod.

"I'll see you later, Camille." Ronnie kissed her on the cheek and went back to the bathroom.

"I think it's time for me to go." Camille got up and Diane escorted her to the door. "Hang on to her, Diane. Don't do anything you'll regret."

"Do you realize when she's forty-seven I'll be sixty-five?"

"And I'm sure she'll be happy to pour your prune juice for you."

"Now there's a pleasant thought."

She kissed Camille good-bye and shut the door, the words Ronnie had whispered still echoing in her ears.

22. The Camping Trip

"Tell me again why people find camping enjoyable?" Richard asked, a look of distaste on his face. He pulled a sleeping bag down from the garage shelf and tossed it to Brody, who unrolled it to check for spiders.

"It's called the outdoors, Richard," Brody said. "Some people actually go outdoors for things other than sex in the park."

"Really?" Richard was serious and Brody rolled his eyes.

Ronnie continued to pull stuff off the shelves, including a propane stove, lantern and mess kit. "Who does all this belong to?" She held up some tent poles and began looking for the canvas.

"Most of this stuff is Dave's," Richard answered. "When he met me, he gave up camping. I found better activities for him *indoors*." He tossed her a folding chair, which she added to the growing stack of equipment.

"So where are you going?" Brody asked.

"Far away," Ronnie replied. "We're going with Camille and Judy down to Encinitas for the Fourth of July weekend. At least if we're out of town, Diane might loosen up a bit."

Richard jumped down. "Is all not well in the land of lust and love? Are you having trouble with the good professor?" He opened three folding chairs and motioned for Ronnie and Brody to sit. "Let's have a group session." He crossed his legs, rested his hand on his chin and stared at Ronnie intently. "Begin."

Ronnie sat down and took a deep breath. "Well, in some ways, it's great. We're so compatible."

Richard pretended to take notes on an invisible notepad. "How's the sex?"

"Great."

Richard wrote that down with his nonexistent pencil. "Then what's the problem?"

Brody groaned. "Richard, there's more to a relationship than sex."

"I know. I'm just prioritizing. So what are the issues?"

Ronnie pulled her hair into a ponytail and fastened it with a rubber band. "It's just that we rarely go out. You're not the only people who don't see me. I haven't seen hardly anyone since I got back from visiting my folks in Arizona."

Brody shrugged. "It sounds like she's a homebody."

Ronnie disagreed. "It's more than that. She's really worried that people are going to find out, particularly students."

Richard tapped the air pencil on his knee. "So, what do you two do?"

"We spend a lot of time in bed. Or we read, or talk or take walks on the beach. It's nice. I'm not saying it isn't. But we rarely go out to dinner, never to a nightclub, and only once in a while to a movie, and that's because it's in a dark theater."

"Wait a minute," Brody said. "Didn't you two used to go to the museums or out for coffee?"

156

"That was before we started sleeping together."

Richard stroked his chin. "Maybe she thinks it's obvious now. I mean, when I see you two, I know you're together. It's like the world around you evaporates."

Brody nodded. "I have to agree with Dr. Phil, here, Ronnie. He does have a point. You two have great chemistry."

Richard laughed out loud and slapped his knee. "Chemistry? I'm surprised that people at Carlson haven't figured it out. How do the two of you manage to teach in the same classroom without causing an explosion?"

Before Ronnie could argue, a car horn honked. Judy's huge Ford truck had pulled into the driveway. The guys helped Ronnie load everything in the back and the women were on their way to pick up Diane.

Ronnie hoped this trip with Diane would add something to their relationship, which seemed to become more reclusive since the summer began. Both of them had gone their separate ways after the trimester ended, visiting their parents at opposite ends of the world for two weeks. While Ronnie went home to Globe, Diane journeyed to Japan where her father was conducting some financial seminar and enjoying golf whenever possible. They spoke at least three times a day on the phone, sometimes for over an hour, and Ronnie calculated that she would need to put in several extra shifts at the bar to pay for the international calls she'd made. Sometimes if Diane's father realized she was on the phone with Ronnie, he would ask to speak to her, wanting to discuss golf—a sport Ronnie played fairly well. She had golfed a few times with Diane and her parents, Diane growing restless by the sixth hole and excusing herself to the clubhouse.

Ronnie's parents were dying to meet Diane, who promised Ronnie's mother that she would join Ronnie on the next trip. Ronnie couldn't imagine what Diane would think of the tiny mining town where she grew up, and the old blue clapboard house that had been her home for her entire life. It was a far cry

157

from the mansion outside Santa Barbara or the Beverly Hills Country Club. Yet Diane would probably enjoy walking through the historic antiques stores of nearby Miami, Arizona, and she would love the enchiladas at Guaya's el Rey, the best Mexican restaurant in the Globe—Miami area. They would have a lovely time—because they were far away from Carlson.

Brody was right. They used to do so many things, go so many places. It always gave them fuel for discussion or disagreement, and while Ronnie was grateful that they had indeed slept together, it had changed their relationship. She felt her friendship with Diane was being eclipsed by their romantic love and Diane's unwillingness to allow the two worlds to mix. Their most recent outing, a simple evening of dinner, had ended in frustration and anger for Ronnie.

After a week of prodding and pleading, Diane had finally agreed to go out to their favorite Chinese restaurant, a place they had frequented for months before, usually discussing research, often bringing their books and notes with them. Ronnie had hoped the familiar surroundings would ease Diane's anxieties, but without the armor of work around them, she was nervous. They looked like what they were—two women on a date.

Ronnie watched with disappointment as Diane ran her hand through her hair endlessly while they read the menu. She constantly glanced about the restaurant, looking for any Carlson people who might see them together. When the waiter took their orders, Diane sat with her hands folded in front of her, clearly enduring the evening rather than enjoying it.

"What's wrong?" Ronnie asked.

"Nothing," came the short reply. "I'm fine."

"Diane, you look like you're sitting on a bomb and trying very hard not to move. Look at yourself. This isn't pleasant and it certainly isn't romantic."

"What do you want me to do? Hold hands with you in front of the whole restaurant?" she snapped.

Ronnie's eyes widened at the chastising remark. "I guess I just wanted to be with you, someplace other than the bungalow."

Diane closed her eyes for a moment and took a breath. "I'm sorry, Ronnie. I didn't mean to be sharp."

She gave a slight smile, which Ronnie returned. Although she didn't bark at Ronnie anymore that evening, she didn't relax. The evening had been a total loss, and by the time they left the restaurant, Ronnie was equally paranoid, sure that Elliot Michaelson would leap out from behind the giant lobster tank and yell, "Aha!" Since then Ronnie hadn't had the strength to push for more outings.

It had been Diane who suggested the camping trip. She obviously sensed Ronnie's growing restlessness and knew they needed some time together away from L.A. As the truck pulled up to the bungalow, Diane appeared from the garage with a knapsack and a duffle bag. She threw them into the truck bed and climbed into the backseat with Ronnie, pulling her into an embrace for a sizzling kiss.

"Whoa!" Ronnie exclaimed.

Diane's eyes shone with excitement. She traced Ronnie's lips with her finger until Ronnie caught it in her mouth. Diane laughed and slowly pulled it out.

"God." Judy moaned from the front of the cab. "You two better behave back there, or I'll have to move Ronnie up here to the front so we can talk about cars."

"Keep it PG," Camille concurred. "If I don't get any yet, nobody gets any."

"We'll be good," Diane assured them as her hand crept up Ronnie's thigh.

The Friday evening sunset over the ocean was breathtaking. The hues of yellow and orange met the blue water, a band of silver defining the end of the sea and the beginning of the sky.

Ronnie snuggled with Diane on a blanket in the sand, every one of her senses fulfilled. She watched the sunset, listened to the hum of the waves, smelled the sea air and, most importantly, felt the warmth of her lover's embrace and the taste of her mouth, a sweet hint of mint from the candy they had enjoyed for dessert.

"Looking out there makes me realize how small and insignificant everything really is," Camille said.

"I've always loved the sea," Diane added.

"Me too," Ronnie said, "and in Arizona we have an even greater appreciation than you Californians."

Diane smiled at her and touched her cheek.

"So how are things going for you two?" Camille asked.

"Great." Ronnie brightened. "But do you know how I could graduate, like, *tomorrow*?"

Diane poked her in the ribs. "I'm not that tense."

"Yeah, right," Ronnie said, turning to Camille and Judy. "A few weeks ago we came out of a movie and Diane made me hide in the bathroom until a group of Carlson students left."

Judy wrinkled her nose in disgust. "Diane. How could you?"

"Look, Judy, you don't know what it's like for me. Camille understands because she knows the kind of pressure we're under. Don't you read those articles about teachers losing their tenure because they get involved with students?"

"This is college." Judy shook her head. "Besides, that usually only happens when a professor has promised good grades for sex."

"It still doesn't look right, certainly not to the administration." Diane's voice rose. "I've only been tenured for a few years. There's a lot of ways I could be fired. Not to mention that I have to apply for a grant next year. Plus the issue with my teaching evaluation. How do you think this would look to Dean Morgan? It would cause a scandal."

"See, Ronnie," Judy retorted, "you're moving up. Now you're a scandal."

Ronnie smiled meekly at the joke. She hadn't meant to start an argument.

Camille took Judy's hand. "I understand what you're saying, darling. But Diane also has a point. Regardless of Ronnie's age, she's a student at Carlson. We get memos all the time on this kind of stuff. What constitutes fraternization, the appropriate times and places for conferences, how to discuss grades with students . . ." Camille's voice trailed off as Diane nodded in agreement.

Judy held up her hand. "Wait a minute, honey. Whose side are you on? I thought you wanted Ronnie and Diane to be together."

Camille kissed Judy's hand. "Of course I do, darling. I want them to experience the happiness we've known." They rubbed noses and looked lovingly at each other. "They just have to be careful right now, that's all."

Ronnie looked on as the couple abandoned the conversation, enamored with each other. Could it ever be that way between her and Diane?

"Are you sorry we slept together?" she asked.

Diane looked startled, her gaze darting from their romantic friends to Ronnie. "No, of course not," she said.

All eyes suddenly turned toward Diane. The reply had been less than emphatic, Ronnie thought, and clearly no one was convinced.

"I'm taking a walk," Ronnie said, saddened. She jumped up, intending to head down the beach.

"You're an idiot, Diane," Judy said as she joined Ronnie.

They walked along the beach for a while and finally sat down on a pier.

"These professor types. They're all so"—Judy searched for the word—"cerebral. If it's not all explainable, then they don't get it."

Ronnie pulled her legs up to her chin. "Tell me about it." She chuckled. "You know, it's too bad you and I didn't get together. Sometimes I think I have more in common with you than with Diane."

Judy leaned back on her hands. "I know it seems that way, but the fact is, girlfriend, we need those two. Camille is my other half. I know that sounds trite, but it's the truth."

"We'd probably kill each other in the first month." They both laughed at the idea. Ronnie could picture the two of them shouting at the top of their lungs over an article in the newspaper. "I love her, Judy, and I don't know what to do," she said softly, her eyes misting.

"Well," Judy cracked, "Diane's brilliant, but she's a slow learner. She loves you, too, I can see that. She's just romantically challenged."

They both laughed heartily and Judy gave Ronnie a hug. They talked under the moonlight for another hour. Eventually they wandered back to the campsite; Camille and Diane were nowhere in sight.

"We should be able to get some really good nookie out of this," Judy said, heading for her tent.

Ronnie stood outside on the beach, listening as Camille apologized profusely. Their voices soon faded and Ronnie knew what they were doing. Still not ready to face Diane, Ronnie sat on the beach and watched the waves. She remembered the night she had proclaimed her love for Diane, the night of the party. She had been adamant about not leaving one closet for another, but wasn't that exactly what had happened? She had allowed Diane to keep their relationship a secret to protect her job, and Ronnie knew that as out as she wanted to be, she would never jeopardize Diane's career. They were breaking all the rules, and while it was hard for her to remember that, Diane never forgot it. Judy's description of Diane replayed in her mind. Diane *was* brilliant, but she was also a slow learner. Ronnie wondered how long she could be patient.

Realizing she was only prolonging the inevitable, Ronnie crept into the tent. As she slid into her sleeping bag, Diane's arm wrapped around her. "I'm so sorry," she whispered.

"Don't worry about it," Ronnie said icily.

"Honey, we have to talk about this. I can't sleep with this still hanging over us."

Ronnie was poised for an argument. "Diane, I don't really think there's anything to discuss. We obviously view our relationship from totally different perspectives, and that's just the way it is. I can't change how you feel, and you can't change how I feel."

"I just don't understand how you can be in love with me," Diane said. "We've only been romantic for a short while and it just doesn't make sense."

Ronnie groaned. "What? I'm telling you how I feel. Now, the fact that you can't say that to me is your issue, but if you consider me to be a somewhat levelheaded human being, someone who possesses at least a modicum of intelligence, then you'll at least validate *my* feelings." She paused for a breath and forged on before Diane could speak. "But judging from your behavior tonight, though, you obviously think I'm some kind of crackpot, because you have a PhD and know everything." She fell silent, realizing the whole campground probably had heard her little speech.

"Are you through?"

Ronnie nodded. It wasn't very often that she got to light into Diane.

Diane sat up and faced her. "First of all, I'm sorry. I don't mean to belittle your feelings."

"But you don't believe I'm in love with you."

Diane took a deep breath, as if weighing her words. "I think love is a lot of work, and lasting love only happens after time. It's impossible for someone to know she wants to commit to that person for the rest of her life based on such a short time. You just can't know right away."

"Maybe you can't, but does that mean it's true for everyone? Diane, just because you haven't experienced it, or it's not documented in some book, doesn't mean it doesn't exist. How could we believe in God or outer space?"

"That's totally different. I certainly haven't met God, but I have been in love and I've been in relationships, so I do know something," she said, "regardless of my PhD."

She fell right into Ronnie's trap. "So in other words, your experience in relationships speaks for all of us? Diane Cole is the definitive source on love?"

"Shh!" she reprimanded. "You're going to wake the whole camp."

"Well, maybe we should," Ronnie said, refusing to lower her voice. "I'm sure all of these people would like to meet the Love Doctor." When Diane didn't reply, she went on. "But then again, that probably wouldn't be a good idea."

"Excuse me?"

Ronnie wrapped her arms around Diane's neck. "Darling, do you have any idea how much I love you? I would do anything for you."

She smiled. "Ronnie, you're sounding a little maudlin."

"I know. And no one is more surprised than me. I don't get this way about women. I've had several girlfriends, Diane, and I've slept with a good amount of women. I've told a few I was in love with them. No one has ever made me feel the way you make me feel."

Diane brushed her lips across Ronnie's, silencing her. Ronnie suspected she was still uncomfortable about her own feelings, unable to explain how she felt.

Ronnie was philosophical. "It's probably better anyway," she said. "I know you'll never be able to love me in the same way."

Diane bristled. "What do you mean by that?"

"Someday I think you might love me in your own way, but

164

you love from your head, not your heart. And when it comes to love, the heart is always stronger."

"So now who's the expert?" she shot back.

"Look, Diane, we're never going to agree on this, and frankly, it doesn't matter. How we got here isn't the point." Ronnie pushed her down on the sleeping bag and rubbed her hands up and down Diane's thighs. "But could you do me one favor?"

"Anything, as long as you don't stop what you're doing."

"Could you please admit that there is at least the slightest possibility that just maybe I'm right? Just maybe? Especially since I never get to win an argument with you, and this time I actually do have some logical ground to stand on."

"I'll admit that it's possible, but I do so under protest."

Ronnie smirked, knowing Diane hated being wrong.

Her hand slid down the front of Ronnie's sweatpants and the subject was closed.

23. The Calendar

Diane stormed into the office and dropped her briefcase with a thud. Ronnie looked up from the notes she was taking, sure that Diane had once again visited Elliot Michaelson's lair. No one else could make her that upset, and the fact that the beginning of the academic year was approaching meant she had to endure more of his meetings, phone calls and e-mails, raising her blood pressure in the process.

"That damn Michaelson! He made out the schedules. I'm teaching a seven-forty a.m. class! He's punishing me for appealing my review. I just can't believe this. He knows how hard it is for me to get here before nine. I'm not a morning person. I admit it. Sleep is the only part of my personality that isn't anal retentive. And what's worse is that Hank Brookstone specifically asked for a seven thirty class and didn't get it because Michaelson felt it would be better to place my class earlier." She sat down on

166

the edge of the desk by Ronnie and crumpled up the memorandum.

Ronnie gently caressed Diane's back. "Well, darling, there is one consolation. Since neither of us particularly likes sex in the morning, at least you'll be doing something productive."

Diane smiled. "I'd rather be sleeping."

"I know. But when I'm there, I'll make sure you get out the door on time."

"And what about when you're not there? Michaelson would just love to see me be late for class. It would give him a few more pages for my growing personnel file."

Ronnie stared into Diane's eyes. "Then I guess that means you'll need me in your bed every Monday and Wednesday night next trimester."

Diane glanced at the open door and the empty hallway before bringing Ronnie's hand to her lips and kissing her knuckles. "I guess so."

They were still staring at each other when a young man knocked on the open door. They both turned and saw an underclassman with a camera around his neck dressed in Bermuda shorts and a T-shirt. He couldn't have been more than five feet tall and his hair was slicked straight back. He carried a black portfolio case under his arm, and Ronnie noticed his knees were knocking together.

"Excuse me. I'm looking for Ronnie Frost." His eyes went from Diane to Ronnie in about two seconds, and he smiled. "You have to be Ronnie," he said. "Could I talk to you for a few minutes?"

"Sure," she said.

Diane went to her desk and the boy entered the room timidly, his eyes never leaving Ronnie.

"Wow. You are incredibly beautiful."

Ronnie didn't bother to hide her annoyance. "Can I help you with something?" She looked over at Diane, who was thoroughly amused. Ronnie sat up straighter, strengthening her resolve. No one would ever get to Ronnie Frost by acknowledging her looks *first*.

The young man cleared his throat and looked her straight in the eye. "My name is Nick Brown, and I'm studying photography here at Carlson. For my trimester project, I'm creating a calendar of the women of Carlson University. Maybe you've heard of that concept before?"

She was already shaking her head and rising from her chair. "I'm sorry, Nick, but I'm not interested."

"Wait! Please listen to my pitch, if for no other reason than I practiced it for an hour last night. Please?" He clasped his hands in front of him, and Ronnie thought he might get down on one knee.

"Oh, all right." She returned to the chair and crossed her arms over her chest. "You have one minute. Go."

"Okay, here's the thing. I've got to have you in this calendar. When I started asking around, everybody kept saying, you've got to ask Ronnie Frost. You've got to get Ronnie Frost to be in the calendar. And I kept asking, 'Who's Ronnie Frost?' because I had no idea who you are. I mean, I was just a freshman, so how would I know?" He cleared his throat again. "Anyway, everybody said that you were this totally hot grad student and the calendar wouldn't be the same without you in it—"

"Nick?" Ronnie raised her hand. "First of all, you've got to slow down, second, I really don't care what other people think of me, and third, you've used up thirty of your precious sixty seconds. What I want to know is why are you doing this and what's in it for you."

Nick blinked. "Nothing."

Her eyes narrowed. "Excuse me? You're going to do all this work, and you're going to get nothing? You are going to sell this calendar, aren't you? You're not just looking for some cheap thrills and a chance to meet girls, are you?"

"No, no. I am selling the calendar, but the money is going to fund breast cancer research. All of it. I'm just using the calendar for my portfolio and my grade."

Ronnie looked at Diane, who nodded her approval. "All right, Nick," she said. "You've got my attention. Show me your portfolio and prove to me that this isn't going to be a waste of my time, and I'll consider it."

His face lit up and he sat down across from Ronnie. When he unzipped the portfolio, dozens of stills and head shots poured out onto the desk. She examined several and realized Nick was naturally talented. He had already photographed many beautiful women and landscapes. Amid the sea of gorgeous breasts, long legs and high cheekbones was a stark black-and-white photo that immediately caught her attention.

The head shot was of a woman, her face drawn into itself, her eyes sunken. The eyes told the story of innocence lost and unpleasant experience found. Ronnie guessed she was only in her forties, but the haggard expression telegraphed the excruciating pain she must have felt. Slight wisps of hair covered her mostly bald head and she stared straight into the camera, not shying away from her state, no doubt unwilling to let anyone else turn away before they stared into her dark eyes.

"Who is this?" she asked, still glued to the photo.

"That's my mom. She died of breast cancer when I was six-teen."

The Women of Carlson University calendar took one day of Ronnie's life. Apparently Nick's biography touched others, too, because Ronnie was surprised to see an entire crew gathered around Castillo Fountain, the location where she would do her shoot. Nick had recruited professional lighting people as well as a Hollywood makeup artist who gushed over Ronnie's face the entire time she sat in the chair. The stylist weaved Ronnie's hair, and, with her dark skin, she was the epitome of a California girl.

Vandella grinned at the end result. "You look incredible, my friend," she said.

Ronnie had insisted Van accompany her, as her nerves were on edge. She'd even smoked a cigarette that morning, hoping to allay the fear of standing in public and smiling. And there was no more public place on campus than Castillo Fountain, which sat in the center of Carlson next to the Memorial Union. Still everything seemed to be going well, and Ronnie just tried not to think about all of the people who would see her.

She had managed to calm herself until she walked into the changing room and saw the swimsuit Nick had selected, or rather, the three patches of cloth that would cover her most private of parts.

"Nick!" she yelled.

He came running into the room, not even bothering to knock.

Ronnie stood there waving the very skimpy silver bikini at him. "What the hell is this?"

"Um, well, you're going to play in the fountain."

"I'm what?"

"I even got special permission from the dean," Nick blathered, pulling a piece of paper from his shirt pocket. "He said it was okay."

She grabbed the paper from him and ripped it up. "You are crazy if you think I'm wearing this or that I'm getting into the fountain."

"But you have to, Ronnie. You're the last one. I'll be short a whole month without you. Who'd buy a calendar without June? Not to mention the fact that I'll fail photography. Do you really want me to be a failure?" Nick's voice was cracking and he looked as though he might cry.

There was a knock on the door and Diane stuck her head in. "Hey, what's all the yelling?"

"Wonderboy wants me to wear practically nothing in public."

Ronnie tossed the bikini to Diane. Standing behind Nick, she smiled seductively, and Ronnie scowled at her.

"Ronnie, you have to do this. Please!" Nick whined. "Everybody's here. They're all waiting."

"No fucking way!" Ronnie poked him in the chest with her finger.

"Nick, why don't you let me talk to Ronnie, okay?"

Nick nodded and left the women alone. Diane examined the flimsy pieces of silver material. "Well," she said with a sigh, "it's not a thong, but I'd still like to see you in it."

"And I'd be happy to wear it just for you," Ronnie replied. She stuffed her things in her duffle bag and turned to the door.

Diane popped the lock and held up the bikini. "Put it on for me, now," she whispered. She wrapped her arms around Ronnie's neck and kissed her. "I want this on you." She began unbuttoning Ronnie's shirt.

"You're not getting me to do this, Diane."

Diane touched Ronnie's chin. "I think you should do it because you promised. And Nick picked this outfit because, frankly, darling, you're going to sell a lot of calendars. You look amazing and everyone's going to know it."

"No, everyone's going to *see*," Ronnie said, her anxiety surfacing. "All those people looking at me, Diane. In this! I can't do it. Even if it is for a good cause."

"Yes, you can. You just need to pretend that I'm the only one who can see you. It's all for me. Because it is all for me, right?"

Ronnie nodded.

"Imagine that we're alone, and show me how much you desire me."

Diane's eyes were smoldering, and Ronnie nodded again, still unsure if she could really exhibit her body in front of hundreds of bystanders who passed by the M.U. Diane handed her the bikini, kissed her softly and left her to change.

Despite being a geeky sophomore, Nick had enough fore-

171

sight to leave Ronnie a sheer robe so she could be partially covered while the crew adjusted the lights or changed the water flow of the fountain. When she emerged from the changing room, her eyes alternated focus between Nick and Diane, who had positioned herself to Ronnie's right. Wearing a slight smile, the professor nodded her approval.

It was all for her, Ronnie thought. She stripped off the robe and followed Nick's directions as he set up the first several shots. Even though he was slow, he knew what he wanted and Ronnie respected that. The poses were seductive, exposing much of Ronnie's cleavage, the curve of her buttocks or the inside of her thighs. With every crane of her neck or shake of her hair, Ronnie thought only of Diane, and the idea of making love to her broadened the smile on Ronnie's face.

"Absolutely perfect!" Nick called to her, his finger jamming down the shutter, capturing a multitude of images. He moved in close. "Don't smile," he said authoritatively. "But don't frown. Just look into the camera."

She did so, imagining that she could see Nick's face through the lens.

He dropped the camera to his chest, and Ronnie blinked. It was as though a hypnotist's session had ended. "We're done, Ronnie. Great job!"

She found the robe, covered her body and started toward the changing room. Something was different but she hadn't noticed it before, too focused on the camera and too eager for the whole experience to end. She glanced back toward the fountain from the changing room and finally comprehended what was happening—a huge crowd had assembled around the fountain and they were chanting her name.

Three weeks later Ronnie found a square manila envelope on her desk, a significant bulge sticking out from one side. She held it up to Diane, who shrugged. She ripped open the flap and with-drew—herself. She was staring at her own face on the cover, the blue eyes iridescent and, she thought, even seductive. It was a great picture. She plopped the calendar in front of the book Diane was reading and the professor gasped.

"Jesus, Ronnie. That's an incredible photo." Diane opened the calendar to June and swallowed hard. "God, I remember this shot. I thought I was going to have an orgasm right there on the mall."

Ronnie stared at the person in the photo, someone she couldn't believe was her. She'd been leaning back on her left elbow, her body horizontal on the fountain wall. A sheet of water covered her face, and her mouth conveyed total ecstasy. Nick had stood above her looking down, the swell of her breasts jut-ting toward the camera, the fingers of her right hand splayed over her abdomen, suggesting a trip southward. While there was nothing explicit about the picture, it was highly erotic.

There was a note in the envelope too. *Dear Ronnie,* she read. *Thanks for posing for me. I got an A on my portfolio, and the calendars are now in their second printing. We've made over ten thousand dollars for breast cancer research. I should also tell you that three different modeling agencies have phoned and I've included their numbers in case you want to call them back.*

"Yeah, right," she said under her breath. Diane continued to stare at Miss June, totally ignoring her. She cleared her throat to gain the professor's attention. "Um, excuse me. I know you're totally engrossed in that picture, but I've got a question for you."

Diane looked up and smiled. "What is it?"

"Why would you settle for imitation when you could have the real thing?"

Diane looked momentarily puzzled until Ronnie pulled out the silver bikini from the envelope and dropped it in her lap.

24. The Necklace

It was different this time. Diane couldn't explain in words what had happened or why tonight was a milestone, because Ronnie's touch always ignited a fire throughout her body, even when she wasn't in the mood. She could be standing in the kitchen, mad as hell at Elliott Michaelson or thinking about inane topics like the best olive oil, and Ronnie could come up behind her, kiss her neck innocently, and Diane was ready for sex, wanted sex and, often, demanded sex. *Demanded* was a bit strong of a term, since Ronnie never refused an opportunity for the two of them to jump into bed, but Diane's sex drive stunned both of them. She had never been like this before, and although she could easily dismiss her horizontal urges as a statistical stereotype of a woman in the throes of midlife, more than likely her desires sprung from her current partner.

She and Ronnie were a perfect fit.

She'd known that from the first kiss. When Ronnie had leaned across the bar that night, Diane's shock lasted a mere nanosecond before she willingly parted her lips ever so slightly and pressed them firmly against Ronnie's. Onlookers would never have rated the kiss as passionate, Ronnie's incredible control fooling the rowdy bar patrons. The kiss was innocent, but there was sex in Ronnie's eyes and only Diane saw that. It had been the most lustful moment of her life, witnessed by a hundred people, and none of them had been conscious of the raw desire emanating from the two women. She had told Ronnie it was brilliant, and it truly was. In fact, *brilliant* described Ronnie perfectly.

Diane grinned in the darkness at the memory. She stretched like a cat, leaning back fully into Ronnie's embrace, pressing against Ronnie's chest, her arms over her head and wrapped around Ronnie's neck. She lay prostrate while Ronnie's fingers trailed across her skin, cooling the heat of her passion in the afterglow, sculpting her body into a different shape of desire. She sighed and parted her legs, knowing that Ronnie would reclaim her soon.

"You're ready again?" Ronnie teased.

Diane laughed. "It seems that way. Pretty unbelievable for a woman my age, huh?"

Ronnie rolled over on top of her and kissed her neck and earlobes hungrily. "Consider me your personal aphrodisiac, your libido activator or, my favorite, the fire of your desire."

Diane pulled Ronnie toward her and their tongues and lips collided roughly. Their bodies immediately reacted to the contact—hips, legs and arms finding comfortable rhythms that brought them both pleasure. The familiar slight touches, kisses and breathy moans were a step away from ecstasy.

Ronnie abruptly stopped and faced her. Diane sobered immediately and swallowed hard. "What's wrong?"

A sly smile crept over Ronnie's face. "There's nothing wrong.

In fact . . ." She reached into her bag and, with no ceremony or warning, withdrew a long, slender jewelry box.

"What's this for?" Diane's heart pounded from excitement and fear. At least the box wasn't small and square. She couldn't handle a proposal.

Ronnie only shrugged. When Diane opened the box her jaw dropped. Resting on the velvet was a slim gold chain attached to an incredible diamond wreathed in gold. She was speechless.

Ronnie lifted Diane's chin and their eyes met. "I wanted to give you something special, and I wasn't going to wait for a special occasion. Every day is special with you."

"This is far too expensive, Ronnie. You can't afford this."

"It doesn't matter what it cost." Ronnie took the necklace from the box and placed it around Diane's neck. They moved to the full-length mirror and admired the glistening stone against Diane's tanned skin.

"It's unbelievably beautiful," Diane said.

"No, *you're* unbelievably beautiful." Ronnie wrapped her arms around Diane's waist and hugged her tightly. "And not just on the outside," she whispered. "I love your mind, your heart. I love that you are everything I want to become."

Hot tears streamed down Diane's face. Ronnie gently kissed her cheek and returned to the bed.

Diane remained in front of the mirror, fascinated by the diamond, turning it from side to side. The moonlight washed over her and cast a glow against the stone. She turned to her lover, unable to lock her emotions away any longer. "I love this," she said, "and as corny as it sounds, I'll never take it off."

Ronnie's smile filled the room. "Good."

Diane stared at her as she had so many times before, amazed at her beauty, mesmerized by her deep, blue eyes and the perfect physique that had been bestowed upon her. Diane slowly closed the distance between them and stood over Ronnie, the diamond swaying gently between her breasts. "I'm petrified. You know that, don't you?"

Ronnie nodded empathetically. She reached for Diane's hand and placed it against her heart. "I love you, Diane."

For the first time, Diane recognized her own power, the desire she fueled in Ronnie. For the first time, she believed what Ronnie told her. "I love you, too, baby."

25. The Party

The sociology department loved to party, giving new meaning to the term "animal behavior." As the unofficial social committee of Carlson University, the twelve-member department organized everything from formal teas to Wild West Nights. Any occasion was a reason to celebrate, and the fall trimester merited a semi-formal affair at the dean's house in Malibu Canyon.

Doctor John Morgan and his wife Mary lived on a sprawling twenty-acre ranch complete with stable and tennis court. When he wasn't playing tennis, Dean Morgan was often spotted riding his horse Desdemona on the beaches and roads surrounding Carlson. A devoted equestrian, it was not uncommon to see Desdemona on the campus, since Dean Morgan believed horseback riding to be the ultimate mode of transportation.

"Wow" was all Ronnie could think to say as they pulled up to the enormous house.

"Do I look all right?" Diane asked, checking her face in the rearview mirror.

Ronnie cast an admiring gaze at her. "You look amazing, darling."

Diane smiled. "I'm not sure I can trust your opinion. You're a little biased."

"Love can do that, but you look absolutely stunning." Ronnie brought Diane's hand to her lips while her gaze followed the curves of the navy blue cocktail dress, the same one Diane had worn the night she appeared at the restaurant.

"I love you," Diane said.

"I know you do. Shall we go in?"

"Do you think people will suspect?" Diane asked, grinning.

Ronnie could tell the concern over their relationship had vanished from Diane's mind, replaced by a mischievous satisfaction. She shrugged and opened the car door. "Who knows?"

They advanced to the massive entryway, Ronnie stumbling several times on the horrid spiked heels that matched her dress perfectly.

The inside of Dean Morgan's house was as impressive as the outside, but not ostentatious. He had always struck Ronnie as an earthy guy, and his house reflected that personality. No antiques, no Ming vases, just lots of nice furniture and walls filled with family photographs and memorabilia from his trips around the world.

He and Mary greeted them at the door. A short, stout man of about seventy with silver hair and a handlebar mustache, he looked like he belonged in *Gunsmoke* repeats. Mary, though, did not look like a cowboy's wife. She was elegant in a flowing pink dress that easily knocked off twenty of her sixty years.

Diane introduced Ronnie to Mrs. Morgan, who said, "I've heard about you, Ms. Frost, and I've seen the calendar. I guess you're the reason that so many have sold. You are truly more beautiful in public than in print."

"Thank you, Mrs. Morgan," Ronnie said, certain her face was

already turning red.

"Tell me, Ronnie. Do you shoot pool?" the dean asked.

"Oh, John." Mary sighed.

"Actually, Mr. Morgan, billiards was a part of my misspent youth."

"Wonderful!" he exclaimed. "I'll see you down in the basement later."

Diane and Ronnie followed the flow of traffic into the living room as the dean and his wife turned to greet the next arriving guests. Diane seemed to fade into the world of her colleagues, minus Camille who was home with a cold. Several of the professors cornered Ronnie about the calendar, encouraging her to do more modeling and kidding her about the record-breaking amounts of money that had been made. At an appropriate interval, she excused herself from the room of academics. The sociology department she could stomach, but not when they mixed with the linguists, the political scientists, the mathematicians and the philosophers. That was just too many degrees for her to handle.

She worked her way back out of the living room just as Stacy Armbruster was entering, Elliot Michaelson right behind her. They both saw Ronnie at the same time. Michaelson stared as if he was undressing her, and Stacy gave a slight smile. She looked either upset or embarrassed, but Ronnie wasn't sure. Michaelson whispered something to her and vanished toward the back of the house.

Ronnie smiled and greeted Stacy with a hug. "Hi. How are you?"

Stacy nodded. "I'm okay." She looked around, amazed. "This is really incredible. I can't believe the dean invited all the lowly TAs, too."

"Yeah," Ronnie agreed. "I was surprised."

Suddenly Stacy seemed distracted, her mind clearly on something else.

"Are you really all right?" Ronnie asked.

Stacy's smile broadened. "Of course. Listen, I'm going to go look for something to drink, and I need to catch up with one of the other TAs, but maybe I'll see you later."

Ronnie watched her walk off. Something wasn't right, and although the two of them had become friends, Stacy still did not readily confide in her. Ronnie wandered around the ground floor, and after grabbing a beer from a waiter's tray, she found the stairs leading to the basement. Gathered around Dean Morgan's pool table were three of her favorite sociology professors.

"Ronnie!" Professor Croft called. "Come join us."

For the next hour she shot nine-ball with the three of them. Other party guests filtered in and out of the basement, but none wanted to play. Ronnie was happy to be out of Diane's way and in the company of polite, intelligent men. They were racking the balls for a new game when she felt a hand on her shoulder.

"Hello, Ronnie."

She turned to find Dr. Michaelson staring at her chest. He was wearing the same clothes he always wore to school—button-down shirt, khaki pants and red bow tie.

"You look smashing," he said, continuing to ogle her. "Do you think I could join the game?" he asked.

"Sure," she said. "You can take my place."

"Actually, I'd like to play against you," he said, and she understood his meaning.

The three professors willingly stepped aside, leaving Ronnie with no choice. She certainly didn't want to make a scene, and, thankfully there were other people present. She racked the balls, conscious that Michaelson was standing right behind her. She could feel his gaze on her buttocks and a cold shiver swept through her. She thought about excusing herself, but when she looked over at the three sociology professor still standing in a circle, she was reassured. She didn't want to aggravate Michaelson any more than necessary, especially if he directed the

181

anger at Diane.

"You break," she said, motioning to the table.

Michaelson wasn't very good, his mind evidently occupied by her chest and her ass instead of the fifteen little balls on the table. Halfway through the game, the sociology professors wandered back upstairs, and Ronnie's anxieties immediately increased. She pretended not to care, realizing she was probably being stupid. This was *the dean's house*. There were a hundred people one flight above them. Only an idiot would try to pull something.

She sunk her next ball, ignoring Dr. Michaelson and trying to end the game quickly.

"Excuse me, Professor, you're in my way." She waved her pool cue slightly, indicating where she intended to shoot.

"I'm sorry, Ronnie."

He moved behind her, out of sight, and she lined up the shot. As she brought her stick back, his hands wrapped around her front, fondling her breasts. She whirled around and met his embrace, dropping her pool cue in the process.

"Dr. Michaelson, let go of me." He had a firm grasp on both of her arms, pushing them against her body in a vice grip.

"Ronnie, I want you. You're a beautiful woman. You're always in my thoughts. That calendar spoke to me. I have to have you." He pressed her backside against the pool table as he attempted to shove her down.

"Dr. Michaelson, let go of me right now. Let go, and we'll pretend this never happened."

He kissed her hard, releasing her arms but taking her face firmly between his hands and wedging her between him and the pool table. She tried to pry his arms away from her face, but as she did, his hands pressed harder against her cheeks until she thought he might break the bones in her face. She had to find a weapon, something to get him off her. His torso ground against her, and she could feel his rock-hard erection. He lifted her up over the edge of the pool table. If she didn't do anything, she would be on her back with Michaelson on top of her.

She wiggled her legs, the only free part of her body, and felt one of the heels scrape her calf. *Those damn shoes. Those damn wonderful shoes.* She slammed her right heel into his soft loafer, the spike landing squarely on his arch. He yelped and fell to the floor.

They glared at each other, and Ronnie had the presence of mind to grab a cue stick, just in case. Noise floated down the stairs. People were coming.

"I wondered where you'd gone," Diane said, smiling. Dr. Cable and Dr. Marks, two other sociology professors, followed her, but their smiles faded when they saw Michaelson on the floor, Ronnie holding the pool cue over him, like a guard watching a crazed prisoner.

"What's going on, Ronnie?" Diane asked.

"That bastard tried to rape me."

Michaelson laughed. "Ronnie, you exaggerate so." He hobbled over to a chair. "I gave her a kiss," he told the jury of three, "and she reacted violently." He turned to Ronnie. "I'm very surprised at you, young lady. After what you said in Dr. Cole's office, I thought kissing was the least of what you wanted from me."

Her eyes widened. "What?"

"Ronnie, stop the charade. You came on to me first." He nodded at the others. "She did. She told me that if she were ever going to be with a man, it would be an older, mature man, preferably an accomplished academic. My God, Diane, she practically threw herself at me right in your office!" He was beginning to believe the lie himself, and so were the two male professors.

They looked to Ronnie for a response, but she was speechless. Michaelson had lied so effortlessly that she wondered if he'd prepared it in advance, in case he got caught. She looked at Diane, who alternated her gaze between the floor and

Michaelson.

"Do you want to say anything, Ronnie?" Dr. Marks asked accusingly.

"Only what I said before. That bastard tried to rape me. He pushed me against the pool table, forced himself on me, and if I hadn't stepped on his foot, you all would have seen me spread-eagled on the table when you came down here."

Dr. Marks said to Diane, "What do you make of all this? She's your research assistant. Does she have a tendency to lie?"

"I'm not lying," Ronnie shot back.

Limping slightly, Dr. Michaelson approached her, a look of forgiveness on his face. "Well, Ronnie, you can call it what you want, but you're certainly not telling these people the truth."

"I suggest you stay away from me, Professor, or I'll shove this stick up your ass."

He stopped moving. "Ronnie, I'm willing to forget this whole incident if you'll just tell these three what really happened. You had a moment of craziness and attacked me. Granted, I shouldn't have tried to kiss you. For that, I'm sorry. It was unprofessional, but after all of the phone calls and love letters, I thought it was what you wanted. I just couldn't help myself." He turned to Marks and Cable. "I don't expect Dr. Cole to understand, but surely you gentlemen can see why my emotions got the best of me."

Ronnie watched all six beady eyes explore her body.

"This girl is a temptress. How many other faculty members have you been involved with, young lady?"

The weight of Michaelson's questions sucker-punched her, and suddenly protecting Diane was more important than the truth. She couldn't look at her lover, and she had no idea what Diane's reaction was to Michaelson's question, but she had to be worried to death that the male professors would figure out their relationship.

Ronnie flew up the stairs not looking back. She whipped by

184

Stacy on her way out the door and didn't start to cry until she was seated in Diane's car. She was sobbing uncontrollably by the time Diane got into the driver's seat and pulled her close.

"It's okay, honey," she whispered. "It's okay."

"I want to kill that bastard!" Ronnie screamed into Diane's shoulder.

Diane pulled her tighter and kissed her forehead. Her fingers smoothed Ronnie's hair and eventually the sobs ceased. "Do you want to go to the police?"

Ronnie shook her head. "I don't know. I don't know what to do. Nothing like this has ever happened to me."

"Then let's go talk to someone who does know."

It was almost one o' clock in the morning by the time Ronnie had relayed the event of the evening to Judy and Camille. As a rape counselor, Judy was trained to evaluate situations and present victims with options. She took meticulous notes, often asking Ronnie to back up and answer the most trivial of questions. Camille only interjected twice, and Diane was silent, stoically sitting on a stool and sipping her coffee.

Finally Judy set her pencil down and locked eyes with Ronnie. "Here's what I think. I believe every word you've told me. I don't think you've exaggerated a single detail, and I'm absolutely sure the bastard has done this exact same thing to other women." She took a deep breath and gave Ronnie a sympathetic smile. "However, it's not that easy. If you file criminal charges against him, it will undoubtedly go to court, and it sounds as though it will be your word against his."

"But Diane and the other professors came down the stairs and I was holding a pool cue over him," Ronnie argued.

"Yes, but he already explained that. He tried to kiss you and you overreacted, and he even apologized for that. The fact is, Ronnie, you have no marks of a struggle on you because he was very smart about the way he touched you, and he created a somewhat plausible story right on the spot. You also need to remember that the most disgusting part of rape cases is that the victim is truly the victim. Michaelson will fight this charge because he has to; his freedom and professional life are on the line. He'll hire a great attorney, and most likely your sexual past will become an issue. Not only will they start asking you about the number of lovers you've had, but it's also likely that your relationship with Diane will surface and be questioned."

"Do you really think they'll find out about Ronnie and Diane?" Camille asked. "I mean, I haven't heard any talk."

"It will come out because Ronnie will be asked if she has ever been intimate with a faculty member, and her choice will be to tell the truth or commit perjury."

Ronnie stood up. "Then we're not doing anything. I'm not risking Diane's career over this."

Judy touched her arm and she sat down again. "Ronnie, you need to listen to me. I know the picture I've painted is rather dim, but I'm a rape counselor for a reason. The only way we stop rape is to prosecute the people who do it. My advice to you is to prosecute that bastard as far as you can, because if you don't, he'll do it to someone else."

"And what's to say he hasn't already?" Camille added. "Your dirty laundry won't be all that gets aired, Ronnie. Michaelson's skeletons will come out of the closet."

"But he has no hesitation about lying," Ronnie said, frustrated. "He already did it tonight, and very skillfully, too. I'm not willing to lie."

They sat in silence, and Ronnie glanced at Diane, who looked utterly miserable, her face drooping behind the cup of coffee.

"Diane, what do you think I should do?"

Diane just sat there, taking deep breaths. She closed her eyes for a moment, then said, "I don't know what to tell you to do, Ronnie. You have to decide for yourself."

"I do think Diane should distance herself from all of this," Judy advised. "If you can handle it, Ronnie, there will be less suspicion cast if you both stay away from each other for a while."

"I agree," Camille said.

Ronnie hated the idea of separating from her lover, even for a short time, but Diane quickly said, "My parents have been badgering me to join them in Europe for a month. Maybe I should." She looked at Ronnie, who nodded slowly.

Diane turned to Camille. "Will you cover my classes and take care of Claude?"

"Of course."

Judy squeezed Ronnie's arm. "What are you going to do?"

"I'm not sure. I'll need to think about it."

"Well, you'll need to make a decision fast. I'm sure the other professors have already told the dean what they saw in the basement," Judy said. "You should go visit him tomorrow."

Ronnie understood. She got up and hugged Camille and Judy. Diane followed her out the door. They rode silently in the car, and Diane automatically drove Ronnie home and not to the bungalow. Ronnie already felt a distance growing between them, one she couldn't control.

Diane put the car in park, leaned over and quickly kissed her on the mouth. "I'm so sorry about everything that happened tonight."

"I know."

She pulled Diane to her and held her until Diane broke away. "I'll call you when I arrive in London, okay?"

"Sure," Ronnie said, doubting if there would ever be a phone call.

She got out of the car and watched Diane's black BMW drive away. In the distance, thunder sounded, and Ronnie felt the drops of rain begin to pound her head. She remained motionless, watching the taillights fading into the dark night, small pinpoints that disintegrated into nothing.

26. Left in the Rain

Rain and thunder pelted the house. Ronnie let herself in the front door, the lightning show and sounds from the street flooding inside momentarily until the lock clicked into place. She kicked off the stilettos and sank to the floor, drenched from the downpour. Her body started to shake but she didn't care. She remained motionless for a long time, too exhausted to move. She cried until she fell asleep. Hushed voices floated across the room in the darkness, and her eyes fluttered open. Standing over her were Brody and Randy.

"Help me get her up," Brody said.

"I've got her." Randy easily cradled her in his arms and carried her up the stairs. Ronnie stared at the kind eyes that met hers. "It's okay, Ronnie."

Van took over when they reached the landing. She stuck Ronnie in a shower while Randy and Richard made tea. Since most of Ronnie's clothes had found their way to Diane's bunga-low, Brody found some shorts and a T-shirt she could wear.

The roommates hovered over her until Vandella kicked them all out of the bedroom and sat down on the bed next to her. She held out a steaming hot mug. "This ought to help. Randy made it from his grandmother's recipe. I guess it's got a little more kick than orange pekoe."

Ronnie took a sip and felt her lungs close momentarily, the spice of the tea balanced by a heavy dose of brandy. She groaned out loud and her eyes bulged. The effects were short-lived and within seconds a comforting warmth engulfed her. "God bless Randy." She sighed, then took another sip. "So are he and Brody . . ."

"Yeah," Van said, smiling. "It's great." She looked at Ronnie, her caring, motherly eyes doing the talking for her.

Ronnie told Van everything about the attempted rape, Judy's advice and Diane's departure for Europe. She cried again and Vandella held her. She kept sipping Randy's concoction, recog-nizing that it was sliding down her throat like honey.

"What are you going to do? Are you going to call the police?"

"I don't know. It's like Judy said. If I push it, I'll go on trial, and so will Diane."

Van took her by the shoulders. "You have to stop worrying about Diane. This is your life, too. She made a decision to get involved with you, despite the rules."

Ronnie felt her eyelids getting heavier. "It's not that easy, Van. I don't think I could ever do anything to hurt her, nothing at all." She felt her body collapsing, and at some point, Van put a light blanket over her. Sleep was calling her when her cell phone went off.

Van answered it. "She can't come to the phone right now." There was a long pause as she listened, nodding. "No, she's okay, but I'll give her your message."

Ronnie closed her eyes, remembering Diane's car driving

away as she stood in the rain, unable to move. She wanted a movie ending, the part where the heroine returns after a change of heart. She saw herself there in the rain, waiting for it to materialize. The harder it had rained, the more she believed that it would happen, so she remained on the pavement. Why she decided to come inside she couldn't remember, but she had hoped the rain would melt her, wash her away down the storm drain.

She did melt. Back to the basement, holding the pool cue over Michaelson. He was yelling, "How many faculty members have you seduced, young lady?"

Diane was there, shaking her head. "Only one, Elliot. You are such a bastard. Even if Ronnie was interested in men, she would certainly have higher standards. But the fact is she's a lesbian, and she's my lover."

Michaelson sunk to the floor at the announcement and the rain melted him into the carpeting. Then his hands were on her cheeks, pushing the bones of her face together, bruising and breaking her.

She awoke gasping. Her whole body was shaking and she was covered in sweat. She looked around, recognizing her room, remembering the dream and what had really happened. She went to the bathroom and threw up. The tile felt so good against the heat of her body that she peeled off the drenched T-shirt and sank to the floor.

She woke up to Vandella hovering over her. "Hey, sleepyhead. That must have been some drink, that's all I can say. You need to get up now. It's a new day. No more crying, no more whining. Besides, you don't make a very good shower mat."

Ronnie smiled and took Van's hand. She looked in the mirror and was shocked. The night had definitely taken its toll.

"Oh, by the way," Van said as she stepped into the steaming hot water. "Stacy Armbruster called last night right before you went to sleep. She needs to talk to you immediately."

190

27. Truth and Consequences

"Dean Morgan will see you now," the secretary said.

Ronnie and Stacy rose from the couch where they had waited for nearly thirty minutes and followed the woman through the large oak doorway. She quickly retreated back to her side of the door once Dean Morgan greeted them.

Ronnie's gaze swept across the room. Dean Morgan's office was exactly the opposite of his home. It wasn't comfortable or inviting; it was official, and it projected exactly the image that befitted a university president. Glass cases full of artifacts and antiques lined one wall, and several framed plaques proclaimed his degrees, honors and accolades. Included were a dozen photos of Dean Morgan glad-handing various politicians and celebrities. A brick fireplace covered much of the opposite wall, encircled by comfortable sofas and end tables. Ronnie imagined it was here that Dean Morgan did most of his reading, rather than

191

behind the power desk that commanded the corner of the room and was backed by floor-to-ceiling windows that overlooked the entire campus. It was to the sofas that Dean Morgan led Ronnie and Stacy.

"Ladies, I've already spoken to Professors Croft and Marks this morning, and I understand Dr. Cole was present as well; however, I've been unable to reach her. She's apparently gone overseas. My intention is to gather the facts, hear Dr. Michaelson's side of the story and, if it is warranted, take action against him. Of course, Miss Frost, you have the option of speaking to the police."

Ronnie nodded. "I know that is an option, Dean Morgan, and I may pursue it; however, I understand that it will be my word against the word of a tenured university professor. I'm not sure I'll be believed—"

"You will if it's true."

Ronnie offered a slight smile. She very much liked the dean, but he clearly didn't understand the ramifications of a woman crying rape. "Well, I know it's the truth, but I've brought Stacy Armbruster here with me today because she has a story to tell."

Ronnie and the dean looked at Stacy, who had yet to say a word. Ronnie took Stacy's hand and smiled at her encouragingly. She squeezed Ronnie's hand and began. "You probably know that I'm Dr. Michaelson's research and teaching assistant. When I started working for him last year, it was very professional. Everything was done in his office, the hours were legitimate, and I felt proud of my accomplishments. I guess that was the point. Professor Michaelson was bonding with me, creating a relationship. I admired his intellect, and soon he started asking me about authors I read or music I liked. And after about six months the lines became blurred. He would bring in postcards he had seen of paintings I admired, or he'd find books I wanted to read. It was still innocent enough, but it was definitely moving from professional to personal. And part of me liked it. He gave me atten-

192

tion. Now that I can analyze the whole thing, I'd say he made up for the father I never really had. Anyway, things started to change. We'd meet at his house and work there. Sometimes he would cook, and we'd look like the model of domesticity. Then, eating led to drinking, which led to touching. Of course the first time he ever kissed me, I balked, but only for a moment. By then I had grown quite fond of him."

Ronnie glanced at the dean, who listened intently.

"Then one night he asked if he could paint me, naked. He'd introduced me to ouzo and it affected me quickly. I hesitated but he helped undress me and positioned me on the bed, because of course his easel was in his bedroom. It was when he sat down that I realized he was only wearing a robe, but he seemed involved in the painting, so I assumed everything was still platonic. He kept talking about the beauty of my breasts and the thickness of my thighs, all sorts of sexual remarks that began to make me uncomfortable. Periodically I'd take another drink of ouzo, and I was having trouble holding the position he wanted because I was drunk." Stacy paused. "What I remember is falling onto the bed and Elliot appearing over me, his robe removed and a big smile on his face. His hands were all over me, and he was whispering in my ear, telling me how beautiful and desirable I was. I was drunk and partly believing him, and yes, it felt good to have someone touch me. I let his hands roam, but when he opened my legs, I said no. I told him to stop."

Tears streamed down Stacy's face, and the dean handed her his handkerchief. She blotted her eyes and composed herself.

"I was a virgin," she said simply. "Afterward, Elliot gushed about how wonderful it had been and what a capable lover I was. Even though I had resisted, he was complimentary, effusive. He told me he was in love with me. And somehow, amid all of his talk, it made it okay. I forgot about what he had done. So the next night, I gave myself to him willingly, and as physically painful as it was, I didn't let him know how much I hated him on

193

top of me." She shrugged. "It went on like that for a few months, but Elliot started to get bored with me. I think he was fantasizing about Ronnie, because he constantly talked about her, and he would look for reasons to go to Dr. Cole's office. And when that calendar came out, he went ballistic."

Ronnie shifted on the couch. The idea of Elliott Michaelson being aroused by the calendar made her queasy.

"I was sitting in his office, and he stormed in, the calendar in his hand. He locked the door, and before I could say anything, he'd grabbed me and pulled me to the couch. In two seconds his pants were undone, and he reached under my skirt, ripped off my underwear and pulled me on top of him. It was so violent." Stacy shivered, clearly disgusted by the memory. "He came quickly, and then pushed me aside. Once he'd zipped his pants up again, he unlocked the door and left. That was the last time we had sex. I'd been trying to break up with him for the two weeks prior, but I was afraid of how he would react, and if he would hurt my standing at the university. Then when I heard that Ronnie had stood up to him at your party, I wanted to come forward."

Dean Morgan patted her hand and went to his phone. "Call Elliot Michaelson to my office, now."

The three of them sat in silence for the five minutes it took Michaelson to appear. He had only taken two steps into the dean's office before he stopped and the color drained from his face. As much as he tried to compose himself, his journey to the sofa only belied his anxiety. Ronnie looked at Dean Morgan, power emanating from his being, his strong jaw and steely eyes. She admired and feared him at the same time.

"Elliot, you will explain yourself now."

Michaelson looked from the dean to Stacy and Ronnie. "John, I don't know what stories these girls have concocted, but I assure you—"

"Damn it, Elliot, I don't have time for stories. The truth,

now."

Michaelson's mouth started to quiver, but he wouldn't budge. "John, as someone who has known you for years, I'm telling you that this is all a misunderstanding. These women have aligned themselves with Diane Cole, and she would do anything to disparage my name."

Dean Morgan sighed. "This has nothing to do with Diane, Elliot. Leave her out of it. Did you or did you not try to rape Veronica Frost?"

"Absolutely not."

"Did you have an affair with Stacy Armbruster?"

"Of course not. It's against school policy."

"Liar!" Stacy cried. She clenched her teeth, her face full of hate. "You used me, you seduced me, and when I said no, you kept going. The first time, you raped me!"

Michaelson's indignation seemed believable. "The *first* time? Are you suggesting, young lady, there were multiple times?" He looked from Stacy to Dean Morgan. "John, I'm not sure where this is going, or whose side you are on, but I'll be contacting the faculty review board and an attorney. We'll get to the bottom of this and expose these young ladies for the malicious slanderers they are." He glared at Stacy and Ronnie before strolling confidently to the door.

"I'm pregnant," Stacy announced.

Only then did Elliot Michaelson's shoulders sag in defeat.

Ronnie gunned the engine to sixty as she found a straightaway on Highway 1. The Mustang's top was down and she was rolling with the curves, tapping the brakes as little as necessary. It was a game she played when she was upset—drive fast and dangerously. She shifted the wheel from left to right and back again as the road wound up the mountains. The sun had set long ago, blackness around her, only adding to the thrill.

She found the familiar turnoff and slowly maneuvered the car over the bumps, careful not to damage the chassis. When she reached the gate, she parked the Mustang and headed into the woods. There were so many rocks, dead tree limbs and stumps that she was amazed she and Diane had not been thrown from the motorcycle at least once before. At one point her ankle caught in a hole and she fell to her knees. She shook her head, never having noticed the hazards at twenty miles per hour. She walked slowly, realizing she was in absolutely no hurry. She no longer had anyone to answer to, nowhere to be and no obligations to fulfill.

It took thirty minutes to get to the edge of the cliff, a cool breeze blowing from behind her. She looked down at the rocks below, a perfect place for a suicide, if she had been melodramatic and so inclined, but she wasn't. She pulled a piece of paper from her back pocket and unfolded it. The official Carlson crest sat at the top, along with her name and a list of all the classes she had taken and the grades she had received. It was impressive, she thought. More than halfway through her master's program, she was carrying a 4.0 grade point average. Most students could not boast such an accomplishment. Unfortunately, she no longer cared.

Across the course titles and grades earned, in large, red, block letters was the word *WITHDRAWN*. Ronnie stared at the paper and crumpled it into a ball. She hurled it out over the cliff, already turning away before it landed in the sea.

By the time she had returned to the car, she desperately craved a cigarette. When she opened the glove box, much of the junk she had piled inside spilled out, revealing an old pack of smokes and a lighter tucked in the very back for emergencies. She dropped her seat into a reclining position and just stared at the stars, the only light source around, save for the glow of the ember from her burning cigarette. It surprised her that she was so calm. She had still not told her parents that she'd dropped out of school, but they would understand, because they understood everything. It was her life, not theirs. They were the only parents she knew who truly got it. Still, they would be worried about her, about her future, her life course, all of those things that gave older adults ulcers.

Ronnie, however, was at peace. She stubbed out her cigarette and began piling years of car registrations, insurance cards, old napkins from a multitude of drive-throughs and everything she had ever thought she'd lost back into the glove compartment. She fired up the last cigarette and stared at the business card she'd retrieved, the slick gold writing shimmering in the moonlight: *Nola Monroe, ALM Modeling Agency.*

28. Crash Landing

"We are now beginning our descent into Los Angeles. At this time the captain asks that you return your seat to the upright position and turn off all electronic equipment."

Diane quickly finished the e-mail she was writing to her publisher and followed the voice's instructions. Once her laptop was stowed, she reached for an abandoned *New York* magazine, the current issue, stuffed in the seat pocket. She hated flying, and she craved distractions to help her forget that she was thousands of feet in the air, sitting in a little metal canister.

She skimmed the table of contents, looking for an interesting article to read. It soon became apparent why the magazine had been left on the aircraft. It was one of those fashion magazines that Diane detested—full of advertisements and smelling of three different types of perfume. There was perhaps one interesting photo spread about Italian fashion, and since she had just spent a month in Italy, it would hold her attention.

She flipped three-quarters of the way through the magazine and found the photos. She barely noticed the models and their attire, her focus on the scenery behind them. The pictures were breathtaking, reminders of the last seven days she had endured in Rome with her mother, staring at cathedrals, walking up and down cobblestone streets and looking at artwork. Prior to that they'd been on the coast not far from Pisa. There had been enough mother-daughter bonding time to last her for another year. Although her father had been present for brief parts of the trip, it didn't take him very long to map out the ten golf courses he wanted to play and disappear every morning for his tee time.

The first two weeks had been hideous, Diane's mind wallowing in the images of the night she left Ronnie standing in the rain after Michaelson's attack. The shame she felt consumed her. She was a coward and a selfish bitch, and it reached a point where if Ronnie entered her thoughts, her own self-loathing eclipsed all the memories they shared together. She stopped thinking of Ronnie, hoping to protect the moments she cherished, coveting them for another time in the future, when her heart had healed. Her strategy made the last month bearable. She had not checked her messages, called Camille or initiated contact with anyone else except with her publisher. They'd formalized their agreement and Diane had committed herself to a September release for her book on homosexuality and school culture. Thoughts of the book quickly shifted to thoughts of school—how her classes were going, where she would find a new TA and Elliot Michaelson's fate. She'd walked out on her life, and now that she was returning to it, she was filled with anxiety.

She decided the trip was a mistake. She'd run away from her problems and spent a month answering her parents' questions about her relationship with Ronnie. They loved Ronnie and pried endlessly until Diane finally told them they had split up.

Her father had been livid. "I don't understand how you could have let such a classy dame get away from you" were his exact words. Diane had remained silent and taken his abuse. There was no point in telling him anything about what happened and the potential retribution Michaelson could inflict upon her.

Her mother's comments, although more reasonable, almost drove Diane over the edge. She wasn't angry, just totally perplexed.

"What don't you understand, Mother?" Diane asked.

"The two of you just seemed perfect. You were so happy, and I've never seen you smile so much."

"Well, sometimes it just doesn't work out," Diane said, resorting to clichés to end the conversation.

"I know. I'm just surprised. I remember when we were visiting the two of you, and Dad told you how much he liked Ronnie. You were beaming from ear to ear."

"Well, Mom—"

"No, let me finish," her mother had insisted. "I was watching Ronnie. Her expression, well, it's so hard to explain." Her mother stammered with the familiar sounds Diane had heard her entire life whenever her mother couldn't verbalize her thoughts. After a deep breath she said, "When you smiled, I could see the love pouring out of her face." Her mother had laughed. "It probably sounds silly, huh?"

Diane closed her eyes as the plane touched the tarmac. The rush of pressure and noise sweeping through the plane caused her to lose her place in the article, despite her efforts to focus. She thumbed back through the pages, knowing it would still be a good five minutes before she could disembark.

A face caught her attention as one of the slick pages slid through her fingers. Something immediately held her, but she didn't know why. It was probably a splash of color on the page, a way to make a certain advertisement stand out. Still her curiosity demanded that she see whatever it was. She worked backward until she found the picture, a woman in a long flowing black gown with a plunging back that revealed much of her flawless skin and sensuous curves. It was an advertisement for a new perfume, but the woman, not the product, covered the page. Her blond hair was pulled into a severe bun, and she wore evening gloves that ran above her elbows. She stood in front of an off-white background, her body turned to the side to display her impeccable figure. What held Diane's attention when she gazed at the photo was indeed a splash of color, two of the bluest eyes she had ever seen. Against all of the dark elements in the picture, they shone like topaz, and they seemed to look right at her.

She knew those eyes very well. They were the same eyes that sparkled into hers every time they had made love.

Everything was different when she pulled into the garage. The Harley rested in the corner, the gray cover fitted snugly over the metal frame. Inside she found the empty drawers and hangers, indicating another person had once shared her life. Sitting on the entry hall table were the spare keys to her house and the Harley, and the extra garage door opener Ronnie had used. Gone was Ronnie's trademark baseball cap that she readily flung on to the table whenever she entered the bungalow. Diane smiled slightly as she remembered all of the times she had picked up the cap and placed it on the adjacent hook, gently chastising Ronnie for her slovenliness.

She had finally given up one day when Ronnie challenged her. "What's the big deal if it hangs on the hook or sits on the table?"

"The table isn't so cluttered," Diane responded logically.

"Yeah, but then I can't do this." From twenty feet away, Ronnie had flicked the cap through the air and watched it land perfectly on the oak sideboard.

"If you can do that again," she told Ronnie, "you deserve to keep your hat on the table."

Ronnie retrieved her hat, moved five feet farther back than she had been and tossed the cap in nearly the same spot. "It stays on the table," she said, pulling Diane against her for a long kiss. "You ought to see me toss the rings at a carnival."

Diane had laughed hysterically as Ronnie tickled her, kissed her and finally picked her up in her strong arms, carrying her to bed. At one point during their lovemaking, Ronnie bounded over to the table for her cap, sending them into endless peals of laughter again.

Diane sat down on the couch and reached for the *New York* magazine. Claude jumped on her lap, and she stroked his back while she checked her messages, her answering machine indicating that she had twenty calls to screen. Several of them were from friends who knew nothing of her impromptu escape from the country, six were from Camille, telling her to call immediately and two were from the dean. *Oops.* She cringed at the thought of upsetting him, and she actually had no idea if she was still employed. Depending on Ronnie's course of action against Michaelson, their whole affair could have been exposed, and Diane would need to retune her résumé.

She punched in her best friend's number, wondering if in fact she had guessed correctly.

"You know, when you get e-mails that say 'urgent' in the subject line, you really should answer them." Camille had obviously read the Caller ID and declined to start the conversation with a hello.

"I just didn't want to talk to anyone."

"I'm not just anyone and neither is Dean Morgan."

"So, is he angry?"

"No, he's fine. I explained that you had to get away, and he understood. After that whole horrible thing with Michaelson, I think he would have forgiven anyone in the sociology department for anything."

"And what did happen?" Diane thumbed through the magazine and found Ronnie's picture. She lay back on the couch and stared at it. She hadn't noticed some of the finer details before, like Ronnie's blood red fingernails and her sculpted eyebrows.

"Diane, are you listening to me?" Camille was clearly annoyed.

Diane closed the magazine and focused. "I'm sorry. I'm a little distracted. What happened? Am I still employed?"

Camille sighed. "Yes, you're still employed, and I've made sure that your classes are going fine. As for the other matter, Ronnie didn't go to the cops at first, but she went to Dean Morgan and told her story."

"Why did he believe her over a faculty member?"

"Because Stacy Armbruster went with her, and it seems Stacy and Elliot were engaged in some strange sexual relationship that revolved a lot around psychological and emotional control. How's that for a sociologist's perspective?"

"Stacy and Elliot? I'm shocked."

"We all were. Anyway, the dean couldn't prove Ronnie's attempted rape, but he could prove that Elliot had an affair with Stacy, because she was pregnant."

Diane's jaw dropped. "You're kidding!"

"No. So, the end of the story is that Michaelson is fired, and Dean Morgan has asked Diane Cole to be the department chairperson."

"What? Why not you?" Diane was flabbergasted. "You should be the chair."

"No, no. I don't want to deal with all of that, honey. I'm three years away from retirement. You're the best choice, and we all voted for you. It didn't hurt that you weren't there to say no, and since you weren't answering your e-mail . . ."

"I'm not sure whether to be elated or really pissed."

"You'll be great." Camille paused. "So how was your trip?"

"Fine. Camille, where's Ronnie?" Diane flipped the magazine open to the right page.

"Well, honey. That's a little harder to explain. The whole thing with Michaelson and you, it was too much for her. She left."

"What do you mean?"

"She quit school. You know that modeling agent that kept calling and calling? Ronnie contacted her. The woman was ecstatic and took Ronnie to New York almost immediately. I hear she's doing very well and is the talk of the town."

"She quit school? To be a *model*?" Diane was stunned. Nothing registered in her mind. Everything she knew about Ronnie, how much she loved academics and hated superficiality—none of it made sense.

"I hear she's doing some ads."

"Yeah. I'm staring at her in a magazine right now."

"Is it the one in *New York*?" Camille asked.

"Yes. She's unbelievable."

"I'm sorry, Diane," Camille said softly.

Tears streamed down Diane's face. "Well, my love life average remains the same. I guess no one should be surprised. And since Michaelson got fired for bedding a student, then I'm better off, and I also get to be right. That would sure bother Ronnie." She laughed for good measure, but Camille did not join her. "Um, I'll see you tomorrow, okay? I'm sure I've got a lot to learn about this new position."

She didn't wait for a good-bye before she hung up.

29. Veronica

"Are you sure you don't mind going alone?" Marcel asked for the fourth time.

"When have I ever minded?" Ronnie replied. She flinched as Zenon, her sadistic hairstylist from hell, pulled the French twist into place. She sat as still as possible while he finished, and Claudette, her makeup artist, lined her lips with the newest shade. When they both backed away, she looked in the mirror at the person she could barely recognize. The first time Nola transformed her from Ronnie to "Veronica" had been a total shock, almost repulsive, since Veronica was fake. She thought the makeup looked clownish, being so unaccustomed to wearing anything at all. Even when she realized the secret to makeup artistry was to create a natural look, she could never appreciate it.

Ronnie still wasn't prepared to see herself as a brunette, even if the shade was a light brown. The coloring changed her entire look, which was exactly Nola's intention for Ronnie's next shoot. She couldn't remember why she needed to be a brunette, and she couldn't even remember where she was going tonight, but that was Marcel's job.

Marcel had proven to be the greatest personal assistant in the world. A slight, gay man, he reminded her of a cross between Richard and Dave. He may have looked like Richard, but he had Dave's steady personality. She desperately missed her friends, but Marcel was an acceptable stand-in. He lived nearby, and while he couldn't afford the rents of Greenwich Village, where Ronnie's loft was located, he could be at her place in ten minutes. That was exactly how Nola had arranged it.

She realized Ronnie would be high maintenance, but not because Ronnie was demanding. No, in fact, Ronnie was exactly the opposite. Ronnie could have cared less, and she told Nola so the first time they met in her office.

Nola had been overjoyed that Ronnie wanted to model, but Ronnie quickly squelched the mood. "Let's get everything straight. I'm doing this because it will give me financial security for the rest of my life, if in fact you're right, and I'll be successful. I do, however, have my rules. First, I will never pose nude. Second, I will not accept work that I don't want to do, and third, I sign nothing. I make no promise to you for any length of time, but I will give you my word that when I quit—and believe me, someday I will—that I'll give you six months' notice."

Nola had readily agreed to all of Ronnie's terms, because she knew she could make Ronnie into a star or so she said.

Working with Nola had also given Ronnie a backup topic when she informed her parents that she'd quit school.

Her mother had been thrilled. "My God, Ronnie! I always told you. It's your gift. You were born to model, and school will always be there, but your looks will someday abandon you."

Unlike her mother, her father had been much less pleased. "I guess if it's what you want to do," he said. "But I just hope you go back. You're too smart to let your mind go to waste. I really can't imagine you not in school. Don't you think you'll get bored? And don't you think Diane will come around?" He was much more intuitive and not blinded by the modeling opportunity.

Ronnie's father also knew what Ronnie feared—she hated to let her mind go idle, which was why the walls of the loft were filled with bookcases and books. She read constantly. She always had three books in her bag at a shoot—one novel, a book of nonfiction and whatever sociology text Camille had recently recommended.

"Are you sure you don't want me to go, Ronnie?" Marcel asked one final time. "I could pose as your escort again. You know Nola likes to see you with someone at these events."

"I appreciate the offer, Marcel, but I really hate the setups, no matter what Nola says. I'm going to go to whatever this is, get interviewed and come home. What is this, anyway?"

Marcel opened his PDA and tapped the screen. "Let's see. This is a benefit concert for the New York Philharmonic. You'll walk down the red carpet, run the press gauntlet and sit for an estimated two hours of classical music."

"Is there any part of that description that you're making up or exaggerating?" Ronnie hoped her expression conveyed her total displeasure about attending events in which she had absolutely no interest, and classical music was one of them. Now, if it were a Harley show, she would be happy to do cartwheels down the red carpet.

"No, that's the event. There will be lots of press present, and a few of the large fashion houses will be in attendance. The idea is to be seen."

"When is that ever *not* the idea?" Ronnie said sarcastically, rising to leave. She reached for her bag, checked herself in the mirror once more and gracefully walked to the elevator, Marcel close behind. She wished she could retreat back into the warmth of her loft, make a cup of tea and curl up with a book. How anyone could stand the brittle cold of a New York winter, she didn't understand. Most New Yorkers would tell her that November wasn't cold, but as a true desert rat, she thought different.

"Okay, now, while we have a few minutes, let's review next week. You have a shoot here in New York Monday and Tuesday, and then you board a plane to Mexico City for a summer magazine shoot. That'll last two weeks." Marcel looked over at her, but she was already losing interest and staring at her long red nails. "Then you go straight to hell," he added for good measure. She continued the inspection of her cuticles, never responding to his joke.

They arrived at Lincoln Center, Marcel in tow, hiding in the limousine. He would have plenty to do for the next few hours, since Nola had apparently left a five-minute message on his phone. Ronnie knew that every piece of information would be noted in the PDA, every shoot scheduled and every errand completed, since Ronnie did very little by herself or for herself. Nola wanted her in front of the cameras. The rest was frivolity that anyone could do, and she had said so. Taking care of Ronnie was his life.

Ronnie emerged from the limo and was escorted to the red carpet by a hired valet, a beautiful New York boytoy that Marcel was surely ogling from behind the frosted glass window.

"Veronica! Look over here!" a photographer called from outside Avery Fisher Hall.

Ronnie twirled around, the silk skirt billowing around her, exposing most of her upper thigh through the long side slit. A multitude of flashes popped simultaneously, blinding her in the process. She just kept smiling and walking, doing exactly as Nola had taught her.

She advanced another ten feet when another series of flashes erupted around her. She held a pose, continuing to smile, her mind removed from the entire event. She was in another place, on the top of the cliff at Diane's parents' estate. The waves battered the rocks below, ceaselessly, rhythmically. She imagined the foam rolling to the shore as the tide slowly shifted.

More smiling, more waving. No one noticed she was disconnected, set apart from the glamour, the attention and, most of all, the cameras. When it came time for her to talk to the nosy reporter from one of the tabloids, she focused long enough to be coherent and pleasant. She was no longer Ronnie Frost, but Veronica, print model and soon to be runway model. That was another Nola wisdom: perception was critical to jobs. Veronica had a stellar reputation, and her star was only rising, or so Nola told her. She was never late, rude to anyone or difficult to work with.

Her career ascended straight up, exactly as Nola had predicted.

After only a week in New York, she'd had her first photo shoot. The whole process proved extremely laborious and distasteful, but the $5,000 check readily made up for the boredom she'd endured in the tight black gown and the three days she'd spent on a set designed to be a Turkish bathhouse.

The most uncomfortable aspect, in Ronnie's opinion, had been the changes Nola demanded regarding her behavior. While Ronnie possessed natural beauty, she had no grace, and she did nothing to preserve or enhance her looks. Nola changed all of that, hiring a manners expert and a team of assistants who created Veronica, because Nola quickly realized that in at least one way, Ronnie was a typical lesbian, lacking any sense of fashion. She couldn't tell the difference between perfumes, or a French twist and a French braid, and even more frustrating for the agent, Ronnie had absolutely no interest in learning.

She thanked the tabloid reporter and went inside to the event, having already forgotten what it was. Nola insisted she appear in public once per month, adamant that the exposure was critical to her becoming more than just a model who caught people's attention momentarily. She darted into the ladies' room and checked her makeup, another Nola lesson. Ronnie had needed beauty lessons, learning what creams to apply, when to frequent the spa and, most importantly, how to survive on her own when Claudette wasn't present.

Ronnie reapplied her lipstick, only slightly conscious of her surroundings.

"What color are you using?" a voice nearby asked.

Ronnie blinked, realizing she was being addressed. She glanced in the mirror at the woman next to her, an exquisite dark-skinned goddess in a red evening gown. "I'm using what-ever color I was told to use," she replied.

The woman laughed and took the tube from Ronnie. "Orgasmic Midnight. Hmm." She leaned closer to Ronnie, as if examining her lips. "It's perfect on you."

Ronnie's heartbeat quickened and the woman returned the tube. "Thanks."

"My name is Tania."

"I'm Ronnie. Veronica."

"I know who you are. I saw you at the shoot in Milan. All the other models were jealous because the company wanted you the most, and they gave you the best clothing."

Ronnie shrugged, apathetic to the jealousy of others. "I just show up."

"Come with me," Tania instructed. She took Ronnie's hand and they darted into the vacant handicapped restroom just as a throng of women walked through the door. She engaged the lock and pressed Ronnie against the tile wall. "We'll need to be quiet," she whispered. Her fingers quickly made her intentions clear.

Due to the lines of the gown and the high slit up the side, Ronnie's dresser had forbade her from wearing underwear, which presented Tania with easy access and Ronnie with her first orgasm in ages.

"I've watched you," Tania whispered, her fingers still deep inside Ronnie. "You seem so isolated, distant. It's as though you don't care about anything, except when you're in front of the camera. Then it's different."

"I don't want to talk about myself," Ronnie said hoarsely. She pressed against Tania and suppressed a scream.

Tania held her and caressed her neck, not allowing their heads or faces to touch for fear of smearing makeup and ruining hairstyles. Ronnie's hands disappeared inside the low-cut front of Tania's dress, her thumbs circling Tania's nipples, staring into her brown eyes. They were very intelligent eyes, of this Ronnie was sure, and for a fleeting second she was reminded of Diane, the unflinching gaze or the vacant stare that indicated when the professor was deep in thought.

"See, you're doing it right now," Tania murmured, removing Ronnie's hands from her breasts. "You're not really here. You've gone somewhere else in your mind, and all I have here with me is your physical shell. As much as I'm enjoying this, your beauty is not enough for me."

Tania disengaged herself from Ronnie, and Ronnie followed her to the sink, still reeling from the encounter.

"I'm sorry," Ronnie apologized, not attempting to lie.

"Where do you go?" Tania asked, her voice free of judgment.

Ronnie felt compelled to answer honestly. "To the past."

"What's in the past that's so important?"

At first, Ronnie couldn't answer. She didn't know what to say. Then she blurted, "Happiness."

"I see." Tania took Ronnie's hand. "We must go in, but I would like to talk again. You are not only beautiful but enigmatic."

"Thank you. I'd like to see you again as well."

Tania smiled seductively and left Ronnie in the restroom. Ronnie closed her eyes for a moment, then headed for her seat.

People stopped her several times, introducing themselves or complimenting her, and she was gracious to every single one. They were oblivious to Ronnie's tryst, her life of ennui, for it was Veronica who stole into the hall ten minutes late, her façade restored.

30. Happy New Year

Diane took a long toke on the joint before passing it back to Judy. Her eyes settled on the hanging light above. Diane was sure she could reach out and touch it.

"What the hell are you doing?" Judy asked.

"Touching the ceiling," Diane replied, waving her hand.

Judy laughed and plucked the joint from Diane's fingers before she dropped it and burned a hole in the carpet. "You're stoned, D."

"No, I'm not," Diane slurred. "If I am, you are, too."

"Sorry, I smoke this stuff somewhat regularly, a holdover from the past. What I'm feeling is a pleasant buzz." Judy rose from the couch and joined Diane on the floor. "Now you, on the other hand, when was the last time you smoked weed?"

"Hmm. It's been a while."

"Yeah, like when Carter was president."

They passed the joint back and forth in silence. Diane studied Judy and Camille's small house, which hadn't changed in fifteen years. And there was no reason it should. It was beautiful. Raised by a carpenter, Judy had grown up holding a circular saw and understanding how to build a tongue-and-groove joint. Her success and skill was visible just by looking at her house. She had designed and built every piece of furniture, including the oak staircase. The carved railings and banisters led up to a loft, which served as a bedroom and an office. What was most evident, and made Diane supremely jealous, was that the house was more than just a place, it was a home. She and Camille had worked hard during their fifteen years together, and it showed. All of the wall hangings, pictures and knickknacks they had purchased as a couple, symbols of their life and memories to treasure. Diane had nothing like that, except for the few pictures of her and Ronnie, ones that Ronnie had left. She hadn't taken anything to remember their relationship, a fact that stung Diane deeply.

When Diane mentioned that she had no desire to spend Christmas or New Year's with her family, who would inevitably grill her for details about Ronnie's rise to stardom, Judy offered her company, and Diane had readily accepted the offer of drinking and drugging their way through New Year's. Camille, of course, did not approve at all, and had opted to go to her sister's house.

Judy reached for the necklace around Diane's neck. "This is lovely."

Diane felt suddenly overwhelmed with sadness.

"Hmm. Beautiful, intelligent and has exquisite taste. What more could you ask for?"

Diane said nothing, but she rose from the floor and went to the couch, putting her head into her hands.

Judy joined her on the sofa and patted her on the back. "Diane, it's New Year's Eve. Why are you here?"

Diane's thoughts clouded. "I hate my life."

Judy pulled Diane into an embrace and kissed her forehead. "Then I have one piece of advice for you, darlin'. Stop fucking it up." Diane started to object but Judy held up her hand. "Listen to me. I know you're afraid."

"I'm not afraid," Diane spat.

"Yes, you are. Diane, we've known each other a long time, and now's the time for the truth. You've never really had a meaningful relationship. From what I can tell, every woman you've been with has been nothing more than a friendly fuck, yours truly included," Judy added with a sweep of her hand.

"I don't have to listen to this shit." Diane jumped up. The room started to sway and she landed back on the couch.

Judy grinned. "Yes, you do, unless you can move your ass off of this couch and out of this house."

Diane moaned. Her head was starting to pound. She closed her eyes and hoped her annoying friend would go away.

Clearly feeling no pity, Judy went on. "See, Diane, here's how it is. This woman is different. Not only does she love you more than any of us ever did, but she'll put up with your shit."

"You make it sound like I'm some sort of horrible monster." Diane moaned.

"No," Judy disagreed, "just rather self-serving. You want her but you don't want the work. You don't want the rumors, the fighting, the pointing, all the stuff that's likely to happen because you fell for a student." She put her face up to Diane's. "And it scares you shitless."

"You're forgetting one simple fact. We broke up. There isn't anything to be scared of. It's over," Diane said smugly.

Judy flicked the joint into the ashtray. "If it's over, then why are you here drowning your troubles in Maui Wowi and Jim Beam?"

"I'm not. I'm here because you're helping me select the dust jacket for my book." Diane pointed to the two samples haphazardly thrown onto the carpet.

215

Judy chuckled. "That decision took about two minutes, before we began our recreational activity."

Diane looked away, focusing instead on a picture that hung over the fireplace. After a long pause she asked, "Does she ever mention me?"

"Only in passing. She'll make a joke, and then she'll wonder what you would have thought of it, or she'll say something about the two of you having gone somewhere or attended something."

"But only if it's part of the conversation," Diane concluded. "Does she ever ask about me specifically?"

Judy smiled empathetically. "No."

Diane chuckled and reached for the joint. "You know, it really is ironic how everything turned out. When Dean Morgan asked me to take Elliot's place, I felt as though I had to tell him, since I was guilty of exactly the same thing as Elliot."

"That's not true," Judy said, her voice sharp. "Elliot was a rapist. That's not anything like your relationship with Ronnie. So what did John say when you told him?"

Diane cracked a smile and shook her head. A small laugh escaped her lips. "He said he had suspected as much. He'd watched the two of us conduct class, and he's bright enough to know chemistry when he sees it. He wasn't surprised, and he didn't care, despite the rules. Pretty ironic, huh?"

Judy grinned. "Oh, so the great Diane Cole was *wrong* about something."

Diane could only shake her head, the marijuana making her lightheaded. "He said it was different because in his liberal mind, no one was taking advantage of anyone else."

"I can't believe you told him. Does Camille know?"

"Yeah. I had to tell him, Judy. I violated the rules too. Besides, I had to know if I'd given it all up for nothing."

Judy shrugged. "What do you mean?"

"I had to know if I threw our relationship away senselessly. I was so worried about what everyone would think, who would find out, how I would be punished if they did . . ." She wiped a tear away. "Well, I got my answer, and in the process I treated Ronnie like a second-class citizen. For that I will always be truly sorry."

Judy stared at her as Diane studied the joint in her hand. "Maybe you should tell her that?"

Diane shook her head and put the joint down. "She doesn't care about me. She already has a girlfriend, that African-American model. They are together, right?" She closed her mouth, suddenly realizing how jealous and paranoid she sounded. She had no claim to Ronnie or her life. *She* was the one who had broken up. She was the one who had abandoned her lover after she was nearly raped.

Judy relit the joint and took a hit. "I don't know. I think they're somewhat involved, but Ronnie always says she doesn't have a girlfriend, and the tabloids are having a field day with her sexuality. I think she spends as much time hiding in the closet as she does anything else."

"I just never thought of Ronnie as someone who would hide."

"She only does it for her manager, who is convinced Ronnie's career would tank if she came out."

Diane snorted. "Right. It's every heterosexual man's dream to imagine himself with two women. She'd just be adding to their fantasies."

"Exactly," Judy agreed. She leaned very close to Diane and whispered, "Which is why she's going to come out next month, whether her manager likes it or not."

"She is?"

"Yes," Judy said conspiratorially. "She told me that she's sick of it, all the pretend boyfriends and the uncomfortable questions. She and Tania—that's the woman she's been seeing—are going to attend an event together and have a big kiss."

Diane felt her stomach turn over. She wasn't sure if it was the alcohol, the pot or Judy's information, but she stumbled to the bathroom and found the toilet just in time.

31. Pillow Talk

Tania's body was flawless. Although time was still on her side at only twenty-six. There wasn't a single imperfection that Ronnie could find on Tania's incredible figure after endless nights of touching and exploring someone new. Not a blemish marred her skin, no callous roughened her heels and no ounce of fat hung from any of her limbs. Her perfection, though, brought Ronnie little delight, but rather discomfort. She couldn't help comparing herself to Tania. Since they were both models, vying for the same jobs and the highest paychecks, she studied Tania's body while she savored every part of it with her lips and fingers.

Tania had no physical flaws, but she did have a weakness—cocaine. Her habit sat on the border of serious recreational usage and addiction, and the line between was always blurred. Much of her paycheck went for blow, and she encouraged Ronnie to partake with her, which Ronnie did readily, having never shied away from a new experience, but the Friday night frat parties had not prepared her for the daily offerings of cocaine in the fashion industry.

Ronnie learned it was endless, the drug of choice that served as a party favor for any function, the paraphernalia easily hidden inside a purse. Tania herself had a custom-designed compact, and although it looked perfectly innocent, inside were a vial and a tube, hidden within the contours of the panels.

The first time she did coke with Tania was the night of their coming out, where they kissed each other in front of the press.

"Nervous?" Tania had asked as they sat in the line of limos at a downtown club, waiting for their turn to exit.

Ronnie looked at her hands. She'd been wringing them anxiously and her palms were sweaty. "Just a little," she admitted.

"I know how to fix that," Tania said. She opened her purse and withdrew the little vial. Ronnie watched as she scooped the powder into her pinky nail. "There is a definite advantage to being a femme," she joked. "Now, let's take the edge off of that tension."

Ronnie put her hand up. "That's okay, I don't need it."

Tania held her pinky close to Ronnie's face. "I know you don't need it. You're a very strong person, and one little toot isn't going to make you an addict. Besides, I'm starting to get a complex that you'll never party with me." She laughed a little and smiled. "Now, are you going to use this, or do I get to keep it all for myself? I am generous, you know. Mama taught me to share."

Ronnie chuckled and leaned forward. Tania's fingernail disappeared inside Ronnie's nostril. After two quick snorts, she did indeed feel much better, able to face the crowd as a lesbian. The coke had given her the confidence she needed, and she began to seek its assistance more often, certain she could control her usage and not become a statistic.

That had been several weeks ago, exactly how long Ronnie

wasn't sure. Her awareness and control of her world had disappeared, and she floated in a vacuum while everything spun past her, intangible and unknown. What she did know was that Tania was practically living in her loft and they were using cocaine daily. If she needed confirmation of the truth, all she had to do was roll over in bed. Tania's silk black negligee lay discarded on the pillow next to Ronnie, its owner already out the door to her shoot. Ronnie glanced at the nightstand, the mirror and razorblade sitting in front of the digital clock, the red numbers staring at her. It was already noon?

Ronnie sat up in bed and rubbed her eyes, trying to wake up and shake the grogginess from her body. Unlike Tania, cocaine numbed Ronnie, relaxed her, whereas Tania became energized and unconquerable. Ronnie stumbled to the bathroom and washed her face. Her eyes were those of a stranger's, foggy and distant. The twinkling blue stars, as Diane had always called them, were gone. She held the sides of the sink, long enough to put Diane out of her thoughts and allow her legs time to acclimate to walking like a real human being.

Tania had made coffee and left a note, the subject of which was their next cocaine buy. Deke would come at two and Ronnie should give him the cash in the drawer. Ronnie could only imagine how much they had spent on their entertainment, but she was sure it was a lot. She sat on a stool and gazed around her loft. She had no idea how much it had cost either, since Nola and Marcel had arranged its rental. When she had arrived in New York, she had been dazed over losing Diane, and she didn't care and she didn't want to know about anything. It amazed her to think that she had turned into a helpless child—one who knew nothing of her finances, the activities that consumed her hours, the constructed friendships Nola had designed or, indeed, the course of her life. The precious days were evaporating one by one, and she was caught in a cycle she had always vowed to avoid. She had boasted to Diane that she lived life on her terms, but now she didn't have any terms, or a life. She laughed out loud, noting the irony of an epiphany spurred by her cocaine usage, forcing her to examine her life from many facets.

She glanced at the book titles clustered on the shelves against the walls. She thought of Diane's book and wondered when it would be published. She'd given up reading in favor of partying, whether it was during a shoot or afterhours with Tania. She'd stopped carrying books in her purse in favor of her own special compact.

The pictures on the wall came from a gallery in SoHo, but she couldn't name the artists, and the more she absorbed their meaning, the more she realized that she didn't care for them at all. She went to take them down but was drawn to the wrought-iron bed. Had she really picked it out? It matched the loft, but certainly not her personality. She much preferred a large oak frame, like the one at Diane's bungalow.

Her legs buckled and she sat back down on the bed. She was numb, but its point of origin was her soul, not the nerve endings or brain waves ravaged by her constant drug usage. She had given her life away, to whom and for what she did not know. It wasn't as though anyone was taking advantage of her, misrepresenting her or abusing their influence. No, if anything, it was the other way around.

Just then the phone rang and the familiar voice made her smile.

"I just thought I'd check up on you, honey. Frankly, Judy and I have been a little worried. You sounded really out of it when we spoke on the phone last week and, well, I'll be honest. When Brody came back from visiting you last week, he came to visit me. He said you spent most of the time pretty wasted. Is that true?"

Ronnie took a deep breath and sighed. She could barely remember anything about Brody's weekend in New York. "Yeah, it probably is. I really don't remember."

"Is this out of control? Do you need help?" Camille asked simply.

"I don't know. I was just sorting through everything when you called. I need to make some changes, Camille, but I'm not sure what to do. Have you got any ideas?"

"Yes."

32. Reunion

Signs of the coming summer were ever present, especially at the ocean. The sun hovered much longer over the horizon, unwilling to set. Diane found herself remaining at her office later and later, wanting to time her drive down the coast each evening with the eruption of color that inevitably enveloped her windshield. No matter how chaotic her day had been, the sunset comforted her, its resolute strength untwisting the knotted strands of problems she faced as department chair, providing clarity and peace by the time she pulled into her garage.

She didn't mind the added responsibilities, and in fact, she relished the challenges to manage the department. Also, it gave her purpose on the weekends and during the evening hours. The work was endless, the difficult issues constant, and only fatigue forced her to close a book or drop a file out of her hands, sometimes scaring her awake from her momentary nap. More often than not, she dozed on the couch, never bothering to change into the nightshirt she had purchased since Ronnie's departure and climb into her bed, which no longer felt warm and comfortable. Weeks would go by, the comforter undisturbed, the only occupant of the bed Claude, who refused to sleep on the sofa with her. She may have been ridiculous, but he was not.

Diane did not need Susan Skaggs or a self-help book to analyze her behavior. Keeping her mind busy was critical to side-stepping the unavoidable self-loathing that sat like a land mine over her heart, frequently reminding her of what she had done and the betrayal Ronnie must have felt. She had cast a hundred scenarios, each one more heartbreaking than the one before, envisioning Ronnie's response to her abandonment. Replaying that evening would send her into a freefall of depression that could distract her for days, affect her classes, drive her to a drunken stupor and, worst of all, collapse the delicate web of normalcy and routine she needed to survive.

Now that her book was completely finished and with the publisher, her anxiety heightened as she looked toward another project to fill the time absent of students and classes. Her friends offered their company often, but all of them were in couples, and it was apparent when her presence was desired or when she was the victim of a well-intentioned act of charity.

Tuesdays provided a slight break in the routine. On her way home, she'd stop at Lou's Super Mart and replenish the gallon of whiskey she consumed every seven days and, more importantly, purchase all of the fashion magazines that Lou's distributor restocked every week. The first few times she had tried to browse through the magazines and only purchase those that included Ronnie, but it was terribly time-consuming, since Ronnie was a constant fixture. It was just easier to buy all of them and spend a few hours perusing the many ads and occasional articles that featured her. Diane had become Lou's favorite customer, bolstering his profits with her regular stops for booze and periodicals. She rifled through endless advertisements, all socio-logical studies about the vulnerability of women and their fears about obesity, body odor, ugliness and aging, anything that would make them less appealing to men.

Nothing in *Cosmopolitan* this month, which didn't really sur-prise her, given the fact that Ronnie had been the cover girl for April. She picked up a new magazine and saw that one of the articles previewed summer swimwear.

Ronnie was the centerfold. Two pages were devoted to her, specifically her mostly naked body, which would explain why the editors hid her deep within the magazine. Parents would have complained had their ten-year-old sons seen Ronnie on the cover while waiting in a grocery line. As usual the photos rode the line between raw sexuality and soft porn.

Her hair, returned to its natural blond state, was severely pulled from her face in cornrows, which matched the simplicity of the bikini she wore, made of hemp. Her body was bronzed, either from makeup or a long stint at the tanning salon. Only her most private of parts were covered, and Diane could definitely see the outline of Ronnie's nipples through the thin cloth of her top. Water poured over her from a waterfall, and in Diane's favorite picture, Ronnie's head was tilted back in ecstasy, her hands reaching for the water, and her breasts thrust forward.

Two other magazines featured Ronnie in ads for various products, including a cosmetics line. She had posed for them before, and Diane was beginning to wonder if Ronnie had signed a contract with them. More often than not, they referred to her as "Veronica" in bold marquee type. It was obvious Ronnie wasn't just a face anymore, but a woman making her mark.

Diane saved everything, a table in her garage filled with Ronnie's image, dozens of glossy pictures, many of which Diane admired periodically. It provided her with a timeline of Ronnie's short but brilliant career and she could trace Ronnie's life since she left L.A. She piled the magazines on top of last week's, her

225

eyes still glued to the swimsuit spread. She looked carefully at Ronnie's eyes, at something disturbing, something familiar. They were vacant, not conveying their usual electricity, but rather an intense dislike of herself, it seemed, something Diane saw every morning when she looked in the mirror.

She flew down the stairs of the Social Sciences building, her Courtship and Marriage notes tucked under her arm. She had seven minutes to get to class, just enough time to ask Camille some questions about the upcoming oral defense schedule and still make it across campus for her lecture.

Camille's door was shut, and an impeccably dressed gay man in his mid-twenties sat in the chair outside. It looked as though he was talking to himself, but Diane saw the black hands-free headset that trailed from his ear to the front of his mouth. He held a PDA and was tapping the stylus against the screen at a maddening pace. He only glanced at her, and she somehow felt she should know him. She thrust open Camille's door, hoping she wasn't being too rude to the student who was deep in conference with her advisor. "Camille, I'm sorry to interrupt, but I've got to finalize this schedule," Diane said.

At the sight of the woman next to Camille, Diane lost her grip on the stack of papers and they fell to the floor. It was Ronnie. Dressed in an Armani pantsuit, she sat perfectly erect, her legs crossed and her beautifully manicured nails resting on her knees. Her hair was shorter now, pulled back from her face and held in place by a hairclip. When she turned to acknowledge Diane, she smiled with her entire face, one that was perfectly sculpted and worth millions. Diane was drawn to her eyes, for it was there that she saw a shadow of the Ronnie she had once known. They were bright and vibrant, twinkling like stars.

"Hello, Diane."

Diane was speechless, shocked at the sight of the woman she

had lost. She wasn't supposed to be here, and Diane's inability to process Ronnie's presence was no doubt evident.

Ronnie rose slowly, with a grace and elegance Diane had never witnessed, and glanced at the notes. "Here, let me help you," she said, bending over to pick them up.

"Oh, no, I'll get them." Good manners brought Diane back to the present, and she also squatted to the floor. In the process, her necklace freed itself from her shirt collar, and the diamond swung freely in front of Ronnie, who took it between two French manicured nails, as if unable to believe Diane was wearing it.

Ronnie said nothing. She simply stared into Diane's eyes while her fingers caressed the stone and the gold chain. At one point, Ronnie's hand brushed against her collarbone, and Diane thought she would fall over from the touch. Diane smiled, and suddenly Ronnie's face shifted, the façade of grace destroyed. She looked away and stood awkwardly. Diane looked at her, puzzled by the change in Ronnie's demeanor.

"Ronnie, we have to go," a voice from the doorway said. Diane assumed it was the efficient young man with the PDA.

Clearly flustered and unable to look her in the eye, Ronnie handed Diane the stack of papers.

"Ronnie, I know you have a plane to catch," Camille said. "You go, and I'll try to explain everything to Diane."

Ronnie nodded and returned to Camille's desk. They whispered softly while Ronnie packed her book bag, Diane staring at Ronnie's striking image.

She turned from Camille and smiled warmly at Diane, evidently back in control of her emotions. There was no residual anger or hatred, and Diane sensed she was forgiven, which made her feel worse. Forgiveness meant Ronnie had moved on and Diane was forgotten.

"How are you?" Ronnie asked.

Diane nodded. "I'm fine."

"I hear the book will be out soon—September, Camille said. Congratulations."

"Thanks."

"Ronnie, the plane leaves in two hours." The young man moved toward her and took the book bag. She nodded and smiled once more before she exited, the scent of her perfume lingering behind.

Once Diane heard the door shut, she fell into a chair and closed her eyes. The act was over. It was only her and Camille, and Camille had much explaining to do. She controlled her voice as she asked, "Why didn't you tell me?"

"Ronnie didn't want you to know. She didn't want to complicate things for you."

Diane's mind whirled. She tried to grasp a thought or idea, but all she could see was Ronnie's brilliant face, smiling at her.

Camille sighed. "There are some things you should know, since you'll probably be running into her."

Diane stared at her. "Don't you think I would have noticed? I am the department chair, you know?"

"Calm down, honey. I was just looking for the right time to tell you. Now, I know you need to go to class, so why don't we meet in front of the library at one?"

The phone conveniently rang and Camille answered it, excusing herself from the conversation and delaying her explanation for four hours.

Diane went through the motions of class, her anger and feelings of betrayal increasing with every thought of the situation. She pictured Ronnie flying into L.A., secretly meeting with Camille and Judy, probably having dinner with their friends, spending time together while Diane sat isolated in the bungalow staring at two-dimensional pictures. Ronnie had put Diane out of her mind, of this she was sure.

By noon, Diane had already started to walk toward the library, which was undergoing remodeling. She sat on a bench across from the entrance as burly workers in hard hats erected the large marble nameplate, officially renaming the Carlson library "Armbruster Media Center." It seemed Stacy's father had yet again guaranteed his daughter's continued success, but she really didn't need it, Diane thought. Stacy was an excellent student in her own right, when she tried.

Diane watched as the workers struggled to guide the sign into place, barking orders at the crane operator, who moved the marble slab to the left then the right as it precariously teetered on its side. A jackhammer drowned out the shouts of the men, who resorted to hand signals. After several attempts, the workers centered the sign permanently.

As the tower bell struck one, Diane watched as Camille leisurely came toward her, hands stuffed inside her skirt pockets. She lowered her large frame next to Diane on the bench and patted Diane's arm.

Diane was still fuming, feeling duped by her best friend or, if she was being honest, cheated. "How long has Ronnie been in L.A.?"

Camille leaned back and crossed her arms over her chest. "Two months. She moved back in with Vandella and the guys. She travels most of the time, but at least when she comes home, she feels as though she belongs."

Diane shook her head, unable to believe that Camille had kept this from her. She thought of the endless nights she had imagined Ronnie in her New York loft. All along, or at least for a while, Ronnie had been less than ten miles away.

As if reading her thoughts, Camille began her story. "I called her one day because I'd heard stories. She broke down and told me everything. She was terribly depressed, she'd given up most everything she cared about, and she'd started using cocaine—seriously."

"What?" Diane couldn't picture Ronnie as an addict.

"Apparently her friend Tania is quite the cokehead, and she

229

started to drag Ronnie down with her. Fortunately, Ronnie had enough sense to recognize what was happening. She had to get out of there, and she desperately craved an anchor, something to make her feel grounded."

"School," Diane concluded.

"Yes," Camille agreed. "I talked with Dean Morgan and explained the situation. She wanted a degree, but she couldn't attend the classes in a traditional way, since her traveling wouldn't permit it. I told him that I would be her advisor, and that I thought a few of the professors would be willing to meet with her on a regular basis, and she could complete the coursework on an independent study basis."

"And he went along with it?" Diane was astounded.

"He had reservations at first," Camille admitted. "But I managed to convince him. He always thought very highly of Ronnie, and I think he always believed her version of what happened with Elliott."

"That doesn't matter. She's not following a regular program of study with rigorous coursework and, most importantly, class discussions."

"No." Camille shook her head. "Ronnie's actually working harder than most of the students, reading more literature and doing more assignments. If anything, Marks and Croft are working her harder than anyone just to make a point."

Diane shook her head vehemently. "It's not right. This is a prestigious university, not some paper mill where students can phone in their education. I've never heard of something so unorthodox. Dean Morgan would never agree to something like this." She looked at Camille, who shifted on the bench, suddenly silent. "There's something you're not telling me," she said.

"Well, as I said, he did balk initially. But then Ronnie made him an offer he couldn't refuse."

"And what was that?"

"She made a large donation to the building fund."

"How much?"

"Two million."

Diane sat there quietly. The amount alone was shocking. She remembered when Ronnie was just a starving student trying to get by on tips from bartending, and now she was contributing to the endowment.

"What are they building?" she asked, not really caring.

Camille pointed across the street.

"The library? But Armbruster's name is on the front."

"That's exactly the way Ronnie wanted it. She'd helped Stacy a while back, and Stacy was happy to return the favor."

"Stacy helped Ronnie?"

"Yes. They've become good friends since they banded together against Michaelson, and then Ronnie helped Stacy get through her abortion."

Diane stared ahead. "So he agreed to put Stacy's family name on the library so Ronnie could go to school. Unbelievable!" She rose, unwilling to hear any more. "She bribed her way into the university. And you condoned it? I'm floored."

Camille's eyes narrowed. She pulled herself up and pointed a finger at Diane. "Don't pull this pious bullshit on me. In the first place, Ronnie is one of the best students who ever enrolled at this school. She was in trouble and this place saved her. For that I think you should be grateful. And since when does Diane Cole, champion of students, avoid helping one? You are a teacher who goes to the wall to make things happen for them. Hell, I've learned it from you." She started to walk away but turned around. "We both know why this situation bothers you so much. It's not Ronnie's financial persuasion, or that she's earning her degree in a different way. No, you're upset because you're jealous. I've been seeing her since March and you haven't."

Diane returned to the bench and sat down. She wanted to cry, but the last thing she needed was a group of students to walk by and see their professor sobbing.

231

Camille rejoined her on the bench and put an arm around her. "Diane, I love you, but you're miserable. You need to let go. I think it's for the best. Ronnie will always be in your heart, but it's time to move on."

Diane looked at her, tears in her eyes. She nodded. "You're probably right."

Camille hugged her tightly. "I know I am. What you need is a good date, and I know just the woman for you. She's brilliant, she's your age, and she's unattached. I think you'd really like her."

"Maybe after the book is published, okay? I need at least a few more months."

"Maybe," Camille conceded. "But I'm not letting you slip into some hole of despair and turn into an academic recluse who wears her pajamas all the time and stares out a window."

"That couldn't happen, Camille. I don't own any pajamas."

33. Rehearsal

A little girl smiled at Diane, wisps of the girl's white-blond hair kissing her face in the breeze. Her little white bathing suit was covered in yellow daisies, the skirt rippling up and down. She held her tiny hands in front of her and giggled endlessly, as though she had the hiccups. She suddenly turned and headed for the surf, Diane trailing after her, worried that the riptides would swallow the unsuspecting child. The girl looked back, and seeing that Diane was behind her, she shifted course and started running down the shoreline, the ocean forgotten. Despite Diane's quick stride, the child distanced herself until she was almost out of sight, and Diane had to follow the small footprints left in the sand. She worried that the little girl would once again head toward the sea, which was growing more violent by the second. Black clouds were forming in the distance; a storm wasn't far away.

She had walked almost a mile when the footprints disappeared. A feeling of dread swept over her as she looked about for any clue of the child's whereabouts. A high-pitched squeal from above a nearby dune resonated over the sound of the waves. Diane trudged through the sand, once again seeing the outline of the tiny footprints. When she reached the crest of the dune, the little girl was there, her arms outstretched, spinning in circles like an airplane. She paid no attention to Diane, engrossed in her giggling and twirling and the delight of it all. Diane joined her and they spun together until Diane was terribly dizzy and fell into the sand on her back.

When she awoke, it was with a smile on her face. The dream had been lovely, certainly the sweetest dream she had experienced since Ronnie left, and for the first time in a long time, she felt refreshed after resting, even though she had only been sleeping for an hour. She sat up, adjusting the black sheath that hugged her body and looking for her shoes.

It had been an eventful evening with all of Carlson University invited to celebrate the publication of her book. Although the actual release wouldn't occur until fall, Dean Morgan took full advantage of the opportunity to open his home again in honor of Diane's accomplishment. The party had done wonders for her self-esteem, the guests a mutual admiration society, all published scholars who empathized and applauded one another's efforts. Most of them would never read the entire 412 pages, since they hailed from other disciplines, isolated in their own specialties, encapsulated in their own particular building on the Carlson campus. Of course, her department would do her the favor of generously skimming the book, and Camille, her best friend and friendly academic rival, would read every word.

One blurb for the book called it exceptional, and already it was receiving kudos from literary scholars; several book reviews were scheduled. There were even whispers that it would cross over into the hands of the general public. Diane couldn't think about that happening, for it was very rare, and if it did, the credit belonged at least partially to Ronnie for all of the work she'd done.

No one seemed to notice Ronnie's absence from the party, or if they had, they did Diane the courtesy of feigning ignorance. For Diane, the party was incomplete, merely a responsibility of work. Any true joy could have only come from having Ronnie at her side. Diane had left the party and come back to the office, unwilling to go home, dreading the empty bungalow.

The clock read two o'clock, and she rose with a sigh. It was time to go. When she peered through the window, a full moon greeted her, and she knew her drive home would be beautiful. Armed with her shoes and purse, she descended the four flights of stairs barefoot, enjoying the perfect solitude and silence of the old building.

As she came around the corner of the ground floor, she saw light streaming out from the lecture hall near the front doors. She looked through the small glass pane in the hall's main door and her heart skipped a beat. Ronnie stood on the small stage, pacing back and forth in front of the one hundred empty seats, talking to herself and pointing to invisible charts and graphs. At times she would pause and freeze, thinking of what to say, and then her diatribe would begin again.

She wore a pair of stretch pants, a tank top and the baseball cap that Diane loved. Even dressed in casual clothes, Ronnie was still poised and beautiful. When she bent over to pick up one of her notes, Diane inhaled deeply, staring at the firmness of Ronnie's derriere against the tight-fitting fabric. She closed her eyes, commanding herself to walk away and out the door. She was spying, and she had no right to be there, but her feet wouldn't move and she remained leaning against the door, watching Ronnie rehearse the oral defense of her thesis, which Diane knew Camille had scheduled for the next day. If Ronnie successfully completed her defense, she would earn her master's degree, and then, Diane realized, she would no longer have any ties to Carlson.

Suddenly Ronnie sunk to the floor of the stage, burying her head in her hands. Diane focused on the beautiful long fingers and French nails that pressed against her skull in despair. It was Ronnie's trademark position of frustration. Diane had seen it many times when Ronnie was upset. Like Diane, Ronnie needed control, and when she was a victim of circumstances, she felt helpless. Diane realized that defending her thesis was something Ronnie couldn't control, and it must have frightened her immensely, since so much was at stake.

Without thinking another thought, Diane opened the door to the hall and went in.

Ronnie looked up from the floor in disbelief. "What are you doing here?"

Diane descended the steps until she stood in front of Ronnie and sat down in the first row. "I was here working, and I fell asleep."

Ronnie blinked and arched an eyebrow. "In that outfit?"

Diane blushed, suddenly remembering her attire and, more importantly, why she was dressed in a cocktail dress. "Um, well, it was the party for the book."

"Oh," Ronnie said. Her face remained expressionless as she processed the information. "How was it?"

"Fine," Diane said with a shrug.

The silence between them now was painful, Diane thought, so unusual and uncomfortable, unlike the lazy pauses that had always punctuated their conversations while they processed ideas.

"What happens if I fail?" Ronnie asked quietly.

"You are not going to fail," Diane said. "If anything, I'm positive that you are more than ready, and now you're having a case of nerves."

When Ronnie finally looked at her, she smiled.

"Don't worry," Diane whispered in a voice that had always calmed Ronnie in the past whenever she was anxious. Diane tried to convey a tone of compassion and command. After all, she thought, she was older and more experienced, the voice of authority, assuring Ronnie she was right, and she was always right.

Ronnie massaged her temples and took a deep breath. "It's not that Camille and I haven't discussed my defense, but I just feel unprepared, like there's something I'm forgetting to consider. I keep imagining Marks and Croft will ask me a question, and my mouth will drop open but no words will come out."

Diane couldn't suppress a chuckle.

"Diane!" Ronnie exclaimed.

"I'm sorry. It just sounds like a dream I would have."

"It does, doesn't it?" Ronnie smiled.

A pleasant laugh from both of them masked the awkwardness caused by the casual reference to the past and the intimacy it implied.

Diane ran her hand through her hair. "Look, here's what I can tell you. I've sat through several oral defenses with all three of them, and it's very predictable. Croft will focus on your literal understanding of your thesis. Do you really know what you wrote and what you believe? He'll expect you to have it practically committed to memory. Marks is exactly the opposite. He'll want you to extend all of your arguments and he'll challenge your intellect. Camille just expects you to explain and justify your hypothesis."

"So, I need to be all things to all people," Ronnie said, another note of frustration resonating in her voice.

"It won't be that bad. Just try to get some rest and clear your mind."

Ronnie's audible sigh caused Diane to bite her lower lip. Ronnie only sighed like that when she was under great stress, but instead of breaking into sobs, which was Ronnie's usual past

237

behavior, she extended her legs, brought her long arms around over her head and touched her toes, holding the position for several seconds. Diane suspected yoga was now a part of Ronnie's life, and when she raised her head, she was indeed smiling.

Ronnie sighed again, this time with relief. "Okay. I'm fine. Thanks for the advice. I should learn to deal with my anxiety better."

Please don't, Diane thought. *Then you might still need me for something.*

"Get some rest," Diane repeated as she rose from the chair. Ronnie nodded, staring out into the empty seats, the silence interrupted by the black silk of Diane's dress rustling against the chair as she stood. "Well, I should go. I'm sorry for barging in on you."

She headed back up the steps, sensing that Ronnie was watching her, and a shiver went through her.

"Diane?"

Diane paused, her foot on the next step. She knew that whatever request Ronnie made of her, she would perform, whatever question Ronnie posed, she would answer. The simple fact was that she was no farther along her path of forgetting Ronnie than she was the night she drove away in the rain. The realization came in an unexpected instant and she nearly lost her footing.

She took a deep breath and turned, hoping she'd worked her facial features into a deceptively pleasant look.

"You look amazing," Ronnie said.

Diane smiled slightly and hurried toward the exit.

34. The Last Word

"So, how did it go?" Brody asked when Ronnie walked through the door with Marcel, who had agreed to go with her and wait outside for moral support. Dave, Van and Richard sat at the table waiting for Ronnie's verdict about her oral defense.

She smiled and nodded. "I passed," she said, throwing her briefcase onto the sofa. Brody let out a whoop and picked up Marcel, who seemed rather taken aback. Ronnie raised an eyebrow when she realized neither of them was letting go.

"This calls for an appropriate celebration," Richard announced. "I say we go invade Simply Understated and dance on the tables."

Brody shook his head. "No, Richard."

Richard put his hands on his hips. "Hey, I have no problem going into that place and making a scene, not after Randy dumped you."

Brody continued to hold Marcel in his arms. "It was a mutual split, Richard. You don't need to defend me."

"That's not what I think. You were devastated, Brody. That man used you. In fact—"

"Richard, honey," Dave interrupted, "you need to get a clue." He pointed at Brody, who was nibbling Marcel's earlobe.

"Oh," Richard said. "Then I guess we should go to Dusty's."

Ronnie grabbed the discarded briefcase and headed for the stairs. "Really, you guys, I just want to hang out here. I need to pack."

Hearing a mention of Ronnie's schedule, Marcel pulled away from Brody and withdrew his PDA from the breast pocket of his jacket. "Yes, in fact, Ronnie, our plane for Melbourne leaves at nine in the morning. And you have a shoot the following day."

"Followed by two weeks of vacation," Ronnie added. "Make sure that's in your calendar."

Marcel tapped on the screen some more while Brody kissed his neck. "Well, darling." Marcel giggled. "So much for keeping our romance a secret."

"I don't care who knows!" Brody yelled and squeezed him tighter.

Ronnie grinned, happy that her friends had found love, and she'd only had to do a little matchmaking along the way. She trudged upstairs, Vandella following behind.

"Congratulations," Van said.

"It felt really good. Diane was absolutely right. Croft was so literal, expecting me to practically recite my thesis, while Marks kept asking me to expound. And then there was Camille, in the middle, just playing the referee between the two of them."

"You talked to Diane about your defense?" Van was clearly surprised.

"It was weird. She was still in the building at two in the morning, and she just appeared in the lecture hall," Ronnie said softly. "She was really very helpful."

"How was it talking to her? Was it strange?"

"A little," Ronnie conceded. "Sometimes it was very awkward, and I sensed there were things that were left unsaid between us. Maybe it's for the best."

"Maybe," Van murmured. "But before you write her off, you probably should read this."

Van handed her an advance copy of Diane's book, which Van had opened to the dedication page.

Ronnie noticed the italic font, and the mention of her name immediately caught her attention. Diane had bared her soul.

For Ronnie
You taught me more about life and love
than any book ever could.
I love you forever.

Before she headed for her car, Diane checked her in-box for any department mail that might demand her immediate attention or serve as a preview for her morning tomorrow. She liked to be prepared, and she hated unwarranted surprises.

At the top of the stack sat the examination sheet for Ronnie's defense, Camille's flowing handwriting proclaiming that Ronnie had passed. Diane skimmed the comments, noting words such as, *insightful, articulate* and *professional*. Diane smiled and let the form waft back into the box, covering the mail that lay beneath it.

She no longer cared. She stood in front of her desk, keenly aware of the silence around her. It was after five on the final Friday of the trimester. Next week was graduation. The work was done, the assignments completed and the grades recorded. The silence echoed the finality of the term. Everyone was gone for the weekend, but Diane remained in her office, wondering if she hadn't received the memo and the joke was on her. *Maybe it's buried in my in-box*, she thought. For the first time in her life, being alone in the old building equated to loneliness.

"Damn," she whispered to the empty corridor, unable to believe that her one place of security and comfort, the sanctuary of her mind, was now polluted by the despair in her heart. She willed the feeling to pass and knew it would not.

All the way home, she busied her mind with a checklist of urgent matters—or rather, issues she rationalized were important and needed to be addressed. Her other choice was escape, perhaps a long vacation, like a cruise, where she would be forced to interact with strangers and forget her own problems, but that would put her in a position she hated. She hated new beginnings, including first dates and blossoming friendships. She was the introvert, and Ronnie was the extrovert. She breathed deeply, noting the circles of her logic, and Ronnie was everywhere.

Diane realized what hurt the most, and she knew where the largest void existed in her heart. While the gentleness of Ronnie's touch and the twinkling of her eyes mesmerized Diane every day, the simple cadence of life actually provided the greatest gift. She missed the banter, the familiarity, the lack of pretentiousness that was embedded within the sex and the passion.

She didn't miss the relationship nearly as much as the friendship. Hindsight afforded her the chance to think about what would have happened had she listened to her internal warning signs and exercised some self-control, spurning Ronnie's advances. Hindsight, though, required honesty. She had wanted Ronnie almost immediately from the moment they shared that brilliant kiss. Attraction preceded friendship, which preceded love.

She was so preoccupied with her thoughts that she drove on autopilot, until the BMW cruised up to the driveway. Diane hit the brakes before she crashed into a sleek, new Harley sitting in front of her garage. The chrome glistened in the sunlight. It was the handsomest machine Diane had ever seen, and she only knew one person who could afford such luxury.

She placed the clutch in reverse, the instinct to flee overpowering. She couldn't see Ronnie, who she imagined was waiting for her on the deck, watching the ocean and basking in the sun. She got as far as the stop sign near the main road and put the car in park. She was being ridiculous. This was her home, and if she wanted Ronnie to leave, all she had to do was ask. Ronnie was reasonable, rarely prone to make a scene.

Her logic in place, Diane returned to her driveway and quickly went around to the back of the house. Ronnie was indeed enjoying the sun on the porch swing, her long legs stretched out in front of her, reading Diane's book. She lay there with no regard to grace, slouched into a position of sheer comfort. It was how Diane remembered her before she became a model.

"How long have you been sitting in the driveway?" Ronnie asked as she turned a page.

"Not long," Diane replied. When Ronnie continued to read, her eyes never leaving the page, Diane added, "Of course, I did drive away once before I decided I was being silly."

That drew a smile from Ronnie, who sat up and shut the book.

Diane eyed her body; the tight jeans and fitted cotton shirt met with her approval. "Why are you here?" she asked, not sure Ronnie could hear her over the surf.

"Let's go for a ride."

Diane looked away and down at the floorboards of the deck. She shook her head no, unable to look at Ronnie. "I don't think that's a good idea."

Ronnie chuckled and Diane couldn't help but gaze up at the million-dollar smile that had adorned at least a hundred advertisements.

"Oh, don't worry. This will be strictly professional. I just thought you might want to know what I thought of the book, particularly the weak places."

Diane blinked. "Weak places?"

Ronnie shrugged and reopened the thick text, ignoring Diane.

Without a word, Diane disappeared inside the bungalow and searched for suitable clothes. She strained to hear the rush of the sea, but it was her heart, beating at a deafening level, she heard instead. Her whole body was warm, wrought with anxiety, and she debated whether she should just lock the door and wait for Ronnie to leave. Before she could make a decision, she was dressed and standing before Ronnie, who sat on the balcony rail, her back against one of the posts, her eyes closed.

"Ready?" Ronnie murmured.

"Yes."

Ronnie hopped off the balcony and headed for the Harley, Diane trailing behind, moving slowly. Ronnie slid over the back of the seat and tossed the keys to Diane.

The purr of the motor released Diane's anxiety and they were off. She concentrated on the feel of the machine, the hum of the motor, trying to ignore Ronnie's hands at her waist and the nearness of her body. The sun was heading over the horizon and Diane sped up, determined to reach the cliff before the horizon burst into color.

They made record time and parked the bike just as dusk announced its presence, and the ocean shimmered in silver.

Diane climbed off and went to the edge of the cliff while Ronnie pawed through the saddlebags. Diane turned to find her holding a bottle of expensive Champagne and two plastic Champagne flutes.

"What are we celebrating?" Diane asked.

"Well, I can think of three reasons to celebrate," Ronnie said. "Your book and my defense are two of them. I know that I passed," she said secretively. "Camille told me."

"I know you passed, too. All I have to do now is sign the examination paper, and you're done."

Ronnie battled a very tough cork, and neither of them could

repress a laugh when it finally flew over the cliff.

"I thought you were leaving for Australia."

"I am, just not today." Ronnie sat down next to her and filled their glasses.

Diane watched Ronnie tilt the glass to her lips and the liquid slowly descend into her mouth. She lowered the plastic flute as though it were fine crystal, her fingertips curved around the stem in a perfect arc. Her every movement seemed deliberate and purposeful.

"You're very different," Diane said.

Ronnie laughed. "Am I? Camille said the same thing. I guess that as much as I despise being Veronica most of the time, some of her is bound to rub off on me. At least, I hope it's only the good parts," she added quietly.

"What's it like being a model? Do you like it?"

"It's very lucrative," Ronnie said bluntly. "It will also be temporary. I have no intention of doing this for any significant length of time, maybe another year."

"I'm sure your career could go much longer than that."

Ronnie only shook her head. Silence fell between them, and they listened to the surf and watched the sun as it finally dropped below the horizon.

Neither of them felt compelled to speak, and Ronnie realized that for the first time in months, she was totally relaxed. She glanced at Diane, who was staring at the sky, resting back on her elbows.

This was how it used to be between them, and the link to the past made Ronnie smile. She turned to Diane, who was staring at her.

Diane suddenly pulled herself up and crossed her legs underneath her. "I just want you to know how sorry I am, and I hope we can still be friends."

"Friends?" Ronnie asked.

Diane nodded and smiled pleasantly. "I know that things didn't work out, but we're both mature adults. That should count for something."

Ronnie stared at her shrewdly. "This is your usual pattern, isn't it? You get involved romantically, then you break up, but somehow you always remain friends."

"And that's a bad thing?" Diane gripped Ronnie's arm, her voice filled with sincerity. "I do want us to be friends. I want you to see that I'm not some horrible person. I hope you can forgive me for the cowardly way I broke up with you, never calling, never giving you an explanation. Can we be friends?"

Ronnie stared straight into Diane's dark brown eyes. "No, we can't."

Diane's lips started to quiver. "Why not?"

"Because my friends are honest with me, and they're honest with themselves. You are neither. How these other women—Judy and Susan and all the rest—how they stomach your behavior, I'll never know, but I won't. I doubt you can even have an honest discussion with me now."

"I can." Diane's voice was pleading. Her eyes were filled with tears, and she seemed stunned by Ronnie's remarks.

Ronnie stood and picked up her helmet. "Somehow I doubt you can." She headed toward the bike, her whole body trembling.

"Ronnie, please!" Diane cried. "You always said you'd be there for me. Well, I need you now. I don't want you to walk away like this."

Hearing her own words used against her, Ronnie threw the helmet back down and marched back to Diane. She picked her up and forcefully turned her around, pulling Diane against her. "Then tell me right now," she whispered, "how you felt about leaving me that night."

There was a long pause, as if Diane was searching for a word. "Relieved," she said. "There, are you happy? I said it." She pulled away and hugged herself. "I was so relieved. I could breathe again. I could put my life back in order and not have to worry about your wants or needs. It was all about me." She took a breath. "I actually drove home humming to the radio. It was so weird."

Ronnie waited, knowing she wasn't done.

"But it didn't last. The last year has been hell. Instead of enjoying my simple life again, which oddly enough never seemed so dull and pointless before I met you, I just kept comparing everything I was doing to our life together. It was like looking in a mirror and seeing all the flaws. I missed our discussions at Sunday morning breakfasts. When I tried to walk on the beach without you, all I heard was the blaring of the surf. I'd never noticed it before because we were always talking and whispering to each other." Diane hesitated. "Probably the absolute worst thing, though, is that since I took over for Elliot, I *can't* afford to think about you. I've got to stay focused. It's taken every bit of energy I have to push you out of my thoughts, and I'm just beginning to get there." She walked to the edge of the cliff and stared down, the tide crashing against the boulders below. "So there it is. I know you're too compassionate to gloat over someone else's misery, but if I could undo the pain I've caused you, and carry it with me instead, I would in a heartbeat."

Tears streamed down Diane's face. Ronnie untied a bandanna from her belt loop and handed it to her.

"I can't believe I'm letting you see me like this. I'm a blubbering idiot!"

"I've never seen you cry," Ronnie said, holding back an increasing urge to take Diane in her arms.

"I try not to do it often. It makes me look even older."

Ronnie looked up to the sky dramatically and held out her hands. "Oh! The age thing again. If it hadn't been so difficult with your job, would the idea of us being together be so absurd?"

Diane dabbed at her eyes and nodded. "Let's see. I'm almost

forty-two and really starting to show it. A fun evening is a good book and a Mozart CD. Every relationship I've ever had has wound up as a test of endurance for us both. The only bright light in my existence is my career, and even there, I'm a workaholic with few social graces." She suddenly froze. "Oh, my God! I'm worse off than I thought."

Ronnie laughed at the realization and wrapped her arms around the professor.

"I'm glad you think my shortcomings are so funny," Diane said, her pride clearly hurt.

"Well, you've forgotten a few. You're neurotic, paranoid, have a totally skewed view of yourself. You hog all the covers in bed—"

"I do not!"

"And lest I forget the greatest character flaw you possess— you're a fraud. You don't know anything firsthand about relationships. The classes you teach are a front. It's all got to be from a distance for you. That's why all your lovers wind up being your friends. The bottom line is, professor, you have no real experience in your field."

Diane closed her eyes as if letting Ronnie's words sink in. When she opened them, they blazed with emotion. "That's where you're wrong. I've learned volumes in the last year."

"Is that what you meant by dedicating the book to me?"

"Yes." Diane nodded.

Ronnie pulled away and walked to the edge of the cliff, looking down at the rocks, her hands in her back pockets. "Didn't it surprise you that I became a model?"

"I was shocked—after everything you'd said and everything that happened to you when you were a child. I couldn't believe it, especially after the calendar."

Ronnie smiled, thinking about that day with novice Nick. She'd certainly come a long way since then. "There's one reason that I've been able to model. Everytime someone points a camera at me, everytime I walk down a runway, I imagine you're there, and I'm doing it all for you. Just like the day with the calendar. I've thought of you every day at least a thousand times, imagining how you would want me to pose, what you would find sexy. So, no, I don't want to be *just* your friend. I can't handle it. I love you too much, and I couldn't lie to myself about it."

Diane shook her head in disbelief. "How can you still love me? After the way I treated you, I would have thought you hated me."

Ronnie cracked a grin and sauntered over to the saddlebags. She rustled through the contents and removed Diane's book. She opened it to the dedication and pointed at it. "You still love me, don't you?"

Diane's eyes shifted from Ronnie's to the page. "Yes," she whispered.

"You haven't asked me about the third reason."

"What?" Diane asked, clearly puzzled.

"I told you we had three things to celebrate. The first was your book, the second was my stellar performance at my defense, and the third reason is about both of us. The third reason we're celebrating is that we're still in love with each other. Despite everything that has happened, all the time and distance that has separated us, we're still together."

Ronnie advanced toward her, standing as close as possible. Diane inhaled Ronnie's cologne, and she was sure heat radiated off the simple cotton shirt, which was only buttoned halfway up and exposed the curves of her breasts.

"Diane, look at me."

She stared at Ronnie's shiny leather boots, but her gaze drifted up the contours of Ronnie's calves, thighs and crotch, up to the tanned skin between the open folds of the crisp, white shirt. Ronnie's fingers gently tipped her chin upward, and Ronnie's lips met hers. It seemed impossible, but Ronnie's kiss was an exact reproduction of the kiss at the bar the night they met, full of passion, assurance, full of introduction. It was over as quickly as it had begun, its duration, Diane was sure, the same as the first. It was brilliant.

"Marry me."

35. Ronnie and Diane Make a Life

Daylight slipped away before she could finish her notes. Diane tossed the stack of papers onto the redwood table and gazed toward the sound of laughter that had provided a pleasant distraction from her work.

Emily, green plastic bucket in hand, toddled through the sandcastle, collapsing the towers and walls she had just constructed with her mother. She squealed with glee, and Diane laughed from the porch. Emily swung her blond towhead from left to right, searching for Ronnie's approval of her destruction. Ronnie clapped her hands and held her arms open until Emily fell between them, unable to keep her two-year-old legs upright in the sand.

Diane studied them together, Emily's smile and blond hair a youthful version of Ronnie's. From a distance, Emily's sparkling blue eyes seemed bluer and brighter than her mother's ever had

251

been. Ronnie held Emily on her lap, listening to her excited, rambunctious babble, talk that surprised her parents constantly. Her vocabulary, Diane thought, developed from seemingly nowhere.

Every day was full of beginnings. Diane never could have imagined she would enjoy parenting, all the new experiences and the incredible rush of love that occurred each time they watched Emily discover a new first.

Emily smiled and gestured with her little hand. How someone so small could manipulate her thoughts and decision-making amazed Diane. Ronnie was the love of her life, but Emily's existence explained her own, even though Ronnie was Emily's birth mother.

Diane had hesitated when Ronnie announced she wanted a child. Diane was in her forties, comfortable with her job and basking in their selfish, totally pleasurable relationship. They traveled during school breaks and relished new opportunities such as going on a safari or learning to fly an airplane. She didn't want to share her life or her heart with anyone but Ronnie. Yet, her wife had persisted, and her tenacity had unraveled Diane's copasetic world, helping her to see that love could be a room with many doors.

She took a cleansing breath and shifted on the hard bench, her back starting to ache. She had never dreamed she would want to experience childbirth, but the nine months of watching Ronnie bask in happiness and wonder had given Diane the courage and desire to carry her own child. And so Diane, at forty-six, became pregnant with twins.

Ronnie finally managed to coax a stubborn Emily off the beach, the little girl giggling and screaming at the same time. They climbed the stairs to the deck.

"Mommy!" Emily shouted when she saw Diane. "Sandcathel!" She pointed to the beach and jumped up and down.

"That's wonderful, sweetie!" Diane gushed.

"Put your toys away," Ronnie instructed. She handed Emily her bucket and shovel and watched her trek off toward the toy box. Ronnie sat down on the redwood bench, placing a protective hand over Diane's swollen belly. "Are the boys moving around a lot today?" she asked, her eyes still glued to Emily, a child who was prone to mischief.

"They're never still," Diane remarked. "I don't think they sleep."

Ronnie laughed and kissed her on the cheek. She glanced at the stack of papers on the bench. "What are you working on?"

"Those are my old Courtship and Marriage notes. I haven't taught this class in a long time, and I need to refine my views."

"Oh?" Ronnie chuckled.

Diane smiled and shook her head. "You love this, don't you? It means you were right." When Ronnie just shrugged, she continued, "It seems my personal experience has altered my academic understanding of love, marriage and parenting. Are you surprised?"

"No, I'm just glad I was right," Ronnie teased.

Diane placed her hand over Ronnie's, their wedding bands pressed together. They watched Emily, who had managed to remove all of the toys from the toy box and was busily amusing herself with a fire truck. She scooted the plastic engine around the deck, making gurgling noises and high-pitched squeaks. "She looks so much like you."

Ronnie snorted. "God, I hope she doesn't want to model." Ronnie had long since given up modeling and finished her doctorate. She traded in the runways for classrooms and loved being a professor of sociology with Diane at Carlson. There were no regrets, she'd told Diane. With their savings and Ronnie's residuals, money would never be a problem for them, and modeling had afforded her opportunities she never would have known.

"She'll do whatever she wants," Diane said. "It will be on her terms, just like her mother."

Ronnie nuzzled Diane's neck and ran her hand through Diane's hair. "I hope our boys have your dark curls and brown eyes."

"We'll have to see if my genes are as strong as yours," Diane said with a laugh.

Ronnie sighed. "Speaking of genes, your mother called and she can't wait to see the new house. She and your father will meet us there tomorrow after the moving van leaves."

Diane sat up, surprised. "My father is coming? You're kidding!" She shook her head in disbelief.

Ronnie squeezed her hand. "Hey, he's trying. Give him a chance."

"I know," Diane conceded with a nod. She watched Emily as she methodically returned the toys to the box, largest to smallest. Diane was sure she was a genius, but didn't all parents believe that? Her father was in love with Emily and absolutely thrilled that Diane was having boys who could carry on the family name, even if it was hyphenated with Ronnie's last name as well. It was her pregnancy that finally had given them something to talk about. "When are your parents coming to visit?" Diane asked.

"They'll be here on Friday. Mom said she would help us unpack, and I didn't refuse. You're in no shape to lift boxes, and I'm not going to do it myself."

"Brody and Marcel already said they would help, too." Diane added. Brody and Marcel would move into the bungalow at the end of summer. Originally Brody had insisted they pay rent, but Diane was adamant that she wouldn't accept money since she had never owed a dime on the property. It was more important to her to keep it and have it kept up. Ronnie's savings easily paid for the new 5,000 square-foot home just outside the Carlson campus, one that could accommodate three children, many visiting relatives and the dog that Emily was requesting daily.

Diane glanced over her shoulder into the living room, filled with boxes and cartons. The room seemed so empty, their possessions compacted into a corner and stacked high. The feeling of home was gone and only the memories remained. She hated to leave, but it was time to look to the future, and they definitely needed more space. Ronnie had initially thought to add on to the bungalow, but the cost was outrageous and, as it turned out, structurally impossible.

"You okay?" Ronnie ventured, as if reading Diane's mind.

Diane smiled, her eyes misting. "I'm fine, my love. I'm better than I've ever been."

Ronnie touched her cheek and grinned. "Tell me what you've changed in your C and M notes. Let me feel superior, Dr. Cole."

Diane caught the humor in Ronnie's voice. She enjoyed their daily bantering, a symbol of their love that seemed unique and irreplaceable, a secret between the two of them. "Well, Dr. Frost, if you must know, I've learned that you were entirely right, and I was wrong. So you go right ahead and gloat. You've proven that my theories were flawed, and I now agree that love is all about the heart and not the mind. I acknowledge that you are indeed the superior sociologist, and I am humbled to be in your presence." She bowed her head in deference and tried not to laugh.

Ronnie lifted her chin and brought Diane's face close to her own. "You know, you were right, too. You always said love would grow over time, and my love for you strengthens every day. I didn't think that was possible, and it amazes me that the list of what I love about you just gets longer and longer."

They shared a passionate kiss that was interrupted by Emily's attempts to climb onto Diane's lap. She had finally finished putting her toys away. Ronnie smiled as Diane pulled Emily next to her. Exhausted from her play, she immediately rested her head on Diane's belly and was soon fast asleep. Diane brushed the wispy locks away from the child's face, and she beamed at the beautiful innocence of Emily's slumber. Ronnie's eyes were filled with tears. She hugged Diane tighter, while Emily, her blond little head rising and falling with each breath, watched over her brothers.

REALITY BYTES by Jane Frances. In this sequel to *Reunion*, follow the lives of four friends in a romantic tale that spans the globe and proves that you can cross the whole of cyberspace only to find love a few suburbs away . . .   978-1-59493-079-9 $13.95

MURDER CAME SECOND by Jessica Thomas. Broadway's bad-boy genius, Paul Carlucci, has chosen Hamlet for his latest production. To the delight of some and despair of others, he has selected Provincetown's amphitheatre for his opening gala. But suddenly Alex Peres realizes that the wrong people are falling down. And the moaning is all too realistic. Someone must not be shooting blanks . . .   978-1-59493-081-2 $13.95

SKIN DEEP by Kenna White. Jordan Griffin has been given a new assignment: Track down and interview one-time nationally renowned broadcast journalist Reece McAllister. Much to her surprise, Jordan comes away with far more than just a story . . .

978-1-59493-78-2 $13.95

FINDERS KEEPERS by Karin Kallmaker. *Finders Keepers*, the quest for the perfect mate in the 21st century, joins Karin Kallmaker's *Just Like That* and her other incomparable novels about lesbian love, lust and laughter.   1-59493-072-4 $13.95

OUT OF THE FIRE by Beth Moore. Author Ann Covington feels at the top of the world when told her book is being made into a movie. Then in walks Casey Duncan the actress who is playing the lead in her movie. Will Casey turn Ann's world upside down?
1-59493-088-0 $13.95

STAKE THROUGH THE HEART: NEW EXPLOITS OF TWILIGHT LES-BIANS by Karin Kallmaker, Julia Watts, Barbara Johnson and Therese Szymanski. The playful quartet that penned the acclaimed *Once Upon A Dyke* are dimming the lights for journeys into worlds of breathless seduction.   1-59493-071-6 $15.95

THE HOUSE ON SANDSTONE by KG MacGregor. Carly Griffin returns home to Leland and finds that her old high school friend Justine is awakening more than just old memories.   1-59493-076-7 $13.95

WILD NIGHTS: MOSTLY TRUE STORIES OF WOMEN LOVING WOMEN edited by Therese Szymanski. 264 pp. 23 new stories from today's hottest erotic writers are sure to give you your wildest night ever!   1-59493-069-4 $15.95

COYOTE SKY by Gerri Hill. 248 pp. Sheriff Lee Foxx is trying to cope with the realization that she has fallen in love for the first time. And fallen for author Kate Winters, who is technically unavailable. Will Lee fight to keep Kate in Coyote?
1-59493-065-1 $13.95

VOICES OF THE HEART by Frankie J. Jones. 264 pp. A series of events force Erin to swear off love as she tries to break away from the woman of her dreams. Will Erin ever find the key to her future happiness?   1-59493-068-6 $13.95

SHELTER FROM THE STORM by Peggy J. Herring. 296 pp. A story about family and getting reacquainted with one's past that shows that sometimes you don't appreciate what you have until you almost lose it.   1-59493-064-3 $13.95

WRITING MY LOVE by Claire McNab. 192 pp. Romance writer Vonny Smith believes she will be able to woo her editor Diana through her writing . . .   1-59493-063-5 $13.95

PAID IN FULL by Ann Roberts. 200 pp. Ari Adams will need to choose between the debts of the past and the promise of a happy future.   1-59493-059-7 $13.95

ROMANCING THE ZONE by Kenna White. 272 pp. Liz's world begins to crumble when a secret from her past returns to Ashton . . .   1-59493-060-0 $13.95

SIGN ON THE LINE by Jaime Clevenger. 204 pp. Alexis Getty, a flirtatious delivery driver is committed to finding the rightful owner of a mysterious package.
1-59493-052-X $13.95

END OF WATCH by Clare Baxter. 256 pp. LAPD Lieutenant L.A Franco Frank follows the lone clue down the unlit steps of memory to a final, unthinkable resolution.
1-59493-064-4 $13.95

BEHIND THE PINE CURTAIN by Gerri Hill. 280 pp. Jacqueline returns home after her father's death and comes face-to-face with her first crush.
1-59493-057-0 $13.95

18TH & CASTRO by Karin Kallmaker. 200 pp. First-time couplings and couples who know how to mix lust and love make 18th & Castro the hottest address in the city by the bay.   1-59493-066-X $13.95

JUST THIS ONCE by KG MacGregor. 200 pp. Mindful of the obligations back home that she must honor, Wynne Connelly struggles to resist the fascination and allure that a particular woman she meets on her business trip represents.
1-59493-087-2 $13.95

ANTICIPATION by Terri Breneman. 240 pp. Two women struggle to remain professional as they work together to find a serial killer.   1-59493-055-4 $13.95

OBSESSION by Jackie Calhoun. 240 pp. Lindsey's life is turned upside down when Sarah comes into the family nursery in search of perennials.   1-59493-058-9 $13.95

BENEATH THE WILLOW by Kenna White. 240 pp. A torch that still burns brightly even after twenty-five years threatens to consume two childhood friends.
1-59493-053-8 $13.95

SISTER LOST, SISTER FOUND by Jeanne G'fellers. 224 pp. The highly anticipated sequel to *No Sister of Mine*.   1-59493-056-2 $13.95